Sherlock Holmes and

The Dead Boer At Scotney Castle

By Tim Symonds

First edition published in 2012
© Copyright 2012
Tim Symonds & Lesley Abdela

Paperback ISBN 978-1-78092-091-7
ePub ISBN 978-1-78092-092-4
PDF ISBN 978-1-78092-093-1

Published in the UK by MX Publishing
335 Princess Park Manor, Royal Drive, London, N11 3GX
www.mxpublishing.com

Cover artwork by www.staunch.com

Author Biog

Tim Symonds

Tim Symonds was born in London and grew up in Somerset, Dorset and Guernsey. After several years in East and Central Africa in his late teens farming and driving bulldozers he moved to California and graduated from UCLA with a degree in Politics. He is a fellow of the Royal Geographical Society and former member of the Chartered Institute of Journalists.

He and his partner Lesley live in the High Weald of Sussex where the events recounted in *'the Dead Boer'* took place.

To Lesley

Contents

FOREWORD

PREFACE

Chapters

ADDENDUM

FOREWORD

Sherlock Holmes and the Dead Boer at Scotney Castle is Dr John H. Watson's account of the extraordinary happenings which took place in Sussex and Kent on a spacious early Edwardian summer day. Never before had Holmes and Watson come up against a brotherhood like the Kipling League. Dedicated to their Patron Rudyard Kipling, the Poet of Empire, the League's sole allegiance was to England's civilising mission. Its members would allow nothing to get in their way. It is the only chronicle Sherlock Holmes prevented his faithful amanuensis from publishing on the instant. His refusal to allow *the Dead Boer* to see the light of day is understandable. Never had he suffered such humiliation as the Kipling League inflicted upon him, the coterie Holmes referred to (when he could bring himself to refer to them ever again) as the Sungazer Gang.

Despite Holmes' opposition, Watson submitted the manuscript to the Editor of *The Strand* for reasons he explains. It was returned without comment. Was it because Holmes accuses such rich and powerful men of murder – four leading members of the Kipling League? Or had Holmes frightened off every outlet Watson was likely to approach?

Watson's persistent attempts to bring this adventure to his public shook his friendship with Holmes to its core. Even before *the Dead Boer* was completed, Watson came across a desk-diary with 'Notes on the Watson Problem' scrawled on the cover in his fellow-lodger's precise hand, tucked away with a box of Dutch East Indian cigars in the coal-scuttle. The diary contained just two comments, the first a quote from *The Case of The Six Napoleons* – 'Watson, while limited, is exceedingly pertinacious' - and more ominously and with no

1

apparent sense of irony, 'Watson's reports are most incriminating documents. Despite my opposition he continues to compile his narratives to afflict his long-suffering public'.

Within minutes of this discovery Watson hurried to the tin storage-box safeguarding his notes. He emptied the contents into a Russian-leather Gladstone bag stamped on the side with 'John H. Watson, M.D., Late Indian Army' in elegant gold lettering. He took the valise to the vaults of Cox's Bank in Craig's Court. A century and more later the Gladstone reappeared in a makeshift hut in the Weald of Sussex, wrapped in a piece of brown paper and tied round with tarred twine. It contained an archive of many treasures, the paralipomena of Watson's writings - envelopes bearing stamps with the head of Victoria, others that of Edward V11, a copy in Watson's hand of a letter in his name in the *Edinburgh Evening Dispatch* dated September 24 1900, a parchment carrying the signature of a British Ambassador's wife in Peking commencing 'Yuan Shih Kai is the Chinaman of the future', a leather-bound tome embossed with the Karolinska Institute's emblem in gold, a text on the aperient property of *Tamarix gallica*, and two small Moroccan red-leather boxes illuminated with fiery dragons, filled with a mix of powdered jade, cinnabar and hematite, inscribed 'Elixir of Life' in Chinese pictogrammes on the lids.

The Gladstone also contained an Addendum compiled in 1912 in Watson's scribbled hand, headed 'further notes referring to the Scotney Castle matter', now in its rightful place below. In an engaging marginal note Watson writes, 'no collection of my trifling achievements would be complete without an account of this very singular business.' He adds, 'I hope my readers enjoy taking the journey with me as much as its end.'

As do I.

Tim Symonds FRGS
Park Farm Oast
Burwash
East Sussex
March 2012

PREFACE

By Dr. John Watson

A most unusual circumstance has obliged me to write this preface, namely my great friend Sherlock Holmes' refusal to permit the publication of the affair I have titled *Sherlock Holmes and the Dead Boer at Scotney Castle*. Holmes' eyes narrowed when he told me our friendship would be gravely imperilled if I placed these events before my readers. He even ordered me to destroy such notes as I had managed to scribble during that extraordinary day. I refused to agree to any such undertaking.

The Dead Boer is in my estimation the most unforgettable adventure of our many years together, an extraordinary encounter with the rich and powerful Kipling League in Kent and Sussex in the early summer of 1904. If we accept Holmes' own description of these events, no other case or crime was more swiftly but intricately devised, of greater complexity in timing and conduct, or carried through with such ingenuity and aplomb.

From the moment I refused to obey his command, Holmes became much less communicative. Weeks passed without a direct word from him. He began to spend more and more time at the isolated farmhouse purchased two years before near King's Standing, in the county of Sussex, busying himself constructing dew ponds and purchasing Italian bees.

For some months I attempted to keep our friendship alive. I continued to visit him on the farm where in secret I constructed a scriptorium by a cheerful brook (or gill in the local dialect) near to a hatch of Old World Swallowtail butterflies, as far away as possible from the hives of *Apis mellifera ligustica* assembled in his meadows.

4

These hives with their odd, sloping edifices had the appearance of long-departed Roman 'tortoises' or the Square formation of the Brigade of Foot Guards in battle.

I call it a scriptorium because that was its purpose. In reality it hardly deserved to be called a hen-cree. Here I began to turn my notes for *the Dead Boer* into a manifesto if only for posterity. To explain my half-day absences, I carried a gun wherever I strolled, informing Holmes I was shooting for the pot, though the Sussex rabbit seemed tame after the wild goat of the Khyber Pass.

The Dead Boer is more of a chronique intime than many of the earlier stories. I most often call it 'The Perplexing Matter' rather than 'Case' because no formal enquiry was ever conducted after Holmes and I fled in disarray from the débâcle. If I appear inordinately proud of the scientific research which informed the Watson Codex I beg indulgence for a former army doctor's vanity.

To sustain me while ensconced in my hutch, Mrs. Keppell, the same tidy widow who brought Holmes his food, dressed me something filling (and, in winter, warming) – great hunches of bread and cheese and a bottle of cordial confection. She was a daughter of rich soil, a mulier fortis, of ample white hair and a grandly-modelled face, much given to explosions of laughter. With the passage of the seasons (and my shooting) the menu grew more extensive. Venison. Partridge. Over-ripe pheasant. Jugged Hare. For an occasional special treat, Rother Rabbit with broccoli was followed by Lady Pettus' biscakes.

When winter set in, I decided against a grate, terrified that fire would reduce my notes and documents to ash. I made cups of coffee at a spirit-lamp and endured many long cold afternoons, feet inside a pair of cardboard boxes. When completed, I placed the work in my portfolio which I returned to its hiding-place at 221b Baker Street under our landlady's care, alongside the Beaumont-Adams revolver.

When rumours spread that I was attempting to publish *the Dead Boer* against Holmes' wishes, some members of the public wrote to me questioning my integrity, taking his side against me. Why, they wanted to know, did I try to 'spring into print' with the Dead Boer like an eager *Globe* reporter, against the combined wishes of Holmes and the Editor of *The Strand* and even the editors of *McClure's* and *Collier's Weekly*? They asked what triggered this disloyalty? A correspondent from Trincomalee inquired with Buddhist concern, what caused this change in my character? I informed them that they could find the answer to their enquiry in Peter Lely's painting of Oliver Cromwell in the Tate Gallery.

On Holmes' departure for Northern Italy to inspect a dozen hives of a sub-species of the Western Honey bee, I resumed my early interest in paintings and Chinese pottery, attending excellent lunchtime lectures at the Tate. I find from my notebook this was in August 1904. In the course of a lecture, our guide brought us to the portrait of General Cromwell. 'Despite the fashion of the time,' she told us, 'unlike the portraits of Charles the First, Cromwell demanded to be portrayed as he really was, 'warts and all'.' The guide's well-practiced and casual statement jolted me like a shock from the *Electrophorus electricus*, the South American apex predator. I stared hard at the Great Protector. The warts were there for all to see. In that instant I determined my obligation too was to paint Holmes 'warts and all'. I had a mission of trust to my public. It was not my role to be a chanticleer or hagiolater but a Boswell. I would publish Holmes' defeats and imperfections alongside his successes and be damned.

6

At this fateful decision I left the Tate. Back at my lodgings, I withdrew my portfolio and settled down to examine its contents. I laid aside the notes of those cases I could never publish including the 'Foxy' Ferdinand affair. This account of Balkan intrigue would rock the shaky edifice of European monarchy if it were to come to the world's attention. As I leafed through my portfolio, the title I sought leapt from the 'suspended' folder and re-engaged my attention.

I was the more encouraged to ready *the Dead Boer* for publication after my friend Lomax, sublibrarian at the London Library in St James' Square, told me my chronicles were becoming the most popular of the works they held. At one point *The Hound of the Baskervilles* was nearly the equal in bookshop sales to Conrad's Typhoon. One man wrote to me during the Anglo-Boer War, 'The stories are greatly appreciated in the midst of mud and rain and shells, and all that could make life out here in South Africa depressing'. The Editor of the *London Mercury* told me I was outselling all other publications in Kazakhstan and the Falkland Islands. When Lomax added that my chronicles had become the 'birthright of all Britons', my face flushed with pride.

Here follows the unabridged adventure I have titled *Sherlock Holmes and the Dead Boer at Scotney Castle*.

J.H.W.

CHAPTER ONE
A Telegram Arrives

Holmes often stays in his bed until late in the day. At other times he rises with the first glimmer of dawn even before I have glanced at the clock or looked sleepily through my window at the outside world. On these not-infrequent occasions, he selects a coat from his collection as carefully as he chooses a pipe and trips with agility and anticipation down the stairs from the first-floor flat at 221b Baker Street. Sometimes he is gone all day, leaving behind a book by his chair, the pipe with the mended amber stem, and a sense of his presence. East London is his favourite stamping ground though it is undergoing sudden and savage industrialisation. Slavic agitators fleeing persecution have settled in communities around the River Lea, transforming them into principalities of crime. Few Londoners venture without need beyond the Hawksmoor Church of St. George's-in-the-East except for those thwarted in love seeking Chinese love-potions concocted from hashish, geraniums, rose petals, lemon leaves, sugar and honey. On other occasions we will visit Narrow Street in Limehouse on matters concerning the Chinese secret society, the Hung League, that strange group of men who will only communicate with each other by pointing first at the sky, then down to the ground, and last to their own heart.

The area throngs with humanity - cooks from Hainan Island, Petticoat-lane fencers, boatswains from Canton, stewards from Ningpo, men with pointy beards and Homburg hats. Ships of the mercantile marine bring cargo from equatorial climes to London's deep-water docks.

Holmes starts his explorations in earnest at Poverty Corner, walking many miles along the Thames, plunging into the vile alleys lurking behind the high wharves lining the north side of the river to the east of London Bridge. If wet weather prevails, as on the day whose events I now relate, he summons a street Arab and a tilbury, and in the instant is gone. He is as acquainted with St Katherine's, Victoria, South West India, Albert and Tilbury docks as our neighbouring Regent's Park. Fine ships still load for 'Frisco or the Antipodes, the surrounds filled with cackling Creole beldames from Sierra Leone and holy men in turbans and gowns with a reputation for healing.

It was the 27th of May 1904 when the extraordinary and disturbing events of the Dead Boer took place. On referring to my notes I see that though I was living over my surgery at that period, I made one of my not infrequent overnight stays at my familiar old lodgings in Baker Street still filled with most of my clothing and possessions. In the morning I rose by eight o' clock to find Holmes already returned from his sortie and finishing off a plate of the landlady's eggs. He gave me a nod as I took my seat.

Mrs. Hudson's breakfasts were designed more for my appetite than Holmes'. While he readily ate her eggs, he picked in desultory fashion at grilled kidneys, devilled chicken, cold ham and galantine. The kidneys (and galantine in particular) were marched across the table to my plate.

'Holmes,' I began, testing whether he was in a communicative humour. 'What of your day?'

'Watson, I thank you from the bottom of my heart for your great interest and concern. I have had a most charming morning.'

'And,' I pursued, not discouraged by this over-effusive response, 'what adventures among the slop-shops and gin-shops run by

9

rascally lascars, the dark and deep waters of the docks, or murder-traps in streets mournful beyond expression have pursued you like meteors beckoned into Jupiter's maw? Did you obey their notices against smoking, fighting, swearing and spitting?'

I added, 'Would we had a hundred guineas for every poor devil who has been done to death in those vile dens.'

'Adventures none but my discussions at the Blackwall Basin,' Holmes responded in self-satisfied mood. He left the table and threw himself down into an armchair. 'I find much of interest in Dockland, the bowsprits and jib-booms and silken sails of the Australian packets taking the early tide down-river homeward bound. The largesse of the Tropics and the Spanish Main - hogsheads and hillocks of coconuts, indigo, spice, saltpetre and tea. Where better than the Steam Packet beerhouse to purchase the Pipe-fish or the Surinam Toad?

'Where indeed?' I replied.

I had once accompanied Holmes to Schewzik's Russian Vapour Baths, followed by a visit to the aforementioned Steam Packet beerhouse where I obliged the landlord by drinking a mug of tepid brown slop at twopence the pint, beneath a racing calendar punctuated by dead flies. I still recall the smell which comes alone in all the world from long years of herrings cooked on a gas grill.

'Had Darwin spent more time in Rotherhithe or around Tower Hill,' Holmes continued, 'instead of years aboard the Beagle, he might have made a purchase of both tortoises and finches from the Galapagos Islands at the London docks and reasoned the mutability of species within the hour, thus saving himself a lengthy voyage and a year or more of mal-de-mer.'

'As you say, Holmes.'

My companion signalled he was indeed in conversational mood.

'Watson, I shall regret the passing of the barquentine. Each time I am in the upper docks there are fewer of them. They are the most beautiful of ships, possessed of the most aerial and graceful of rigs, the foremast with its transverse spars gives such breadth and balance, steadying the main and mizen poles. Such sheer, like the waist of a lissom woman, finely poised, so sure of herself in profile.'

I duly jotted down the detail of the barquentine on the note-book beside my plate, adding a small sketch.

'Holmes,' I said, pointing to *The Times* left open at the astronomy section, 'is it not fascinating to know that on August 27, AD 2003, Mars will be at its closest to our planet for 60,000 years? Percival Lowell thinks Man will by then get to our sister planet and shake hands with the builders of the Martian canals.'

Alas, I was robbed for ever of one of Holmes' pungent comments by our landlady Mrs. Hudson coming in to remove the breakfast plates, clearing away the remnants - 'crocodile left-overs' as she cheerily called them - to feed an alley cat called Marmaduke, the best mouser in Baker Street, she told us repeatedly in an admiring tone. On this day, after Mrs. Hudson departed with the last of the breakfast plates, Holmes left the room, returning in a green velvet smoking jacket.

'Watson,' he commanded. 'I have a new organic chemical investigation in train. Before I settle in, please be kind enough to approach the window – but with caution, I beg of you.'

My curiosity aroused, I went to the window and bent below the half-drawn blinds, peering out through the copious lengths of Mrs. Hudson's best lace.

'What am I to look at, Holmes? Is some crime of mysterious character taking place right before me?' I enquired light-heartedly.

'Anything odd, my dear fellow? Do you see anything odd?'

I stared down at the bustling street. A diligence pulled by a team of Boulonnais mares, destination Glasgow and ports to the Western Isles, was commencing its long journey. Ragged little Street Arabs known to Holmes and me as the Baker Street Irregulars were playing with home-made hoops along the paving, dropping them to run to the diligence's sides, begging for a coin or fruit from well-dressed passengers tucked under cream-coloured linen dust sheets, cheerily mocking them with offers of farthing buns until the driver's whip made them fall away.

'Nothing odd catches my attention, Holmes, no,' I replied.

'Is there a man with amber eyes - a little above the middling height, sited where he can observe our entryway?'

'Why yes, there is such a fellow but from where he stands he can watch a dozen doorways if need be. Why should it be ours?'

'Please describe him further, Watson. I avoided glancing at him for too long on my return this morning.'

'Collarless cotton shirt, corduroy trousers and a long-sleeved waistcoat reaching down almost to his knees, if that's the man you mean.'

'And selling hares?'

'Indeed. He has one in each hand.'

'And a brightly-coloured handkerchief around the neck?'

'He does wear such a kerchief, Holmes, yes.'

'As to his hat, remind me from your vantage point, does he wear a billy-cock or bowler?'

'A bowler, Holmes. What does such clothing tell you?'

'That the collarless cotton shirt, corduroy trousers and a long-sleeved waistcoat are not the daily accoutrements of a denizen of Baker Street. That should have caught your eye at once. It is obvious their owner is up fresh from the countryside.'

'And the kerchief...?'

'Emphatically a common labourer. It protects the neck from sunburn in the open field at harvest time or against the winter cold, just as you wrap your own throat with a cravat.'

'And you conclude what from the fact he wears a bowler?'

'...that he works on a great estate. A bowler does not start its life in a peasant cottage. Its youth is spent on a well-to-do head.'

I stared down at the watchful man. 'Holmes, what of it? He wears the clothing of a country labourer, possibly from a great estate – why not? What of importance do you read into his presence - he is here to sell his hares.'

'Then answer one more question and I shall release you from your vigil – does his coat still bulge on either side?'

'It does, Holmes, yes, but only from further hares stuffed into a pair of inside pockets, and still alive. I can see them wriggle.'

'Indeed,' my companion replied, reaching for a pipe. 'Those same pockets were a-wriggle when I saw him at sun-up today, fixed to that same spot as by the strongest glue, yet when a passing woman approached him to buy his wares, he waved her on. Why so?'

'And you conclude…?'

'As should you. The hares are a guise for skulking.'

Holmes lit a pipe. To judge by the level of rank smoke already set up in the room it was the second of the day. With affection I watched him puffing life into the shag. I felt nothing in life could ever sever the chain that was around us then.

'We need not worry, Watson,' Holmes continued, smiling. 'We shall watch for him through the morning. I am sure we shall soon discover whether a new game is at last afoot.'

For a while I lingered by the window, looking down on the rushing stream of life. My companion's switch to a smoking-jacket from his

14

outdoor wear signalled he would settle down to his chemical experiment. From out of his alchemical laboratory had appeared crucibles, alembics and a microscope. Our chambers were always full of chemicals, coal-tar derivatives, and criminal relics which had ways of wandering into unlikely positions or turning up in the butter-dish.

Holmes preferred the sitting-room, especially in the morning, with the two broad windows facing east. It offered a cheerful and well-lit space, though in risk of being overwhelmed by a tumble of Holmes' books. His presence in this room was in part a reaction to the clutter of his study, so empty when we had first viewed it, now brimming with mementoes of a full life – billiard cues, boxing gloves and punching ball, make-up table with tiny tongs for curling our magnificent false walrus moustaches, a poison fang of the extinct 100-foot-long Bothrodon of South Africa. Framed newspaper cartoons and pictures of criminals adorned two walls, including the as-yet uncaught cambrioleur Arsène Lupin. One cupboard was crammed with the paraphernalia for our disguises – two huge pairs of shapeless porpoise-hide boots with tabs on, purchased from dustmen, beside a pair of smaller, lighter boots removed for a sum from the living feet of a milk deliveryman

Over the length of my association with Sherlock Holmes we averaged a new case every month. Earlier in the year we had had a run of public and private cases the equal of the *annus mirabilis* of 1895 but the past twelve weeks had been filled with tedium. Such fallow periods prove as irksome for Holmes as for me. It was like watching a butterfly fold up its wings and return to its chrysalis. He put it to me drily, only one important thing had happened in the last three months, and that was that nothing had happened. Like all special gifts Holmes remarkable powers needed a constant burnish

15

lest they corrode through lack of use.

Most cases arrive on the instant – a soft footfall up the stairs followed by a knock at our sitting-room door, or a summons from Scotland Yard. Others lie like a virus in the blood, dormant for years. I am storing a length of parchment received some months before. Over the signature of the wife of a British Ambassador it read:

'Yuan Shih Kai is the Chinaman of the future, and on his success or failure to maintain himself in his present exalted and powerful position depends much of the future of China. He stands almost alone for reform, progress and education. He is honest in money matters, a thing almost unknown in Chinese public life. But his enemies are many and powerful. It is to be hoped he may prevail against them. The present time in China is intensely interesting, and her destiny is rapidly shaping itself.'

She warns Yuan's life might be in danger if he comes to England, any attack designed to provoke an international incident.

Holmes' announcement that a new chemical investigation was in train was not entirely welcome. His engagement in this endeavour made it clear I was in for a pottering day. Perhaps I would walk to Stamford's in Long Acre and pick up the latest maps. Or drop into one of the Bond Street picture galleries, though it was not a very fine morning for a stroll. More likely I would return to one of Clark Russell's fine sea-stories. I opted for my favourite seat at the fireside, tucked under the ornate overmantle laden with Holmes' correspondence. One letter in a bold, masterful hand brought round from the Upper Baker Street Post-office, opened but apparently unanswered, invited him to seek a seat in Parliament for a Party 'whose name and location on the political spectrum you yourself

16

may choose'.

As I settled in I recalled my friend Eddie Marsh asking how I turn my notes into pamphlets. I told him I always started with a dash - some such phrase as 'I had never before encountered such a singular case'. I pepper the pages with 'Inspector Lestrade and John Yates of the Yard (and/or the local police) were baffled' or best of all, 'Our official detectives may blunder in the matter of intelligence, but never in that of courage'.'

Lost in these thoughts and impervious to Holmes' light snore (he often fell asleep pipette in hand), it seemed but a moment later our clocks chimed a quarter to ten. I imply that the several pendulum clocks struck as one at the half quarter but because we usually failed to set each in turn, and we prohibited Mrs. Hudson from undertaking this manly task, they took to serenading us across a length of time, almost continuously, like the chiming bells of the great Cathedral at Rouen when the Dukes of Normandy and Brittany were crowned.

Sharp at eight minutes to ten the last of the quarter chimes ceased. Almost immediately the front-door bell rang.

'What is it, Watson?' Holmes asked, opening his eyes. 'Surely the morning post comes at eight o' clock and twelve?'

We listened to the sound of footsteps coming hurriedly up the stairs and crossing the landing accompanied by audible expressions of excitement upon our landlady's part. One of her crisper knocks followed. At Holmes' 'Enter, Mrs. Hudson!' she rushed in, breathless and excited, holding out a telegram on a brass salver.

Holmes glanced at the envelope and threw it over to me.

'A reply-paid telegram, Watson, and delivered by the district messenger service. As you have your eye-glasses on your nose already, do read it aloud. Mrs. Hudson, please return shortly for our response, and be ready to hasten to the post-office at Wigmore Street.'

Mrs. Hudson departed with unconcealed reluctance.

I took a letter-opener to the envelope. My heart gave a leap when I espied the sender's name.

'Holmes,' I reported, 'you are invited to Crick's End. By the President of the Kipling League.'

A Jacobean mansion in Sussex, Crick's End was the home of David Siviter, a poet (or to some more cynical, 'versifier') whose work was much published in the Westminster Gazette. While not held to be a writer of Rudyard Kipling's genius, he had much talent of the supple kind which lent itself to the popular vein – novelist, journalist, critic or historian as occasion suited.

'I am invited by the President of the Kipling League?' Holmes asked, incredulous. 'Who might that be?'

'Why, David Siviter,' I responded.

'David Siviter?'

'Surely you have him in your great index volume? Rumour has it he rivals Bridges as a future Poet Laureate. They say he is nearly the equal of Rudyard Kipling in knowledge of the East.'

18

'So the President of the Kipling League - acolyte to the great verse-maker himself, and author of many a tale from East of Eden, you say?'

'Yes, Holmes. That is he.'

'Invites me to his home?'

'He does.'

'Crick's End, you say?'

'Yes.'

'Which is where, exactly?'

'In the east of Sussex.'

'And when?'

'At once. He invites you to catch the three-ten train this afternoon from Charing Cross.'

Holmes sat bolt upright in his chair. A look of anger crossed his face. 'At once, you say? This afternoon no less? He who I now recall speaks to the orang-utans and elephants at the Regent's Park Zoo? He demands my presence at once!'

I protested, 'Many of us speak to the orang-utans and elephants at the Regent's Park Zoo!'

'In Malay and Hindustani?'

The angry expression gave way to one of enquiry.

'Watson,' he went on, 'why would this poetaster not send the invitation a week or more ago on featheredge hand-wove or foreign notepaper, in envelopes at a shilling a packet, as parvenus do, rather than by the district messenger service at 3d the half-mile? There is haste in this invitation, surely?'

'I admit it is not a Saturday-to-Monday but your asperity may lie with telegrams. They are the origin of that cousin of brevity – curtness - in us all, at sixpence for each and every word.'

He emitted a further burst of indignation. 'Reply-paid! How kind of this Kipling League to save us five shillings! Is that a courtesy… or contempt? But do go on, my dear Watson,' he urged in a more emollient tone. 'From your expression even a Scotland Yard inspector could see how flattered I should be.'

I returned to the telegram and read aloud. "Dear Mr. Sherlock Holmes, we would most earnestly ask you…" I looked up. 'Hardly imperious, Holmes,' I demurred, repeating, "we would most earnestly ask you…to take the three-ten train from Charing Cross to Etchingham where you shall be met by a motorised barouche with Mr. Dudeney at the wheel'.'

The telegram took on a more confidential note, 'Inclement weather in the form of a thin rain has disrupted our outdoor plans'. This was followed by a witty parenthesis, 'Holding members of the Kipling League together, indoors or out, is harder than herding cats'.

The message ended in an admiring tone, 'Unanimously we have elected to invite you to pass to us some of that insight into the criminal mind for which you are so famed'.

At this recitation, Holmes wrenched the small brier-root pipe from his mouth. He leapt up so quickly from his chair it was as though he spoke in flight. Not known for strength of voice, on this occasion he managed a bull-like roar.

'They have pre-empted my choice of acceptance!' he cried. 'Do you note how he refers to his chauffeur by name? Clearly he assumes we are shortly to be acquainted! 'Inclement weather in the form of thin rain has disrupted our outdoor plans'! They wish me to entertain them like a performing seal? Am I to be a visiting jester or a calf for baiting? Should I attend as though in pantomime at the Richmond Theatre, with an eye-patch, a salt tang about me and a parrot on either shoulder?'

He switched to a grim tone. 'We shall make good use of their reply-paid communication. Watson, take hold of a form and a pencil. Concoct a reply to the following effect ... '

Alarmed at a display of temper that I did not discern was largely dissembled, I offered in a faltering voice, 'Holmes, you have a clear day, it would be great practice for our oft-discussed lecture tours. I am sure you will learn to defend yourself... ', at which words my companion fell back down.

'Sixpence a word, you say? It does not take a strong lens to see he has money to spend.'

He squinted at me through the fug of tobacco smoke. 'Continue,

21

Watson. Tell me more about our host.'

'He is the second-highest paid author in the world, after' Kipling himself. Siviter's work brings him five shillings a word, amounting to more than thirty thousand pounds a year. Even with income tax at a third ...'

'Pray go on...' interrupted my companion, glancing at a large standing-clock, the more accurate time-piece of our collection. 'He says 'We', that is, they... the League...by which he means?'

'Siviter himself, of course. He mentions Alfred Weit and Sir Julius Wernher - and Viscount Van Beers,' I replied.

One of England's most famed Administrators, Stanley, Lord Van Beers had been much in the South African news of late because of the controversy over indentured Chinese labour. During the recent South African War the English cinemas showed flickering film of him in a canteen on a good-will tour of the Veld. His middling years contrasted with a photograph taken during the Anglo-Zulu war a quarter century before. The young man stood smart in his rifleman's green undress uniform, a bandolier over his shoulder, black patent-leather despatch case to hand.

David Siviter's name had come up only a week or two before, on a visit to the Athenaeum for a nostalgic and pleasant evening with a retired Regimental friend. We were soon joined by Eddie Marsh, newly-appointed Private Secretary at the Colonial Office, and something of an alter ego of mine since I found he had been at Cambridge with my boyhood companion Tadpole Phelps. On the evening I refer to, during a discussion of the West End stage and in particular Barrie, out of the blue Marsh said, 'I tell you, Watson, a

22

great actor is lost in Siviter. I was staying with the Desboroughs at Taplow Court and playing the game of guessing historical scenes when Siviter took the stage. I can't recall anyone guessing his subject, which turned out to be the High Priest giving Judas the thirty pieces of silver - that made no matter. The point was the impression he created of something afoot was unutterably sinister and malicious'.

I returned to the telegram and read the post-script aloud. 'And Pevensey hopes to introduce himself'. A famous artist, Pevensey maintained a substantial income painting the landed gentry and their estates. Some decades earlier, at the high-water mark in the great Queen Victoria's reign, Pevensey made his name depicting trials of the human spirit by the demands of duty and honour. His best-known oil titled 'Loyal To The Very End' was a *succès d'estime* at the Royal Academy Summer Exhibition.

'Holmes,' I continued, 'there is a Post Post-script. 'A hamper and a bottle of vintage wine will be delivered to the Pullman car at Waterloo or London Bridge. Cost of same will be born by Siviter, in addition to 'a small requital' for your trouble,' which,' I started to read out for Holmes' delectation, 'amounts to ...'

Holmes' hand rose swiftly, pointing at Mrs. Hudson's shadow by the door... 'a substantial sum and all expenses,' I interposed. 'Holmes,' I exhorted, 'I suggest you get into your country clothes and go.'

He gave a further glance at the grandfather clock. 'They offer great inducements, Watson. Very well. As you are so keen, we shall spend the afternoon in Sussex. Take this down, confirm I shall catch the three-ten train and inform them you will be accompanying me, that is, my dear fellow, if you can tear yourself away from your

23

manifestos. And Watson, bring the latest gazetteer. We shall learn more of Siviter and Van Beers en route.'

I handed Holmes the completed telegram. His long, thin arm shot out backwards.

'Mrs. Hudson, I know you are at our door. Please use the reply-paid envelope and hasten with it to the Telegraph Office.'

He turned his face to me. 'When Mrs. Hudson returns, pray ask her to whistle for a covered cab to take us to the station, a quiet, well-mannered brougham to be precise. I have no wish to get wet twice today, even if in obeisance to your orders I am to commence the life of a circus flea.'

With the man with the amber eyes patently in mind, he ordered, 'And, Watson, ask our landlady to procure not the first nor the second but the third brougham passing by. We must take such precautions as would prevent it being one which has been placed ready for us.'

With a light tread I repaired to my old dressing-room to select the clothing I would wear to Crick's End.

CHAPTER TWO
We Journey To Crick's End

As I dressed, I observed through the window how the first leaves were flourishing on the solitary plane tree gracing the yard behind our house. Standing in the small dressing-room preparing for our journey, I could not have guessed even in a second life-time what we were about to encounter.

Holmes' head appeared around the door.

'Watson, make haste. Now we are on our feet, let us catch the eleven-fifty express. It takes us to Tunbridge Wells. From there we can catch the local train to Etchingham. I would suggest Park Lane and the Mall rather than the Regent's Street and Piccadilly Circus at this time of day.'

At this his head disappeared.

'But Holmes,' I called out after him, 'we can hardly arrive on their doorstep three hours early – surely we must inform them?'

The head reappeared.

'If we are to catch the eleven-fifty we cannot afford to divert to the West Strand Telegraph-office. We shall arrive at Tunbridge Wells quite soon after one o' clock. There we can send a telegram to invite Mr. Dudeney and his motorised barouche to meet us at Etchingham railway station. That will give our host at least a half-hour's warning of our arrival.'

The head disappeared, only to reappear a moment later. 'And

instruct our cabby not to take a main road if a parallel side street will serve our turn.'

The head disappeared, yet again to return. 'And have the cabman face his transport the other way as though we have an assignation on Hampstead Heath or intend to take an hour or two at leisure in the Regent's Park.'

Hurriedly I reached for a pair of Balmorals.

I am a prompt and ready traveller. Hard schooling in the colonial life of Australia augmented by rough-and-tumble Army camps in Afghanistan readied me for the most sudden of trips. In less than the quarter hour I was dressed. The sharp sound of horses' hoofs and carriage wheels grating against the kerb announced the arrival of our transport. In place of the well-appointed brougham Holmes had wished for, the demand for carriages under threat of rain had left us 'beggars choosers'. I descended the stairs to greet the cabman at the threshold where, with trusty leather valise in hand, I awaited Holmes amid the smell of Brasso and Monkey Brand soap and perspiration. On my exit from our lodgings, our amber-eyed observer withdrew sharply a yard or two, like a land-crab at bay. He stood staring intently in my direction. On instruction the cabman turned his horses to face north. I hoisted one shoe to the footboard from which vantage point I could engage him in light conversation on the gossip from Westminster and the density of traffic.

Holmes came down the stairs. He glanced in the long looking-glass in the hall, checking collar and cuff and, with a touch of vanity, the lie of his silver-brown hair. He emerged seconds later, after an inquisitive glance at the Family Herald lying upon the hall-table (the love romances, photographs of pretty horse-breakers and the cookery pages were Mrs. Hudson's favourite reading).

We were lucky to arrive at the station in time. Holmes' train-catching is an anxiety to his travelling companions. It was a signal achievement on the cabman's part, propelling us like the sun god Apollo driving his chariot to light the sky. Down magnificent Park Lane and along the Mall we rattled, ever onward. Our final drive to the departures area terminated in a triumphant flurry of foaming beasts as though preceded by fife and drum and reined in by post-boys in the boot.

The great train pulled away from Platform 6 with a sharp exhalation of steam. Aboard with my travelling companion at such propinquity I could examine Holmes' choice of outer clothing in some detail. He had selected the rare Poshteen Long Coat. The bulky piece with its many flaps and pockets and promise of distant, icy mountain ranges contrasted oddly with the ear-flapped travelling cap clapped on his head where for myself I had chosen a glossy topper. With the Poshteen Long Coat now open, I noted that he wearing his accurate gold watch for only the second time in our long relationship, the watch-key and a gold sovereign attached to a massive Double Albert chain. The watch and chain together with two or three tie-pins and a snuffbox of old gold adorned with a great amethyst at the centre of the lid were as far as I could tell the only heirlooms Holmes possessed, apart from a battered escritoire.

I leant towards him ready to enquire whether he was wearing the Order of the Legion of Honour which would indicate to me his estimation of the occasion but before I could commence my enquiry my old friend took out a pair of black night-spectacles from a pocket sewed inside the cavernous coat. He popped them on his nose, loosened his cravat, and lay as dead for the next ten minutes.

The silence enabled me to contemplate the unexpected and well-remunerated invitation of the day.

'So,' Holmes spoke up suddenly, like a corpse in Shakespeare, quickening and dying and quickening. 'At last we wander in the footsteps of Dickens.'

At London Bridge he removed the night-spectacles.

'I see you have brought Roth's gazetteer,' he remarked with a nod of satisfaction, divining it was the reason I had brought a Gladstone alongside the medical bag containing my armamentarium. He replaced the night-spectacles and fell asleep again.

He awoke as the train arrived at Chislehurst. I remarked how much I looked forward to sight of Siviter's Art collection, especially 'The Mill' by Sir Edward Burne-Jones. In a most off-handed manner Holmes responded, 'I am sure the master of the house will oblige.'

I frowned. 'Are you not in the least interested in pictorial Art?'

'Watson,' Holmes replied amiably, 'no and yes. I am not, yet I am. Art is so much part of the human firmament I would be failing my profession to overlook it.'

With such conversation as I imagine Boswell undertook with Dr. Johnson on their tour of the Scottish Highlands we wound our way into Kent.

Not long past Chislehurst a railway guard went by. 'Sevenoaks next,' he called out. 'Sevenoaks, Sevenoaks. Private visitors for Mr.

Whitehead of Down House alight here. Down House. Alight here for Down House.'

'Isn't that where…?' I exclaimed.

'Yes, Darwin's old abode,' Holmes responded.

At the mention of Down House, Holmes was spurred to ruminate, looking out at the Kentish landscape.

'I shall confess to you something I have not confessed before,' my companion began, in conspiratorial fashion. 'Had Darwin not preceded me, had I not, when very young, devoured *The Origin of Species*, I believe I would have become a Naturalist myself. It was Darwin's theory of evolution by natural selection which led me to develop identical techniques in my own profession. They say Shakespeare killed off a thousand unborn playwrights. It is not too much to declare that had Darwin become a Consulting Detective and not a Naturalist, such was his skill at observation, absorption and induction, I would have been doomed at best to second place in the annals of crime – but then I would have become a Naturalist!'

My companion halted his remarkable epiphany on Darwin. 'Come, Watson,' he said jovially. 'Let us have a brief account of our audience's history and pursuits. Let us attack the gazetteer.'

I reached for the Gladstone and drew from it the large volume, placing it opened at random on my lap.

'First,' he commanded, 'our host.'

SIVITER:

'David (Joseph) Siviter.

Born 1865, Surrey, England.

Poet, short-story writer, journalist and imperialist. Much-admired chronicler of the English colonial experience in India.

Education: Stoneyhurst, Haileybury, and Imperial Service College.

1889, settled in Addis Ababa.

1892, married Abyssinian Princess Burekt. Two daughters.

1900, reported on the Anglo-Boer War.

1902, moved to Crick's End, Sussex. MFH.

London Pied-à-terre No. 3 Gray's Inn Place.

Best selling short-story writer, especially of children's fables.

Publishers Macmillan, Methuen and Putnam's.

Estimated earnings Sterling £30,000 per annum.

Bank, the Alliance.

Offices, President of the Kipling League.

Clubs, Buffalo Club, Rajputana, United Oxford & Cambridge Universities.

'That's the official part,' I informed Holmes. 'The second part is culled from a variety of opinions for which, in no uncertain terms, the gazetteer states it is not responsible but reports solely for our prurient interest.' I paused, raising my eyebrows. 'I must presume this would be of no concern to you, Holmes?'

'Read on, my good friend,' Holmes responded, with an airy wave. 'It is ever the malicious and ill-natured which by habit and profession we so naturally find more captivating than mere age, height, weight and office.'

I continued, 'Heroes: Van Beers, Roosevelt.

Allies in the Press, Gwynne (*Standard*), Blumenfeld (*Express*),

Maxse (*National Review*).
Uncertain relations with the Germans, Irish and Quakers.
Contributed patriotic material to *Daily Mail* during South African War, i.e. 'The Absent-Minded Beggar'.
Leading scourge of Liberalism and democracy.
Lost Sterling £2,000 in the crash of the Oriental Banking Corporation.

Quoted in *Daily Mail* in piece titled The New Jeremiah that England is 'slipping down the broad, easy decline which will lead to our extinction as a Great Power with an influence to exert on the side of the angels, with a civilising tradition to plant all the world over'.'

'That,' I said in conclusion, 'is Siviter.

Holmes dug into a cavernous pocket and took out a tin of Egyptian tobacco, Abdulla's Mix at an aristocratic tenpence the ounce. He preferred Abdulla's even over fine-cut Virginia Leaf or Grosvenor mixture at eight pence an ounce. Holmes had, I reflected warmly, subscribed fully to the Kipling League's promise of fee and all expenses.

He pointed at the open gazetteer.

'Now to Van Beers, if you please.'

'S...T...U...' I muttered, turning the large pages to 'V'. 'Here we are, Stanley Van Beers:
Bachelor. Born 1854. German extraction.
Oxford University.
1880, Published abstract on Julius Caesar's military campaigns, largely the battles of Thapsus, Pharsalus, Zela and Munda.

31

1892, Published *Briton or Hun in Egypt?*, arguing for greater English involvement in Egypt's affairs.

1897, appointed high commissioner for South Africa and Governor-General of Cape Colony. His efforts to gain political rights for British settlers in Boer territories heightened a growing tension between the rival groups and helped precipitate (1899) the South African War.

Developing a doctrine of federalism designed to revitalise the concept of Empire.

1902, Created Viscount. Honorary colonel in the Kaffarian Rifles.

Clubs, White's, Army & Navy etc.

'And the informal?' Holmes enquired.

'Passion for order and efficiency. Love of cut-and-dried solutions. Contempt for British Party politics. Respect for authoritarianism.

Member of The Kipling League.

Heroes: Bismarck, Frederick the Great, Sir Hiram Maxim.

Described by close female acquaintance as 'one moment passionately loving and the next aloof and unapproachable, the most remarkable character of cunning, caution, sophistry and nobility one could imagine.'

Allies in the Press: proprietors of the *Daily Mail, Morning Post, The Speaker, Pall Mall Gazette*. The *Johannesburg Star* (Geoffrey Dawson).

'Imperialist with a missionary purpose.'

To the *Daily Telegraph* his refusal to bend to liberal whim was taken to display 'an original force of character which rejects all moulding by force of circumstance'.

Detractors: *Daily News, Manchester Guardian.*'

After I related this, Holmes asked, 'And does this book of reference have an entry on that little-known personage Sherlock Holmes?'

'Fourteen pages,' I replied with satisfaction, 'full of your awards and sub-titles including Honorary Fellowship in the Royal Society of Chemistry. It even précis your monograph on the hands of slaters, sailors, cork-cutters, compositors, weavers and diamond-polishers.'

He nodded at the valise. 'Did you also bring the Cassell's Concise Cyclopaedia?'

'I did, Holmes,' I affirmed, reaching into the Gladstone for the tome. 'And heavy it is.'

'What does it say about the Kipling League?'

I turned to the 'Ks'.

'Kipling League.
Formed circa 1889 as a cultural off-shoot of the Primrose League (see Beaconsfield). Originally a reading-circle for admirers of Rudyard Kipling's verse and prose.
By 1902 transmogrified into a private movement propagating Kipling's conservative colonial agenda.
Supporters believed to include John Buchan.
Holds discussions critical of Count Leo Nikolaevich Tolstoy, the Russian writer whose philosophy includes non-resistance to evil and the abolition of governments and nationality.
The League is rumoured to have forced the resignation of the 'effete' Joe Chamberlain, and strenuously opposed the election of the Liberal Government.
1903, Rules amended to exclude women from membership.

Rites according to the equestrian order.
Membership by invitation only.
Meetings unpublicised, irregularly held at (London) the Bellona Club and (Sussex) Crick's End. On the Continent at the Flotille in Paris. No minutes kept.'

Holmes stared thoughtfully out of the carriage window. 'Such men exist to do harm to their enemies,' he commented. 'It would be hard to throw light into the shadowed corners of such a league.'

He held up a hand, deep-set eyes upward, as though enquiring of the Deity. 'Does this invitation arise from more than damp weather, I ask?'

'Holmes,' I said, amused. 'Can you not accept we are but a diversion from the tedium of the countryside on a rainy day, what more? You underestimate your fame.'

'Watson, neither Siviter nor Van Beers are idle or uncomplicated men. As to my public speaking,' Holmes continued, looking across at me ruefully, 'you have thrown me to the lions by your insistence.'

'Our Mrs. Hudson, who regularly visits the vaudeville, has given me an invaluable tip, Holmes,' I assured him.

'Which is?'

'Don't turn your back on the audience.'

'Why not?' Holmes asked, mystified.

'That's when they spatter you with rotten eggs.'

Our train entered a lengthy tunnel, damping down the sound of our laughter. Holmes sprang to the window to shut out the smoke and steam. We emerged and immediately pulled to a halt alongside a platform at Tunbridge Wells. A station attendant took the form and two half-crowns and set off for the nearby telegraph office. We crossed a foot-bridge to the local train on a nearby platform. Less than thirty minutes later, announcing itself with a shrill blast of steam, our train arrived at Etchingham.

The small country railway station stood at the bottom of a long, twisting, steep road down the valley side from the village of Hurst Green. Not far from where we alighted rose a sturdy manorial fourteenth-century church topped by a copper vane. Rabbits hopped among the crumbling tombstones. Above us, a kestrel hung in the air, hunting for voles and mice secreted among the thistles and long grass of the river-bank some 30 yards away. Yellow Coltsfoots decked the rusty lines. In the field adjacent to the station, grazing almost to the platform edge, roamed black-faced sheep and dark red cattle. My immediate impression just two hours from the bustle, noise, dust, smell and flurry of Baker Street was of quietness and beauty, a countryside forged with craft and care by the millennial hand of Man. Soon the brantgeese would be arriving from their Arctic home.

We remained for a moment on the platform in front of a large enamelled advertisement exhorting us to purchase Abdulla Superb Cigarettes (Turkish, Egyptian, Virginia). The train left us with a minatory scream.

I looked across the tracks to the village side, reached by a pedestrian bridge. Commercial wagons were assembled in a small public space.

A smart private coach-and-pair awaited its master, the coachman perched high on its box. At its side stood a dray drawn by two dappled horses, their tails tied up with ribbons. Tucked among the disciplined group of horse-drawn wagons like a monster visitor from an alien world stood a large green motor-car, the driver at the wheel. He wore a coat made of dreadnought against the warm light rain. Assuming, rightly, this was Dudeney, we waved to indicate our arrival and began to cross the railway tracks.

CHAPTER THREE
Our Arrival At Crick's End

The car crept towards us through the wagon yard, the low throaty sound of the engine just audible over the whinnies and whoas of the horse-and-cart community. I marvelled at the sight of this open-topped giant.

Dudeney introduced himself with a bob of a leather-clad head as he held open the passenger door. We climbed in and lay back on the extraordinarily comfortable leather seats. Our conveyance would have been at home at a session of the Chamber of Indian Princes – gold- and silver-plated cars, cars with hoods of polished aluminium and bodies of costly woods, cars in purple, lavender, sky-blue, orange, emerald green, vermillion. Cars upholstered in satins, velvets, brocades.

While our chauffeur waited for the horse-drawn traffic to clear, he offered a detailed description of the vehicle, starting with the pre-selector epicyclic gears, working his way with calm enthusiasm to the worm-drive rear axle, tiller-steering and finally the four-cylinder water-cooled overhead valve engine. Siviter had named the Lanchester 'Julia'. In return, I remarked I had read Siviter's cat-and-rat fable and was looking forward to viewing Crick's End electricity at work.

A young newspaper vendor leant over to push a copy of the *Sussex Express* into my hand ('The Paper for Uckfield, Heathfield, Crowborough. Established 1837'). Even as I passed him a coin, Julia leapt forward with a mighty roar, scattering the last of the horse-drawn wagons. Before us bobbed our chauffeur's helmeted head and shoulders, piloting the Lanchester like a Wright Brothers' Flyer. A few more seconds and we passed beyond Etchingham to a broad ridge road. There we gained a small companion. Within inches of my face, a boy peddled hard and with intent, his heavy bicycle and wicker panier emblazoned Thomas Blinks Butcher in gold lettering. In a well-practiced manoeuvre, he obtained a precarious handhold on Julia. By this enterprise he achieved a speedy ride to his first delivery half a mile later, dropping away at a large, dark house set back in a laurel-clumped lawn.

The sweetness of scent enveloped us in sudden great balloons of air. Seated on our vehicle's high bench we had a view over the fresh-trimmed hedges to either side. The run of unusually warm springs commencing with the new King's reign meant the heads of the grasses and wild flowers were heavy with pollen.

Buoyed by the engine's steady roar and the clean, fresh air, I looked out at the serene May countryside, at the profusion of wild flowers and early honeysuckle, contented herds of Sussex Reds resting in the cool shadow of the many great oaks, a tree so prevalent, our driver informed us, it was called 'the weed of Sussex'.

I looked at the *Sussex Express*. A great rat-hunt had taken place on Broyd's farm. Bees killed a dog on Mr. T. Davis' farm.

'Holmes,' I said, amused. 'Listen to this! 'Astounding Doings at lonely Sussex Farm'.

A series of mysterious happenings at a lonely farmhouse in the Sussex Weald has brought about in the neighbourhood a firm belief in the resuscitation of witchcraft. The Walk Farm at Etchingham, in the occupation of Mr. Neil Armstrong, is the scene of its manifestations. A few mornings ago, when Mrs. Armstrong's maid was at work in the farmhouse kitchen, she felt her back was being burned between the shoulder blades. She was not near the fire, and there was no possibility of a spark or live coal reaching her. The girl, who firmly believes 'a witch did it' was considerably burnt and had to be surgically treated. The first suspicion of something uncanny came on a recent morning when several golden sea-bright bantams were found in the fowlhouse with their legs broken. A watch was set that night, but though no one came near the fowlhouse, more bantams were found with broken legs next morning. The next day, when Mr. Armstrong and his family and a neighbour were at dinner, a flower pot on the window sill was seen to be wildly whirling around. Mr. Armstrong ran to the window, but there was no one near, and there was no wind, and yet the pot was still whizzing round. Pans jump up and down on shelves, chairs move jerkily across the floor in broad daylight while no one is near them, brooms dance, and household utensils move while being watched.'

At my side in the comfortable seat Holmes lay back with his hat tilted over his nose. 'This stretch of road,' I said conversationally, having done some cartography on the eastern part of the County of Sussex while Holmes cat-napped on the train, 'is called the Straight Mile, built by the….'

As I spoke these words, our iron chariot ran out of straight road, rounded a sharp bend, and with a crash of its epicyclic gears came to a sudden stop. Close before us a hay-wagon had cast its load. Dudeney left us to assist in the reloading of the bales. The task accomplished, he returned to his seat. He turned to me and said, 'Sir, you mentioned the tale of the cat-and-rat. I'm afraid you will be disappointed. Village children at play raised the sluice-gate and emptied the pond of all its water. The mill-pond is at present too low to run the turbine-generator.'

At this he set off again. I proceeded to give Holmes an account of the origin of the Sussex place-names. 'Holmes, many of the Wealden villages end in '-den'. Did you know that's Old English for 'woodland pasture?'

He withdrew his pipe and answered, 'I did not know that, Watson,' and added, 'I may soon forget it. I have no wish for my brain to emulate our attic.'

Undeterred, I followed up with a description of the South Downs sheep. I was deep into a description of the Sussex Red cattle and about to move on to the Shoveller Duck when I noticed Holmes looking closely at his gold watch. Realising I was boring him with such country matters, I stopped. Holmes laughed and clapped me on the shoulder. 'Go on, my good Watson. I shall indulge you and hear more about the Shoveller Duck, if only to quiet you on the Sussex Red on which I fear I now know too much.'

'Holmes,' I replied. 'No-one can know too much about the Sussex Red. You may find the Shoveller Duck a different matter.'

In this good mood we approached the historic Wealden trading-centre of Burrish. The Lanchester pulled us up a small curving slope and we were on an ancient High Street built when iron was king of the Weald, rich merchants' houses on our left, artisans' dwellings on our right. At its end our driver turned sharp left and we rolled down a steep lane. The view to the South opened up. Large coppices of sweet chestnut and hornbeam spread over the valley sides, cultivated for the charcoal which once fired the many now-lost iron forges of the Dudwell Valley. It made a pleasing contrast with the dims and drabs and slate greys of London.

The Lanchester descended until the lane flattened out at the valley floor. To our left two donkeys stood under a considerable oak in a steeply-sloping field, surrounded by a group of contented, snuffling, small black pigs and one silent, choleric-looking Muscovy duck. On our right loomed the grey stone lichened house. We had arrived at Crick's End.

CHAPTER FOUR
We Meet Siviter And White

Turned to gold in a sudden burst of sunlight, the squat building emitted an air of calm and stability, an English refuge. The roar of the Lanchester's engine dropped abruptly as the vehicle came to a halt, waiting for the handsome wrought-iron gates to open. The gates hung from tall, weather-bitten posts patterned with centuries of epiphytes and surmounted by exquisite carvings of hops. A silver-grey oak dovecot was just visible above the walls and hedges of the house. Crows watched keenly from the great oak on Donkey Hill, their cawing a ceaseless accompaniment to the afternoon.

My companion sat in silence, staring forward at the house. I wondered what first impression he would make on the members of the Kipling League. In addition to his striking appearance, his ancestry (second cousin to the Ulster King of Arms and Chief Herald of Ireland) had bequeathed him a nonpareil sense of the practical and a fertile and retentive mind which sprang alive in the face of the supernatural. So Celtic is he in origins that at a miniature medal affair at Downing Street, after the dramatic solution of a Continental matter, I was asked in a low voice by a British Prime Minister to confirm Holmes' place of birth. The eminent personage felt he must be a foreigner who spoke English well.

'Julia' squeezed between the finely-wrought gates, her voice reduced to a low growl. The grounds of the Armadillo of a building bulged with lines of potting-benches, garages, outhouses and oast-houses built with Staffordshire Blues. Blackbirds atop the yew hedges abandoned their song and flew in alarm to their sanctuaries, giving shrill warning of our arrival.

The vehicle came to a halt before a bronze statue of two defiant drummer-boys. Close to, solid rather than grand, Crick's End looked what its builder, an ironmaster of the 17th Century, had wished it to be, the very image of a manse for the rising Middle Classes.

A servitor of indeterminate age and dark skin wearing a turban waited in the fore-court by the bronze, having seen (or more likely heard) our transport proceeding down the hill.

'Staray mashay,' I tried, placing my right hand over my heart. His head bobbled. With almost a sleight-of-hand gesture he swung his wrist so the palm faced the sky, forefingers slightly elongated. 'Namaskār,' he replied, taking my portmanteau and inclining his head towards the front of the house. 'Or 'Gurdaspu', if you know the Punjab, Sahib'.

Head down, silent, without looking to either side, he walked us towards the entrance.

The brick pathway led us to the Corinthianesque porch. Carved into the sandstone beneath a small oak barometer on the porch's outer left-hand pier were initials which I presumed correctly to be of the Siviter family: RS, CS, ES, and JS, and an unidentified other, CM. The door opened. The clatter of a piano resounding through the house ceased in mid-concerto. A maid-servant with a French accent and a rounded face freckled like a plover's egg stood before us straight from the pages of Lettres de Mon Moulin. In a creaseless white apron and high starched collar she was as filled with grace as a Botticelli Venus. I smiled at her and was about to send her back into the interior with our cards when she was put aside. A man stepped out, dressed in putty-coloured – almost white – broad-cloth and, in surprising combination, a pale-grey patterned silk Ascot tie. It was

43

our host.

Siviter looked of a slightly older age than his true middle or late forties, genial and breezy. His skin was dark by English standards. He sported a luxuriant dark moustache. Goldrimmed glasses over sharp little acetylene eyes were arched by outstanding eyebrows starting to bush with age. One or two teeth were false. At his side he held a brown soft felt hat with a broad, floppy brim and low crown. Stepping forward from beneath the fanlight to join us, he immediately placed it on his head.

In the open air he seemed remarkably small, the crown of the wideawake hardly reaching Holmes' shoulder. I estimated his weight at less than nine stone, a slight amount for a man of his age. Author of the much-loved Heavy Game of the Western Himalayas, it was hard to believe he was the fourth best big-game shot our Eastern Empire had ever produced, a wonder with a 600 Express, a sporting rifle with a recoil so powerful it would break a man's collar-bone if he fired it from a prone position. I marvelled that a man who still wrote extensively about the sapphire skies of India, picturesque buildings, minarets and domes, the camels, deserts, the sense of endless space and endless time should now be living contentedly in so confined a valley.

'How very good of you to come, and at such short notice,' he welcomed us warmly, guiding us towards the door. 'Our patron Kipling himself would be here but he and his wife were called off to Vermont. They are selling up a property there.'

After these civilities we proceeded before him through the porch and open door and entered a dark-panelled hall where my hat, dust-coat and coat and umbrella were taken from me with a bright smile by the same Venus-like maid-servant who greeted our arrival at the porch. Her uniform emitted a slight smell of rose-geranium.

Walking into the Grand Hall from the calm greens of Sussex was like following Aladdin into the Cave of Enchantment. Flowers were abundant, arranged daintily in every nook and corner. We were at once face to face with mounted heads from big game expeditions, at least one in eastern Africa to judge by a long-necked Gerenuk. Burne-Jones' 'The Mill' was flanked by two water-colours by Pevensey of what I took to be gardens at Crick's End. At their side, in remarkable contrast, hung a group of five sepia watercolours depicting Indian trades and professions. Above a fine Coromandel screen was a masterly oil-painting titled Bridge over the Thames at Barnes. It portrayed a choppy and turbulent river in its best grey winter-wear, carrying a red barge towards the interior of London. Next to it, another great waterway was represented by a painting of a dahabiah sailing down the Gambia River. Both were signed by Lesley Abdela, a female artist of Greek descent as yet unknown to me.

We were walked alongside rich and glossy tapestries draping the walls, including one of the lost Titian painting 'Portrait of Isabella d'Este in Red'. Carpets, especially a gold kincob carpet five yards square, gave a touch of Eastern luxury, magnified by the faint smell of tobaccos and spices of India and the sudden, unexpected, sharp clean scent of kaffir lemon grass hanging in the cool dank air. Much of the remaining space was filled with an assemblage of tiny objects, some from the Far East, all from a distant past. Every item had been brought back to England in Gladstone bags specially built for elephants.

In the one step it was as though we were re-entering the Raj or other

45

far-away land, an infinity of all that was beautiful, of utility and in good taste, a space that brought to the senses the cacophony of the sounds of the East – ships' bells, splashing oars, native shrieks, a world where if you stared over the rain you might see Mowgli seated on the jetty, or if you cocked an ear the sound of giant kettle drums from a distant Salute State. I half-expected an Oriental figure to glide towards me, a Hindoo servant clad in yellow turban, with white, loose-fitting clothes and a yellow sash, attendant on his Maharaja, Nizam, Nawab, Khan, Maharawal, Jam, Raja or Rao, potentates whose arrival in villages was feared like the coming of locusts, so large were their entourages which, like those of Tudor and Stuart kings, had to be fed and watered without as much as a silver rupee in compensating payment.

Breaking into my reverie, Siviter told us he anticipated two further guests within the hour. A third, Lord Van Beers, was already in residence or at least on the grounds. He had spent the previous night in a tent in the garden, 'For the sake of his joints,' Siviter added with an ironical expression. 'He tells me the house is too dank.'

The artist Pevensey, grandee President of the Royal Academy, was also for the moment away from Crick's End, 'putting finishing touches to one or two commissions'. He would return around mid-afternoon to a make-shift studio in Park Mill, at the lower end of the gardens, and planned to leave in the early evening, his work completed.

Our talk was to take place in the parlour at three o'clock. There was time for us to be conducted around the gardens. Coats back on, we followed Siviter out of the Grand Hall along a stone-flagged passage and through a side-door on to large terraced lawns where we were greeted by an assembly of leaping, barking, overjoyed Aberdeen terriers and a brace of black, curly-coated retrievers released from their shed, eager for exercise. From their sentry-duty at the front of the house, their ever-watchful eye had spotted what they took to be a stratagem by Siviter to leave them behind.

Millstones punctuated the brick paths. Two gigantic Chinese monals squawked at the dogs, rising near vertically to settle in the branches. The air was filled with the low drone of insects and the sudden sharper note of a bluefly shooting past us with its quivering, long-drawn hum like an insect tuning-fork. The beds bloomed with herbaceous plants and shrubs chosen for their hardiness.

The brick pathway turned to paving stone. The valley air was warming up in the intermittent early-afternoon sun but within the garden it was still cool, with a slight breeze. Overlooking a terraced lawn, stone seats like the sedilia of a church had been pushed into the yew-hedge, facing to the South and West for evening sun and warmth. Tucked away by a hedge we could see Van Beers' tent.

At the sundial Siviter stopped. 'It is my custom,' he informed us solemnly, 'to honour our President by offering a few lines which he composed seated on a canvas chair at this very spot.' With an arm held high, an engaging, almost boyish smile on his face, he sang the antistrophe of 'The Way through the Woods':

Yet, if you enter the woods
  Of a summer evening late,
When the night air cools on the trout-ringed pools
  Where the otter whistles his mate,
(They fear not men in the woods
  Because they see so few)
You will hear the beat of a horse's feet

47

And the swish of a skirt in the dew,
  Steadily cantering through
The misty solitudes,
  As though they perfectly knew
The old lost road through the woods …
But there is no road through the woods!

At that second, daunted by the yap and yelp of the terriers below it, a grey squirrel leapt out of a small tree and bolted across the grass. It had until Christmas to live, Siviter informed us. After that he would shoot it, thereby the filberts the creature had filched from his trees and buried around the estate for winter fare would have a chance to germinate in the spring.

We came to a small clutch of dogs' graves. On one was inscribed with clear affection, 'Our Dachshund Billy 1888-1901, A Wise and Humorous Friend'.
Daffodils, scillas, wood anemones and fritillaries reached up through rough grass.

We crossed a bridge. Some fifty yards further we came to Park Mill. 'Just look at the rabbeting, the mortising, the mitreing, the dovetailing, the joinery,' Siviter exclaimed in admiration. 'And done so long ago.' He pointed at an assembly of wheels, pipes and cable. 'But here, Gentlemen, is a miracle of our age, electric light at the touch of a switch. Put together by Sir William Willcocks, one of the most interesting fellows I have ever met, the very man who built the Aswan Dam and modestly spoke of it to me as 'that trifling affair on the Nile'.'

He added, looking directly at Holmes, 'You may not be a man of Empire but you cannot deny where-ever the English arrive, we find primitive tribal societies. As the President of our League puts it so well, it is England's special duty to fight 'The savage wars of peace /Fill full the mouth of Famine/And bid the sickness cease'. When the time comes for us to depart, we shall leave behind roads, railways, telephone and telegraph systems, farms, factories, fisheries, mines, trained police, and a civil service.'

Subsequently the imperial figure of Willcocks, Siviter told us, 'wandered through Babylon and Baghdad', building dams on the Tigris and Euphrates.

He continued, 'To drive the generator, Willcocks de-clutched the corn-grinding mechanism and installed this turbine. The current is carried by 250 yards of deep-sea cable to batteries in an outhouse. We get four hours of light from ten 60-watt bulbs each evening.'

I saw Holmes begin to look abstracted. To avoid breaking into a roar of laughter which would surely have hurt Siviter's feelings, I burst out, 'Ah, and I assume it takes a fair amount of water?'

'2000 gallons an hour,' replied Siviter triumphantly. 'Through a 14-inch pipe. I would offer a demonstration but as you see, the pond is exceptionally low. We have used it up in supplying extra current for my guests.'

He pointed to the upper floor of the Mill.

'We cleared the mill-attic as a workshop for the artist - you will know of him from his recent appointment as President of the Royal Academy. I commissioned him to paint an oil or two on the Fuseys' estate at Scotney Castle across the Kent border, some twelve miles from here as the crow flies. Lord and Lady Fusey are great friends

49

of mine. Pevensey should be back here shortly to hang the canvases up to dry.'

Our host turned us back the way we came   Led by the dogs we retraced our steps through the gardens. As we picked our way across the Wild Garden Siviter entertained us with an amusing story of baboons chasing him on Table Mountain. This was followed by a more curious happening three years before, at Crick's End, early on the second day of his residence. His wife and children were still in the former home at Roehampton. After a night of recurring fever ('from my days in India', Siviter reminded us) he rose before sun-up to make a cup of herbal tea, no servants having yet been engaged. Outside, a thick mist which rolled in during the night had yet to dissipate. He entered the breakfast-room to find himself staring at a sinister group of grey-beards, wizened monks as at a séance, attired in the black habit of the Dominican Order, immune to a battalion of cockroaches so thick on the stone floor they almost touched each other. To Siviter, not yet recovered from the fever, the monks had the look of uneasy spirits just risen from their graves. One wore a heavy habit enclosing his body like a bell, with a pilgrim's staff and sack, a breviary on his lap. So clearly was such an assembly a ghostly inheritance passed on with the building or the hallucination of his still-disordered imagination and upset sensibility that 'hoping the strange visitors were not too briskly summoning me away in the dim world that lies beyond the grave', Siviter strode on towards the kitchen stove, expecting to walk right through them, but they were solid. He had a difficult apology to make. As they were there for alms he gave them the half a leg of mutton delivered the previous day, some capers, a generous monetary donation, a half-full brown stone jar of overproof West Indian rum, and several bottles of Kops Ale discovered in an armoire secrète. Damp had warped the cupboard's doors and hampered the lock which had to be broken. 'It was from that experience that I wrote the verses of *The Portuguese Monk of the Barefooted Carmelites.*'

It was nearing time for us to sup before we sang, or, rather, to take tea on a velvet lawn near the mulberry tree, at a long table covered by embroidered linen. Our repast would be informal, in the *style anglais* - standing under umbrellas in the drizzling rain. The meal comprised thin slices of bread and butter and a jelly compounded from the half-rotted small brown fruit of the medlar tree. It brought back my memories of Johnston's Fluid Beef.

Siviter and I held a brief, rather conspiratorial chat on our methods of writing before reaching amiable agreement that our styles were Continents apart.

While closing in on the tea and medlar jelly, our host took us on a diversion through the house. On a tiger-skin rug in Siviter's study stood a long, shallow fruit basket of insubstantial wicker-work, filled with a litter of curiosities - ancient broken pottery, delicate papyri, assorted bronze ornaments of Far East origins, a planchette, and such fandangles as a tiger's tooth attached to a bell. Beyond lay a collection of green jade dishes and badly-cracked Imperial yellow rice bowls retrieved from an excavated tomb. Siviter explained Chinese Court etiquette prescribes that when a Sovereign dies, every rice or other bowl adorned with the royal cypher must be smashed, with fresh ones manufactured for the new Emperor. After he interviewed Tung Fu-Hsiang, leader of the Boxer rebellion, for the *London Times* he purchased this collection in the Native City, just outside the Chien-Men gate of Peking.

From such collection of almost unimpeachable authenticity and utmost rarity Siviter had built a European reputation in at least one

51

branch of research, Asiatica, where his power of purse from sales of Eastern tales (nearly the equal of Kipling's) gave him great advantage in the race for fame.

CHAPTER FIVE
We Debut As Public Speakers

Our brief encounter with tea and medlar jelly came to its end. For a moment Holmes engaged Siviter in talk about the richly-woven Persian and Kashmiri rugs spread across the floor of the Grand Hall. My friend's knowledge was gained in Lower Egypt and Persia during the Great Hiatus of 1891-94 when he was thought dead. We ascended the adzed twisted double staircase, through age visibly out of true. Thus we came to the place of trial, our first public speaking engagement.

We entered an entirely different and icier world. By deliberate and extraordinary contrast to the Grand Hall, the parlour exuded an air of mediaeval England. To judge by the smell of many tobaccos, it doubled as a smoking-room. The stiff furniture, chosen for compatibility with the house's age, looked – and proved to be – uncomfortable. In the precise centre, adorned with two mauve antimacassars and positioned like a Princely gadi was a fine copy of a Knole sofa, inspired by the 17th Century original at the great Kent country house of the Sackvilles twenty-five miles to the north. The room was a cabinet of remarkable talismans. Everything was worthy of inspection.

Two chairs were being pulled nearer the fire-place from where first Siviter, then I, then Holmes would speak. Siviter and Van Beers (with whom we had exchanged the briefest of introductions) were talking on the other side of the fire-place in low, confidential tones. Van Beers sat sideways on a chauffeuse, the padded back and seat covered in black material with floral and chinoiserie decoration. In this remote room, on their territory, deep in England's countryside, an air of hauteur had descended. I felt we were discounted, two competition wallahs or subalterns who took soup for luncheon.

I looked discreetly at Van Beers. There was a crispness in his clothes despite over-nighting in the tent in the gardens. His dark blue jacket was made of barathea with silk linings, the handkerchief poked from a sleeve rather than pocket, a characteristic I had only noted among the Imperial Yeomanry. Together with a slight cavalry stoop, he had a cold, bright eye for unhurriedly sizing up an enemy. This same cold, bright eye travelled over my face as though studying a reconnaissance map. There was little extraordinary or peculiar about him, save a pair of fine light cavalry whiskers and a slight stiffness in one leg, caused, he volunteered on first conversation, by a riding-strain; yet what a book it was this man's power to make, whenever so disposed.

It was agreed Siviter would open the proceedings and I was then to introduce Holmes. A maid removed the flurry of Aberdeen terriers with affection and some difficulty. After a glance at his watch and a few further now almost conspiratorial words with Van Beers, Siviter turned about and gave a brief clap. Hands clasped in front of him, he offered a slight and near-formal bow and began his address.

'Gentlemen, we are pleased and honoured to have you with us.' He pointed at the china on the beaufet. 'On the two sides of that pot, in crockery-literature, is written the Chinese precept 'Ask no questions of a guest' but perhaps we can make an exception to-day. Our principal speaker's fame travels years and Continents before him and needs no reinforcement, but such introduction as he may care to allow will be performed by Dr. Watson.'

He nodded towards Van Beers. 'I need not spend time in further introduction. Our other guest is well-known. We expect two more.

54

They send their apologies for being delayed.'

Siviter turned and addressed me directly.

'Dr. Watson, we know your chronicles are like exquisite and fragile vases, perfectly graceful and conscientious works of art.'

At these few but courtly words he sat down.

I rose to confront my demons. 'Gentlemen, it is my privilege to present to you both myself and my comrade-in-arms. My raison d'etre is to record the singular gifts by which Sherlock Holmes is distinguished. I document for posterity the quick, subtle methods by which Holmes disentangles the most inextricable mysteries. He often says that while he remembers the action he forgets the actors. My humble role is to restore them to life by my chronicles. Dare I claim that without my notes the detail of events would slip away.'

Siviter murmured a polite 'Hear Hear'.

I glanced at the notes in my shaking hand and continued: 'My life and manifestos have become a useful row of pegs on which to hang the remarkable insights in detection Sherlock Holmes achieves. If I might add to our host's kind accolade, the personality of Holmes has gained such universal hold upon hearts and minds, and retained that hold so tenaciously over more than twenty years, that his life, his habits and his characteristics have become an object of greater interest even above the adventures he and I have shared. There is a scarlet thread of murder running through the colourless skein of life, and Sherlock Holmes' duty is to unravel and isolate it. No other profession has as supporters a more devoted clientèle, nor as antagonists more irreconcilable opponents. Before I met Holmes, I

55

had no idea such individuals existed outside stories. The unofficial Consulting Detective is a quite separate category from an Inspector of the Yard. It is not the ordinary case which comes to our attention. Whatever is conceived and executed by the duller criminal feeds the mere groundlings of detection. They fall greedily on crocodile leftovers, not the fare of eagles. Holmes is called in by the Yard or Sûreté when all else has failed. The Law Society includes his cases in their curriculum of legal studies. He is the last Court of Appeal in doubtful cases, the elemental force in the Ultima Thule of crime. Many were the times we grappled with the emperor of crime, ex-Professor Moriarty of evil memory, a man of powerful intellect polluted by a wayward temperament, so endlessly bent on upsetting the tranquillity of the public mind. He was defeated in the end only by Holmes' knowledge of baritsu.'

I darted a quick look at Holmes for signs of approval. He was studying the floor.

'Holmes' entry into obstinate cases is sought by Scotland Yard precisely as desperate farmers in the parched Sonora Desert call upon Pueblo Indians to dance for rain. He confronts problems nigh insoluble, of such intricacy as earlier detectives, however assiduous, never dreamt of, but when he started on his life's work there was no work in print on such a system of deduction. Even Sir Isaac Newton declared 'If I have seen a little further it is by standing on the shoulders of Giants,' including Descartes and Copernicus, or as Nietsche wrote, 'each giant calling to his brother through the desolate intervals of time'. A Swedish church, thinking he possesses second sight, implored him to discover Swedenborg's missing skull. Such is his fame that in his absence in Tibet and the Sudan, a hundred bogus Sherlock Holmes of varying degrees of build, height, personation and ingenuity sprang into action. None having met him in the flesh, all tried to fit to their own shoulders the keen face and prescient smile of the Sherlock Holmes they pictured from my chronicles. Three tried to bribe me to vouch for their authenticity. One aspiring Holmes from Stepney Green came to my door sporting a monocle. Another wore on his chest a facsimile of Holmes' award from the Nayeb-Saltaneh of Persia, the green ribbon of the Order of the Lion and the Sun. Each shrank away and made their exit when I said they must prove themselves a Holmes by taking on the nobblers, palmers, smashers, abbesses, rapacious ivory-traders, and dragsmen in the welter of filth which is Stepney and Whitechapel. Christian missionaries prefer to proselytise in Darkest Africa or innermost Tibet than these Stygian wastes closer to home.'

Onward I sped.

'As you know, he works from 221b Baker Street, which I may immodestly call – by dint of Holmes' fame – one of the three best known addresses in London, after His Majesty's and the Duke of Wellington's.'

I may have hoped for a second encouraging 'hear hear' but my audience sat discomfittingly quiet.

'Holmes is a Renaissance Man, a commander of many an '-ology'. As author of the monograph *Upon Tattoo Marks*, his identification is unique outside the Tahitian islands - Berbers of Tamazgha, Māori of New Zealand, Hausa people of Northern Nigeria, the Atayal of Taiwan. He knows the methods of the Black Dragons in Brazil, Peru and America, the practice of Sapo Chino in Bolivia. He can imitate the call or song of almost every bird. He is expert on atonal theory. To my and guests' delight, he replicated in our Baker Street home a whole evening of Alexander Nikolayevich Scriabin at the

Wigmore Hall, the musical equivalent of Picasso – formidable sounds, sharp hisses, explosions, claps of thunder. How well I know the Barcarolle from Offenbach's Contes d'Hoffmann which Holmes strums so admirably on a solo violin. Some call it a dreary tune but it is one which, over time, I assure you I have grown to enjoy. Certainly it is popular on the dancing-floor. And how often he regales me with his disquisitions on Antonio Stradivari or the Arabian Kite...'

At last, to my relief, even Van Beers, a person of rigid calm and impassivity, broke into a guffaw.

'and four ways to varnish Cremona fiddles!'

Louder, almost raucous guffaws followed. Holmes sat completely still, a slight puzzlement on his brow.

I ploughed on. 'I quote my comrade-in-arms, 'I make a point of never having any prejudices and of following docilely wherever fact may lead me'. Those familiar with our chronicles may recall I described my friend at work in *A Study In Scarlet*, published nine years ago, where Holmes whipped out his fine linen tape measure and his magnifying glass, trotted noiselessly about the room, sometimes stopping, occasionally kneeling, and even lying flat upon his stomach. It is often said of Charles Darwin he is different in degree from every other Naturalist. I suggest my great friend Sherlock Holmes is equally different in degree and kind from any other fathomer. The impression left is ineffaceable. The spotted sleuth-hound is as nothing to him. Sherlock Holmes has an unrivalled power of disguise. With nose wax, twisted lips, padded cheeks, the artful use of eye-shadow, within the hour he is the Norwegian explorer Sigerson, or an out-of-work groom – or an old crone. Grease paint is as familiar to him as eggs for breakfast. At will he alters his expression, his gestures, his walk, his manner, his very breathing, his soul. I shall not forget him as a simple-minded Nonconformist clergyman in a broad black hat and baggy trousers, the expression of peering and benevolent curiosity on his mien, or as a decrepit Italian priest when we tried to shake the vile ex-Professor James Moriarty off our tracks in Florence. Famed actors from the Apollo and the Duke of York's Theatre come to Baker Street, pleading with Holmes to teach them skills of an order far beyond the green-rooms of their trade.'

By now I was in full gallop like a well-backed race-horse on the stretch.

'I should add, as my good friend Holmes may not, that on innumerable occasions we have faced frightful danger. For this he has become a Chevalier of the French Legion of Honour. Many have been the times that had he been an officer in the British Army he would have won the Victoria Cross. On more than one of those occasions – I think particularly of *The Adventure of Wisteria Lodge* - I would have rather been up The Grim on the North-West Frontier with the Berkshires, or even at the fatal battle of Maiwand where the heavy bullet of a Jezzail musket fired by a murderous Ghazi grazed my subclavian artery and shattered the bone.'

With long, white, nervous fingers, Holmes began to drum a tattoo on his knees.

I rushed on. 'Holmes is the application of scientific method. His deductive powers are so startling the uninitiated run away in fright. They declare him an elemental spirit on a different psychic plane, or at the very least a necromancer. Enemies swear he communicates

59

with the fearsome voodoo spirit of fertility and war. On exit from the flat on Baker Street I have watched dark-skinned gutter children whisper 'Colonel Samedi!' and take to urgent flight. When closely questioned they aver he is a man who never lived but will never die.'

At this, like a ventriloquist, Holmes whispered from the side of his mouth, still staring at the floor, 'Cut to the chase, Watson! Cut to the chase!'

'To quote the artist confronted by the work of a great master,' I hurried on, 'he is an eagle; I am only a skylark tossing off little songs into the glowering clouds'. Holmes has been called the Master of Disguises, and with every reason. Even I have been fooled. Many a time he has affected disguises from his extensive collection of hats, particularly those with significant brims. And then there are the coats. Take, for example, in Holmes' cupboard, the shiny, seedy coat he wore when solving the matter of *The Illustrious Client*. He possesses two Jaeger Coats, an old Ulster, a Great Coat, a long Covert Coat, a Chesterfield Coat, a fur coat which unfortunately moths have attacked in our attic, a Chinese fur coat which has so far escaped the moths, and a waterproof coat... though his preference is for the long grey travelling-cloak in concert with a close-fitting cloth cap. But, to-day, in recognition of this most gracious invitation, whereas I came in my glossy topper and Ulster ...'

I paused for dramatic effect.

'... Holmes chose to wear the Poshteen Long Coat, last worn by Colonel Francis Younghusband on the notorious trek to Lhasa, which Holmes purchased for no small sum from Perceval Landon.'

To my relief, given I had flung an arm into the air as if 'from

Perceval Landon' was a most remarkable thing, the audience clapped briefly and sharply.

I rippled on at a breathless trot.

'Holmes readily tells a man's trade by inspection of a corpse's knees, his fingers or a shoulder. How easily he interprets the hand of a miner, the lines etched in that blue trade-mark which handling coal leaves on the skin. Upon the instant of our entry into this building, Holmes remarked on the balsamic odour of the Eastern tobacco hanging faintly in the air. Who else can identify at a sniff, touch or glance a hundred and forty forms of tobacco ash, on which Holmes has produced a monograph titled Upon the Distinction between the Ashes of the Various Tobaccos with coloured plates? Or his ability to recognise the 42 different impressions left by motorcar tyres? Why, he could follow Dudeney in the Lanchester to the farthest corners of the Globe. To keep this faculty in perfect shape, he practices on honeys. Our landlady, Mrs. Hudson, complains she has no further larder space from yards of jars produced by bees across the globe – from Tasmanian Leatherwood to Mrs. Peacock's Rotherfield Honey Batch L22.'

At this came a second warning whisper from Holmes' direction. 'My blushes, Watson,' he murmured in a deprecating and firm tone.

But to no avail. Ahead was Beecher's Brook and I was in full canter. Nerves which had forced my face into an involuntary, spasmodic grin now caused me drop my notes. Helpless in the palm of the muse of inexperienced speakers, the Belle Dame sans Merci, I stumbled toward the abyss: 'Then there was *The Adventure of the Blue Carbuncle* where from observing an ordinary black hat

61

Holmes...'

At this, Holmes rose sharply to a crouching position. Like a baleful puppet on a ventriloquist's lap, his head snapped sideways. With a malevolent hiss he commanded, 'Watson! Come to an end, I insist!'

He stayed suspended, menacingly, like a fakir between Earth and Sky. Startled, I backed down towards my seat, my own posterior hovering at a precise level with Holmes' some inches in the air, my eyes locked on my audience in desperate appeal.

I stuttered, 'Like the famous Cardinal Newman my Tractarian mother so admired, after whom I am named, Sherlock Holmes possesses a clearness of intellectual perception, a disdain for conventionalities, and, as you note, a temper imperious and wilful. This is the first time he offers an analysis of his art in public and, I hope, he will allow himself to respond to any questions and interrogations you might have. Not for him the fanciful weaving of ingenious theories miscalled 'intuition' nor the blind acceptance of circumstantial evidence untested by the searching light of cross-examination. I leave you with this thought, there is not a man, from the oldest inspector to the youngest Peeler who wouldn't be glad to shake the hand of Sherlock Holmes and accept a hint or two as to a solution.'

At which final gasp I fell back thankfully into my chair. The slight smattering of applause rang sweetly in my ears. Siviter was at once on his feet, hands together as though at the Mikado's Court, smiling and bobbing in my direction.

'Thank you very much, Dr. Watson, for that very full introduction, might I say, in view of your affection for racing, straight from the horse's mouth. As to your role as a peg, I am certain you are right. To listen to you makes us realise you must lavish a hundred little touches of true knowledge and genuine picturesqueness on the page.'

Siviter turned to my comrade-in-arms. 'Mr. Holmes,' he continued, 'we are especially honoured by a visit from such a famous London specialist. For many years we have been gripped by newspaper reports of your adventures in Wapping and Whitechapel, the very heart of darkness.'

Our host was referring to the many forays Holmes and I made into the most desperate areas of the capital city during this Belle Epoque of crime. Not only Wapping and Whitehall but Mile End, Old Ford, Stepney and Bethnal Green. Every '-ism' known to humankind sprang up in such unpromising soil - socialism, nationalism, secularism, communism, egalitarianism, Panslavism, Zionism, Nihilism, anarchism, pacifism, suffragettism, atheism, the flickerings of Fascism and at least one 'non-ism', free love, courtesy of the Hebrew Socialist Union, all the afterbirth of the Industrial Revolution.

With a light bow Siviter said, 'We now look forward to your lecture.'

CHAPTER SIX
Holmes Gives Clues To His Deductive Methods

Holmes composed himself for a few seconds, with his lids drooping and fingertips together. Then he began. 'Gentlemen, high praise indeed when my friend Watson refers to Charles Darwin and your servant Sherlock Holmes in a single breath. The Century which so recently went its way was dominated by the theory of Natural Selection. I can justly claim one notable similarity between Darwin's work and mine. There is divination in both. In common with Darwin I suffered schooling to every conceivable intent both purposeless - except to tyrants - and worthless for any known profession. The fetters of prejudices from my early education lingered with me for many years. My scholastic career was never filled with promise. Often I was hit over the shins with a wicket. Unlike your literary Master, I was never filled with the joy of literature. Macaulay was not my hero though I was impressed by Edgar Allan Poe. Lack of Greek and Latin or fluency in French and German closed off access to the greater part of Western literature yet a great-uncle decided I should become a poet or author.' He paused. 'Though surely it would be a foolish or a less impecunious man who starts a working life by choosing 'author' for his profession. I learnt far more of substance and value in my short months in rooms on Montague Street, hard by the British Museum, studying all those branches of science which might make me more efficient than in many years at school or two years at Cambridge and Oxford studying music of the Middle Ages and the derivation of the Celtic language. Darwin and I are confederate in one passion - for the facts. I use facts solely to serve my deductions, while Darwin stewed them to produce his magnificent general laws. He would have had nothing but contempt for the effete conventions and hypocrisies of our Edwardian England compared to the vitalising effect of the ruthless but straightforward life-and-death struggles of Nature.'

Holmes paused. He looked towards Siviter.

'But to authors close to home. Who has not enjoyed the verses, sketches, skits and stories of our present host, so full of allusion and quotation, as well as those of your League's namesake, his gift for phrase, the comic intervention, the delight in parody and imitation? Who has not read among Kipling's works The City Of Evil Countenances, Abaft The Funnel, The Jungle Books - and Kim? Kim o' the Rishti who went to the River of Healing, a master work of imperialism, the India of the imagination. Who could forget your literary Master's evocation of Bombay –

'Mother of Cities to me,
For I was born in her gate,
Between the palms and the sea,
Where the world-end steamers wait.'

Your President's patriotism is beyond dispute – think of the tales and poems of the British soldier in India. Who has not visited the Mogul Saloon in Drury Lane to hear The Great MacDermott's rousing rendition of the war song sold to him by Kipling for a guinea? I found his description of Lamaism invaluable. You can never know too much about magic, mysticism and demon worship. I have often addressed a Pathan with 'May you never be tired', a courtesy I learnt from a reading of Rudyard Kipling's works. And might I say, your President and my good friend Watson and I hold to a principle in common – our concern to defend civilisation against brute Nature and the barbarian. One day, when his volcanic voice is stilled, they should name a crater Kipling on the planet Mercury.'

I nodded slowly with pleasure at these words. It was clever of Holmes to pay homage to the source from which he had learned the Pathan greeting.

Holmes' disquisition was interrupted by the sound of voices on the stairs. A modest tattoo was followed by the door opening. The first and tumultuous entry was at floor-board level, a bubbling cauldron of excited, noisy Aberdeen terriers wriggling and rotating like giant brindle caterpillars. They were followed by two aristocratic men around five-and-fifty years of age. Sir Julius Wernher and Alfred Weit had arrived. Both men had been born in Leipzig but chose Queen over Kaiser and settled in England. Both stood about the middle height, dark, with foreign features, attired in the livery of their class, at once recognisable from the window of the Pathé Frères shop near Regent Circus filled with photographs of the celebrities of the day. They were termed, in the popular press, 'Gold Bugs'. Together they held the greatest financial power in the world, their immense fortunes from determined activity in the Kimberley diamond market. They maintained their position through unsleeping vigilance for the affairs of the Rand. The two were mentioned frequently in the society pages of the *Clarion* and the weekly illustrated papers whose reporters so assiduously cull the pages of Debrett, following the lives of the rich, the aristocratic and the Royal, covering the grander dinner-parties in Delamere Terrace or Audley Square. In short, covering the territory in which our income was significantly to be found.

Sir Julius Wernher was the first to approach, radiating suavity, with a silver beard and full moustache. He lifted golden pince-nez to his eyes as he came to the centre of the room like a vieux marcheur, bringing with him a faint whiff of Roger and Gallet cologne. His clothing displayed a delicate touch of individuality, harking back to an older fashion except for the contrasting choice of strikingly fashionable lightweight hat. Made of green felt, the brim rolled slightly inwards on the side, a single crease running down the centre of the crown and pinches at the front.

Sir Julius owned a 3000-ton yacht, The Miloca, always at the ready in Cattaro. Weit's and Sir Julius' great 'palaces' in London were decorated, by all accounts, with imperial grandeur, in the sumptuous taste of Edwardian new wealth, heavily influenced by the Art and fashions of Continental Europe. Sir Julius' Mayfair house was entered by a long flight of marble steps from the drive to the front door, a footman stationed on every third step in knee-breeches and with powdered hair which straggled when it poured with rain. Terracotta statues traced to the tomb of Qin Shi Huang Di, first emperor of China stood inside the entrance. It was reported the bedrooms were as palatial as the downstairs salons, in accord with the opulence and vulgarity of our plutocracy, each with Louis X1V suites picked out with an occasional pink electric light. He had assembled a fine Art collection, including one very large oil-colour by Pevensey. So quickly had he amassed the works they were almost certain to include both masterpiece and fake, like the Tsar's famed collection in St Petersburg. The great names of our time wandered into his palatial homes: Prince Francis of Teck, Sir Thomas Lipton, Lady Sarah Wilson. The latter's courage during the siege of Ladysmith had made her a heroine. The men wore rings on plump fingers and smoked cigars; not a few were owners of Derby winners. A photograph in Collier's Magazine by Catherine Cooke showed great beribboned baskets of flowers, like oblations to a goddess, being delivered daily to Sir Julius' home by horse-drawn vans, coachmen and attendants in livery. Orchids from three continents, malmaisons, and lilies for display in tall, cut-glass vases were scattered throughout the vast construction.

67

For his visit to Crick's End, Alfred Weit had chosen a somewhat rusty suit of black-and-white herring-bone tweed, a tie composed of thin pale blue stripes on a black background, and heavily-brogued shoes and cloth spats. In his left hand he held a pair of yellow chamois gloves. My friend Marsh had mentioned seeing Weit with Van Beers, Sir Julius and Siviter at a private club on Whitehall Gardens at the height of the Anglo-Boer hostilities.

Separating from Sir Julius, Weit crossed the room towards a fine, thick piece of bulbous-headed wood known as a Penang lawyer. For his country residence he maintained Salisbury Hall, a little manor-house near St Albans, with a fine garden surrounded by a moat, once Nell Gwynn's petite maison. He had the face of a Disraeli, lividly pale, with finely-arched eyebrows, though the eyes were beryl rather than intensely black. The eyes spoke of repeated contact with Tropical diseases. Ancient fires flickered in his sallow cheeks.

At their entry Siviter rose to his feet quicker even than I, rushing across to greet them, pursued like a hind by the terriers at his legs.

'Ah, and in excellent time,' Siviter cried. 'Mr Holmes, Dr. Watson. Dr. Watson, I see already you recognise our guests. I might say they have helped me greatly with my investments – more than ten thousand pounds in Kaffirs - or I would never have kept my driving habit alive. As Polonius said, 'Those friends thou hast, and their adoption tried, Grapple them unto thy soul with hoops of steel'.'

He gestured from the two men to us.

'Dr. Watson has steered us safely through to three o' clock, though you must be sorry you have missed his gripping talk on coats and hats. As you may be aware, Dr. Watson is Holmes' panegyrist, Ruth to his Naomi, obliging us by inspiring awe of his colleague's deductive powers to steer a determined course between Scylla and Charybdis. He alone has dissuaded us from transmogrifying the Kipling League into a syndicate of crime, I can tell you.'

At Siviter's words of introduction Holmes stepped forward from the fireside towards the new arrivals.

'We are greatly honoured,' Sir Julius Wernher stated, looking intently at Holmes.

'Most certainly,' affirmed Weit. 'We are well acquainted with your reputation and that of your estimable colleague Dr. Watson.' He gave a courteous bow which I, though not Holmes, mirrored to the inch in Japanese style.

Weit's complexion, while darkened by the sun, displayed a disturbing pallor as though a splash of milk had been mixed in. He would not be the first to have his constitution shattered by living a life abroad. Sensing my eye upon him, he turned to engage me directly. 'And Dr. Watson, as a medical man, can you see from my complexion my health is not the best from too long in Tropical climes?'

I answered his query with a sympathetic nod.

He continued, 'Therefore, as my own doctor is at his best compounding for French horses, may I ask you a question, deeply personal to me, though not to you?.'

I begged him to consider my medical knowledge entirely at his

69

service.

'How much longer would you give me to live?'

I reeled from this unexpected question but answered openly. 'You have suffered a brain attack and have recovered. This may give you a tendency to depression. To avoid a recurrence of the stroke, you must restrict your habitation to altitudes no higher than Chamonix. May I recommend regular visits to Töplitz. As for a tonic, I have particular confidence in the unfailing powers of quassia, obtained from the wood and bark of the Surinam Tree, bitter, it is true, but a fine medicinal drug.'

Again Weit pressed. 'And as to length…?'

'At least the span, if you follow my advice.'

Weit looked pleased. 'I shall do so assiduously, Dr. Watson.'

I turned to find myself under Sir Julius' scrutiny. Upon this cue I responded, 'And you, Sir Julius, like several in this room, have suffered from Blackwater Fever. Its fevers and vomiting put great stress on the human body. I perceive a cataract in your right eye. You must temper the glare of the Tropical sun. Whenever you are outdoors in Africa I advise you to wear a broader-brimmed hat than the one you hold in your hand.'

At this, Holmes broke in.

'Sir Julius, in the matter of headwear, I see you follow our King in your choice of hats.'

Sir Julius appeared startled at Holmes' observation. He looked down at the green felt object in his hand. Before he could reply, Holmes continued, 'though I see you have worn it for the first time today.'

Sir Julius had been taking advantage of the change of speakers to take snuff from a tortoise-shell box, brushing away the wandering grains from his coat front with a large, red silk handkerchief. At Holmes' words his head swung round. There was an indefinable, faint expression on his lips. He began, 'Why, Holmes, how in the name of good-fortune...'

'I assure you it is nothing especially clever,' Holmes responded with an airy wave.

'Perhaps so, but do explain,' Sir Julius requested, his eyes fixated on my companion's face.

'Have you not just returned from the outside, where you spent an hour or two?'

'Why, yes.'

'And in the open air, not confined within a carriage,' Holmes continued, gesturing at a mix of clay and chalk on both arrivals' shoes.

'Quite so,' came the reply.

'In rather inclement weather?'

'Indeed.'

'In which you would be expected to wear a hat?'

'As you say.'

'When you entered this room, you had a faint imprint on your forehead from wearing a hat a half-size too small - the mark already fades. Had there not been rain you might not have worn it at all for it must have pressed upon the temple. Certainly you would not continue to wear it by choice. Closer to your home you would have exchanged it at once. I therefore assume you have worn it for the first time to-day.'

Before Sir Julius could respond, Siviter clapped his hands. 'Bravo, Holmes! Now gentlemen, gentlemen, we must proceed!'

At a clap of her Master's hands, a maid-servant entered to remove the household dogs. Pained expressions brimmed in the terriers' eyes as, even while the door was closing on them, they offered their master a last chance to let them stay. Sensing a malleable soul in the parlour, one of them looked across to me with a most comical cock to his head. His engaging behaviour was to no avail. Siviter pressed shut the door firmly behind them.

Holmes returned to the fireplace and took up a stance, feet apart, straddling two Dutch copper milk pails. He began again: 'I shall try to offer by a few examples an explanation of sorts of the deductive skills by which Watson and I make our way in life. Wholly due to the literary skill of my amiable and long-suffering friend who sits before you, I have gained a reputation I sometimes feel approaches myth, but which myth-building I earnestly encourage.'

Polite laughter and 'hear hear' came from the audience.

'I have watched him writing up his notes in a room full of people talking at the top of their voices, or in a train with the hum of conversation around him, or in a cricket pavilion during a match while waiting for the rain to stop. Before Watson's heaven-sent arrival as my faithful friend and biographer I was alone, attempting to create... at least a decade before I had done sufficient work required for fame... the sort of reputation I felt could best be used to serve the purpose of fighting criminality. I was indeed a Dr. Johnson without a Boswell in sight.'

Again the audience responded with a laugh.

'And,' my comrade-in-arms continued, 'his flattering introduction is but a small instance of the friendship for which I am grateful. If he predeceases me, I shall have *Semper Fideles* inscribed upon his tomb. He has a high and noble love of the right and hatred of the wrong. In all his brochures, epitomes, pamphlets, articles, burlesques or other writings, there is scarcely one word of jealousy or coldness to humanity to leave the smallest smudge upon the mind or soul of any reader.'

Rather than rebuking me for my panic-stricken and over-lengthy introduction, Holmes paid me this generous public compliment. It warmed and cheered my heart. Never before had I heard him speak of the softer passions, save with a gibe and a sneer. Leaving aside his many a hurtful and sardonic 'Well done, Watson!' or 'Watson, you coruscate today!', or 'Watson, your reflection, though profound, had already crossed my mind – last week, I believe', heretofore his sincerest praise had been 'Watson, you handled it fairly well'. More often I was the recipient of his particular humour. 'Watson, perhaps it is your eyes we should examine, not your mind? Shall we say a myopia of four dioptres?' though he knew my eyesight to be the equal of the hawk's, able to spot a puff of gun-smoke at half a mile, or I would have taken the long-arm Jezzail's bullet head-on. I much prefer it when he turns his self-indulgence on the official police, as in *The Sign of the Four* – 'When Tobias Gregson, or Lestrade, or Athelney Jones are out of their depths – which, by the way, is their normal state... '

Few are privy to his greatest secret, his great reliance on cranioscopy. He was brought to this science from reading *A Lady's Life in the Rocky Mountains*, by the redoubtable Isabella Bird, and *Wunderbare Geschichte von Bogs, dem Uhrmacher*, by Brentano and Görres (in the original). He swears this practice enabled him to deduce Moriarty stole the Gainsborough Duchess in '76. Tucked behind his make-up table, amid a clutter of waxes, creams and pastes bought from a theatrical costumier, or sometimes hidden in his cupboard of disguises, he keeps a porcelain bust titled 'Phrenology', manufactured by L.N. Fowler, with an accompanying index headed 'Names, Numbers, and Location Of The Organs'. In private, Holmes' talk is redolent with phrenological asides such as 'Ideality' and 'suavity' which I keep from my epitomes for fear his secret would be laid bare or even that he might be open to ridicule. Or, worse, taken for a spiritualist.

Such mumbo-jumbo runs in concert with Holmes' practical bent. Over the years he has obliged me to conduct several sections of cadavers' faces (provided and watched closely by Inspector Gregson) designed to help in his personations. Once he asked whether it could be possible to transplant a cadaver's cold grey face whole, as the criminal's ultimate disguise, or confuse the official police by building in bits of latissimus dorsi.

A further mention my name broke me from my reverie.

'One secret I must reveal about my great friend Watson...' Holmes went on. 'He makes weekly treks to the Stoppard Lending Library and imports to our lodgings books on heraldry, falconry and armour. I am sure he will invest his characters with the chivalry of Sir Lancelot, the heroism and sagacity of King Arthur, the fidelity of Leander.'

Overwhelmed by this public display of friendship, I bowed my head to cover the tears rising to my eyes.

The pro forma applause stopped and I could turn my attention to our small audience. All four stared intently at the speaker as in the company of some strange animal recently imported. There was fascination and interest in their eye, and the touch of caution commensurate with the speed and strike of a predator's claw.

Holmes now launched into his subject.

'In The Book of Life, in an article I myself wrote,' he commenced, 'I avowed that from a twitch of a muscle or a glance of an eye, I could deduce the innermost thoughts of any man, though in reality the science of Deduction and Analysis is one which acquired only by long and patient study. An involved method is not indicative of a profound technique but a confused one. I merely follow *La règle du jeu*. I find the clues I need and assemble them in order. Never do I spring to a conclusion without possession of a sufficiency of necessary and credible facts. Such success as I have had will point to some small knowledge of the sciences. It is not impossible for a man to possess all knowledge likely to be useful to him in his work. Equally essential to my work is knowledge of the history of crime.

Misdeeds bear a family resemblance. If you have the details of a thousand at your finger's end, it is odd if you are unable to unravel the thousand and first. If every official detective shut himself up for three months and read twelve hours a day at the annals of crime, Watson and I would find ourselves redundant.'

Holmes paused, placing his long fingers together.

'Since your invitation arrived this morning I have given thought how best, within the hour allotted...' (Holmes waved the back of his hand across the room as though giving a Papal blessing or removing a fly from before his face) ... to select from a list of our cases which stretch from that glorious residence of the Pope to the moors of Devonshire. The accursed and terrible history of the Baskervilles is a case from which I can extract the very nub of my art. The key lies in gaining a sufficiency of facts. I confess the events which confronted us in Devon still have the ability to keep me awake at night. When we set off by train for Exeter I had speculated on some South African connection where voodoo reigns – as some among you know, Sir Charles restored the depleted Baskerville fortune by South African speculation, but upon my questioning his medical attendant Dr Mortimer, Sir Charles was described as a shrewd, practical and notably unimaginative man. Nevertheless, I have long understood people may hold contradictory thoughts side by side. It was the sworn word of this same old Doctor, regular companion to Sir Charles, that his patient took the legend of *The Hound of the Baskervilles* seriously. I have been much struck by the power of voodoo. I recommend you read Eckermann's *Voodooism And The Negroid Religions*. To return to the fearful fate of Sir Charles Baskerville, what did we have, what facts were made available to us at the start? Every evening before retiring to bed, all seasons alike, Sir Charles went out from the Hall and walked down the famous yew alley, taking the opportunity to smoke a cigar. One night, at twelve o' clock, on the last round of the day, the butler Barrymore found an outside door left ajar. By that hour all but he should have been a-bed. He lit a lantern and went in search of his master. Footmarks were clearly to be seen between the trees of yew alley. Half-way along the walk a gate led out on to the moor. From fresh cigar ash on the mud, it was clear the smoker had whiled away some time at this spot. Not far along the butler found the body of his employer. Now I can proceed apace. There were no marks on the body, no signs of violence. However, the face was so contorted his old friend the doctor at first completely failed to recognise the corpse. This was explained by the coroner for the benefit of the reporter from the *Western Morning News* as not unusual in the case of death from cardiac exhaustion and dyspnoea. The Coroner came to his finding with unusual celerity, much influenced by the post-mortem examination revealing the deceased suffered from long-standing organic disease.'

Holmes looked around the room. 'So there we were. On the face of it, a case hardly opened, then slammed shut by the desire of the coroner to put an end to ugly whispers of voodoo and black magic in this location on a desolate Moor, as sparsely-inhabited as the Norfolk fens. There it could have rested until a further murder might have taken place ... as I am certain was on the cards... except I noticed a most curious remark in the butler's statement. In seeking his master in the night-time mist, he placed the lantern low while following foot-marks along the damp ground of Yew Alley. For the first part, the footmarks were those of a man proceeding at a stroll, but from the moment Sir Charles left the gate, the observant Barrymore said his master seemed to be 'walking upon his toes'. These are hardly blood-curdling words yet on reading this remark, I asked myself, 'Why would a man walk upon his toes? There was no high fence or hedge to look beyond. And why the grotesque distortion of the corpse's face? As so often happens, when evidence pointing unerringly in one direction is viewed from a slightly altered perspective, it may admit of a very different interpretation. The answer was plain. Sir Charles was not tip-toeing at all. This elderly and infirm man had, suddenly, like a rusty spring uncoiling, begun to run, to run desperately, to run for his life, to run until under this great stress his weakened heart burst and he fell dead upon his contorted face. The direction in which he ran was especially curious. It was away from the Hall, not toward it. What was it which terrified him enough to make him flee - so utterly he lost all his wits? From there we were able to contrive a trap which brought before our pistols the fearsome, diabolical hound given a hellish appearance by means of phosphorus which had frightened Sir Charles to death.'

Sir Julius looked at Holmes quizzically. 'Holmes, if you will excuse my temerity, you were handed the principal clue on a plate – an account of boot-marks of a man which indicated he was running for his life.'

'Gentlemen, then let me inflict upon you one more case, *The Adventure of Silver Blaze*. It concerned the disappearance of a horse owned by a Colonel Ross, recognisable by the white forehead and mottled off-foreleg. One night this valuable animal was led away in secret from its stable. A stranger named Fitzroy Simpson was known to be in the vicinity seeking betting information. He was arrested and accused. When this account was brought to me in Baker Street I cautioned Watson to keep an open mind on the grounds of my dictum the obvious culprit is most likely to be innocent. Nevertheless, we arrived at the training stables carrying with us the expectation the culprit must indeed have come from the outside, as logic and experience would dictate. Theft of important horses in not unknown in that semi-criminal world but why would an owner or member of the stable staff steal the very thing on which their income depended? However, two clues came to my attention, both considered too small to be of interest to the official police. First let me tell you the lads taking the watch over Silver Blaze were brought their meals in the stable and what do you suppose they ate that night?'

No-one ventured a guess.

'Curry,' Holmes announced.

Siviter spoke up with a surprised look. 'Holmes, I must admit I had no idea this dish has reached as far as Devon, but why would that gain your attention?'

'Curry was the first link in my chain of reasoning. It was clear the stable lads heard nothing in the night, indicating they were in a deep and unnatural sleep. Powdered opium is by no means tasteless. The flavour is not disagreeable but it is perceptible. Were it mixed with any ordinary dish the eater would undoubtedly detect it and would probably eat no more. A mutton curry was exactly the medium which would disguise this taste. But by no possible supposition could the stranger Fitzroy Simpson have caused curry to be served in the trainer's family that night. Once I discerned it required knowledge improbably available to a stranger, it immediately circumscribed the culprit to within the stables. One deduction often sparks another. I spotted the further clue which fully amplified my suspicion and enabled me to point to the individual who perpetrated this crime. And there we had it.'

'My dear Holmes,' Weit's high laugh broke in. 'Surely you are not

79

to leave us twisting in the wind! What, pray, was the second clue?'

'Simply the dog that didn't bark loudly in the night.'

Holmes reached into a pocket for the small brier-root pipe. He looked down into the bowl tar-coated from habitual use of the strongest black tobacco.

'Inspector Gregory asked me, is there any point to which I wished to bring his attention? I replied, 'To the curious incident of the dog in the night-time.' The Inspector responded, 'Holmes, the dog did nothing in the night-time'. That was the curious incident, I told him. A farm dog was kept in the very stables from which this horse had been led away, and yet, though someone had fetched out the horse, the dog had not barked sufficiently to arouse the farm. It was clear the midnight visitor was someone the dog knew well. From there it was quite simple, confirmed when later we were to find the culprit, the trainer John Straker, dead, killed by the hoofs of the horse he was trying to nobble at the instance of a criminal betting syndicate. As my panegyrist Watson says, my observation, referred to as 'the dog that didn't bark in the night', has become as well known as the maxim I propounded in *The Adventure of the Beryl Coronet*, that when you have excluded the impossible, whatever remains, however improbable, must be the truth. I should tell you the stable dog benefited greatly from my deduction. So angry had her owner been at her apparent dereliction of duty that had I not intervened with my explanation he would shortly have put this blameless dog down.'

He studied the faces before him thoughtfully. 'I must assume you have read the adventures of Marco Polo?'

The five of us nodded emphatically.

'Of course,' Holmes continued. 'Who among us with a disposition for adventure has not? What do we know about him? Born in Venice some six centuries ago. Went with his father on a Papal mission to the territories of the Grand Khan, to return to Venice after an absence of twenty-four years. Imprisoned by the Genoese. At a loss for money he wrote his fanciful tales.' Holmes paused. 'You are convinced from his descriptions he did indeed reach the Middle Kingdom?'

Siviter's finger darted upward. 'I might say I have some knowledge of the East,' he intervened. 'I wager you fifty guineas if you convince us otherwise!'

'Then,' Holmes continued, 'let me ask you, when I say 'China', what springs to mind?'

'The Great Wall,' Siviter responded.

'Good. The Great Wall would undoubtedly be visible from the moon. What else?'

'Chop sticks,' added Weit.

'Excellent. No Chinaman eats without them.'

'The barbarous practice of binding female children's feet,' I chimed in.

'A very barbarous and wide-spread practice indeed,' Holmes nodded. 'And like the Great Wall and the use of chop-sticks no doubt highly visible to anyone visiting the Middle Kingdom?'

'Indisputably,' we all agreed.

Holmes paused for dramatic effect.

'Then is it not curious that in all his writings about his many years in that faraway and magic place, Marco Polo never mentions chopsticks? Nor does he mention the Great Wall, nor refer to the widespread and barbarous practice of the binding of female babies' feet. Why not? Is it likely when you seek to attain the greatest sale of your pamphlet, where you must entice by the rare and exotic nature of your experience, you would omit such extraordinary things? If I were to publish an account of my two years in Tibet, would it ring true if I left out the giant black mastiffs of the Grand Lama? Or from my visit to Khartoum and Omdurman fail to mention the Khalifa - or the Suez Canal?'

Siviter's mouth fell open in delight. 'Why, Holmes,' he burst out. 'You have convinced me. If what you say is true, he could not possibly have been in China.'

Holmes gave a final, slightly ironic bow.

The small assembly stood up and clapped. Our host was smiling and nodding. I too clapped.
Privately I was chagrined by Siviter's reference to me (picked up by Holmes) as panegyrist - a jibe which seemed designed to denigrate my profession.
As to his use of Ruth to Naomi!

CHAPTER SEVEN
We Meet Pevensey

We had an hour before the Lanchester would transport us to Etchingham for the early-evening train to Charing Cross where a brougham would be waiting to transport us to Baker Street courtesy of our host. The artist Pevensey had not been mentioned again. Ever-keen to add to my knowledge of pictorial art I asked whether our host would permit us to view the commission. After a moment of calculation, Siviter accepted this request. Holmes, the terriers and retrievers and I followed in his wake and once more crossed the chamomile lawn and the Wild Garden to Park Mill.

Leaving the excitable dogs outside, Siviter led us inside. Along the inside walls Watteau garden statues of shepherdesses and Boucher nymphs leaned against each other, jumbled up with stone images of Pan and Adonis. Siviter had collected up and removed the figures from the gardens upon purchasing the estate, together with marble figures of Cupid and Psyche. The centre of the floor was crammed with rococo chairs, fountains, fishing tackle, a chaise-longue, a cornucopia of Ceres, a carriage umbrella, and bicycles for the housemaids and footmen. It was as though at midnight of a full moon, every object would come alive and prance to the music of a hundred Pans.

We ascended the thinnest of stairs and emerged into the mill-attic through an open trap-door. The room was heavily shadowed in the corners but in the late-afternoon sun the centre of the attic was well-lit, a shaft blazing through a small, south-westerly-facing window. At one time the epicentre of the Mill's activity, the arrival of the turbine-generator left the room empty and aloof from every-day work. Just visible, scattered around the uneven floor, were the accoutrements of the artist – stool, sketch-pad, palette and palette

83

knife, a Victorian parasol, a half-empty bottle of turpentine or linseed oil, a scattering of cotton rags and jars and discarded tubes of paint. In the middle stood an easel supporting a canvas depicting a cart and horses in a wagon pond attended by the figure of a wagoner. A further human figure in a wide-brimmed purple-crimson hat surveyed them from the near verge. An immaculate, dainty man stood at the easel's side. He wore the darkest of blue artist's smocks. We were introduced to Pevensey. Away from the easel, almost hidden in the shadows, a second canvas of rather smaller dimensions lay against a wall as though discarded.

Unlike a predecessor at the Academy, Sir Joshua Reynolds, Pevensey seemed of a nervous and excitable temperament, flustered by our intrusion. A half-extended hand, broad and fat like the flipper of a seal, grasped mine coldly. He was not a man whose personality invited confidences from strangers. In my anticipation I had expected him to look the image of Auguste Bréal, bright eyes, pointed black beard, beret, and bubbling with vivacity. Nevertheless, he was a painter of very considerable fame. Great-grandson of a sculptor, son of a successful architect, he had studied in Paris under a disciple of Ingres. His early reputation was founded on large, detailed, academic, rather oriental biblical scenes which, though quietly mocked behind his back in England, had made him a great deal of money in America. Of extreme ambition, it was said Pevensey had advanced well beyond his artistic talents to the point he was parodied as 'the industrious apprentice' in a novel published in 1894, whose protagonist hoped to become 'the duly knighted or baroneted Lord Mayor of all the plastic arts'. Others spoke of him as forever 'busy with his labours among Princes ignorant of art'. With a certitude of opinion, he had endeavoured to become adviser to an assortment of the nobility, among which he included the Earl of Carlisle. The baronetcy duly arrived in 1902. Then to wide surprise he harvested the Presidency of the Royal Academy.

Pulling his hand from my would-be warm embrace, he turned away. Ignoring Holmes, he exclaimed to Siviter, 'It is finished,' adding aspersively, as though blaming his patron, 'I have run out of ordinary linseed oil.'

A silence followed this remark. I broke in awkwardly. 'And how have you enjoyed this extraordinary studio?'

In the compressed space of the mill-attic I retreated to put my back against the wall, head forced forward by the sharp slope of the ceiling. Holmes, less diffident, crossed to the easel and gave the canvas a close inspection.

As though anticipating my attempt at polite chatter, Pevensey replied with a quote from a famed landscape painter. 'The sound of water escaping from mill dams, willows, old rotten planks, slimy posts and brickwork, I love such things.'

To my relief Holmes took on the burden of engaging the artist in conversation, expressing deep interest in his craft. Although it was a social occasion, Holmes reminded me of a pure-blooded, well-trained foxhound dashing back and forward through a covert until it comes across the lost scent.

'Have you painted mostly here indoors from sketches, or out-of-doors?' Holmes asked.

Pevensey replied firmly, 'Almost solely at Scotney Castle. Working out of doors in oils entails cumbersome equipment but assures vitality.'

Feeling a coldness in the air, I was ready to bid the artist a quick farewell and God-speed but Holmes appeared less willing to let him go. I glanced across at our host. For all Siviter's customary cordiality, a touch of reserve had settled on him in Pevensey's presence, as though some friction had broken into their relationship. For an instant, he seemed withdrawn.

'This is a privilege,' Holmes went on, extending his rare attempt at light conversation. 'I have always wondered how the artist commences. Tell me, is it true you first construct a grid?'

'Yes - most artists do,' Pevensey replied. His answer seemed defensive, as though Holmes was challenging him by such a question.

'And then?' Holmes pursued. 'You sketch out the major elements – the cottage and that wagon?'

'Yes. I block in the main features.'

'In broad masses of strong, bright colours, I see,' Holmes pursued.

The length of my comrade's enquiry was causing me considerable surprise, given its frosty reception. Under the circumstances, his interest seemed to me to border upon affectation.

'That is correct,' came Pevensey's reply.

'Please continue,' Holmes requested. 'This is most interesting.'

With seeming reluctance, Pevensey added, 'When that is done I turn to detailed treatment of the landscape, with firm contours and naturalistic colouring.'

'And then, you return to …?'

'…the centrepiece of the commission. The foreground must be lively, sensitive to many reflections. It is above all there that the viewer's attention must be centred.'

'As with that figure?' Holmes pursued, pointing at the figure of the man standing at the wagon pond edge.

'Precisely as with that figure.'

With some puzzlement I observed Holmes' quick glancing eyes and his sharp scrutiny of Pevensey's face, habitually a sign of more than ordinary interest.

'And you completed this when?' Holmes asked, eyebrows raised disarmingly.

'Not long past three this afternoon, I believe,' Siviter broke in unexpectedly, as though Holmes' polite and casual query required an exactness of time. 'As, no doubt, Holmes, you will deduce from the shadow cast by that figure!'

A silence followed. Siviter spoke again, as though Pevensey was not there.

'Pevensey was at Scotney Castle from lunch until after three o' clock today,' he repeated, 'when we sent Dudeney to retrieve him for tea.' With a short laugh he added, 'I have always sensed he feels safer in a studio.'

Holmes absorbed this without comment. He pointed again at the painting.

'And the sheen on that figure and his flamboyant hat? Was that achieved by scumbling?'

'No, not by scumbling,' Pevensey responded abruptly, as though affronted.

'Then?' Holmes pursued in the sweetest of voices.

Pevensey appeared reluctant to reply. Finally, under the sustained press of Holmes' questing look, he responded 'With boiled linseed oil'

'Hum,' said Holmes, 'That explains it. Scumbling is best for half-lights and half-distance.'

My companion gave a self-deprecating smile. 'I confess that while techniques with brush and paint are of great interest, it is the chemistry that excites me most. Why did you use boiled linseed for that figure, may I ask?'

'Why, that's simple, Holmes,' Siviter interrupted. 'Pevensey has already informed us he ran out of his supply of linseed oil. Presumably he called for the next best thing, the boiled linseed we use around the property as a wood-finish.'

A fit of disquiet appeared to overtake the President of the Royal Academy. The atmosphere had grown more unwelcoming. We – or

Holmes' questions - were, I presumed, an intrusion on so self-regarding a painter. The artist turned half-left to face the darkling figure of Siviter.

'Siviter, you will excuse me, I must prepare to return to London.'

Turning back to us, Pevensey repeated, 'You will excuse me. I need to gather up my paints and brushes to go to London or I would offer you further instruction in my art. Perhaps,' he added, with a cold smile, 'in return for some slight instruction in yours. Siviter, I believe I have completed your commission. The canvases are yours. Holmes, Dr. Watson, I anticipate boarding an earlier train than yours lest weighted down with my paints and brushes I run into throngs of hop-pickers and counter-jumpers.'

Pevensey's manner was now cold in the extreme. I smiled politely, more at his excess of snobbery than from a warmth I did not feel, for he would in any case, like us, be in a Pullman car where hop-pickers and 'counter-jumpers' with their trinkets and appurtenances would fear to tread.

Disregarding both my and Holmes' out-thrust hands he turned away. At the opening to the narrow staircase, he threw a final glance at Holmes. Had the thought not been absurd, I would have wagered he was in the grip of fear, certainly someone on extreme guard. He switched his look to Siviter, giving a peculiar nod. With a quick turn and again maintaining a grim stare in Holmes' direction, he descended the steep stairs, his head disappearing downwards like a hanging in slow motion. Holmes looked at me with a glance of comic resignation and gave a shrug.

On Pevensey's departure, Holmes and I left our positions and moved across to look at the second canvas. It portrayed a ruined castle surrounded by a moat, the water as blue as the Blauer See.

'Where is this?' Holmes asked our host. 'I don't recall seeing…'

'No, not here at Crick's End. That is also at Scotney Castle, the ruin itself, a slight departure from the wagon pond. It seemed convenient while we had Pevensey with us to commission him to make it a pair.'

Siviter turned away. His pointing finger redirected our attention to the tiny aperture through which the sunlight flooded.

'Duck Window,' he remarked immediately. 'Until to-day's uncertain weather Pevensey has been hanging his canvases out of this window to dry in the evening sun.'

He pointed through it. 'Look at the view! For two centuries along that river you would hear the ironmasters' hammer resounding loud and clear.'

Siviter stepped back, beckoning us to look out. Over our shoulders I heard him say, 'Down there is Rye Green where Jack Cade, leader of the Kentish Rebellion, was killed in 1450.'

The mill-pond lay immediately below us. The water level was too low to register on the marker at the sluice. Sticks and plant material jutted from the mud, darkening the little water that remained.
With Pevensey no longer in the attic, Holmes stepped within arms-length of the easel. He withdrew a large round magnifying glass from his voluminous coat and placed it over the painting. As if offering a compliment to the departed painter, Holmes remarked, 'One brush is made from the ashy-grey upper half of the Ratel, a

carnivorous animal of the Badger family, found only in Southern India and Southern Africa, though overall I see he is a sable man.'

I caught Siviter's rueful eye in the gloom and gave him a barely-suppressed smile in return.   'Well done, Holmes,' I applauded loyally. 'You surprise me still. I had no idea of your expertise in artists' brushes.'
Holmes scowled. 'My dear Watson, In addition to the fact my grandmother was sister to the French painter Horace Vernet, I took instruction from Roy Perry, Head of Conservation at the Tate.'

He stepped back to allow me to take a closer look.

'I hesitated to mention this before,' I remarked, looking across at our host, 'but this painting is remarkably like...'

'The Hay-Wain by the great John Constable, yes,' Siviter interjected. 'Who else portrays L'Angleterre Profonde so well, though,' he added self-deprecatingly,' hardly one of his six-footers. The owners of the Scotney Estate are to be the recipients of this work. Lady Fusey adores Constable's paintings – she was born and bred up by the Stour. She had her labourers dig an exact copy of the wagon pond ready for Pevensey's arrival,' adding, almost regretfully, 'she eschews all modern schools of '–ism' – Impressionism and Post-Impressionism, or I might have commissioned Cezanne or Vlaminck.

'But in the Constable,' I persisted, pointing, 'this figure....'

'...wasn't there...' Siviter responded. 'Quite right. Instead there was a dog - well remembered. Like the palimpsest there is a dog there still, but I'm afraid I obliged Pevensey to over-paint it.' With a laugh he confided, 'To tell you the truth, I don't feel he is at his best

91

painting our canine friends.'

With the exit of Pevensey our host had returned to his former convivial self. He gave us a disarming smile. 'Gentlemen, though I should not hurry you, an informal meal is being served before your departure.'

Once outside we walked in crocodile formation across the small bridge and reassembled in the Wild Garden. Siviter took up again, 'I have ordered the cook to prepare a special treat. Sir Julius' mother, now some time dead, was a member of the Sephardim, brought up in Constantinople. She taught her son a special dish called Imam bayildi which I believe translates as 'The Imam swooned', presumably with pleasure rather than indigestion. Sir Julius has made me learn the ingredients by heart.'

Cued by his words, I asked, 'And what would they be?'

Crossing back to the sundial and terraced lawns Siviter recited, 'Take an aubergine and split its belly, stuff it with chopped and sautéed tomato, onion and aubergine, seasoned with bay leaves, marjoram, garlic, basil, cumin, and cardamom, add nuts, lemon juice, fruit, wine, rice and cheese, and bake in olive oil in an oven for at least one hour ...'

Companionably he fell back to walk by my side. 'And Dr. Watson, time permitting, in celebration of your years on the North-West Frontier you and I shall retire to the gun-room and wash it down with two bottles each of Burton India Pale Ale - produced at...?'

'Meux's Brewery?'

'Where else!'

Though still remaining in ear-shot, Holmes fell away from the discussion at the mention of Imam Bayildi. He pays slight attention to nourishment with the exception of woodcock and Mrs. Hudson's eggs for which his appetite is voracious. He prefers food which can be eaten at speed, cold beef or simple mutton, tins of corned beef or pilchards in tomato sauce, and a glass of beer. Only once to my recollection did he depart from this frugality, at the time of the extraordinary conclusion to our adventure chronicled as *The Sign of Four*.

As we arrived for our Ottoman culinary adventure Sir Julius remarked that in his opinion there were three great cuisines in the world, of which Turkish was one. In jest, I called to my comrade-in-arms, 'Holmes, you may not be interested in the taste of Imam bayildi but, Gad, the chemistry!'

CHAPTER EIGHT
The Discovery Of A Corpse At Scotney Castle

Standing at the towering cast-iron gates ('from the same forge that manufactured the railings of St. Paul's Cathedral') Siviter saw us off from Crick's End with a cheery wave. The olfactory delight of the Imam Bayildi still swirled in my nostrils.

Once more Holmes and I were enveloped in soft leather in the Lanchester, Dudeney at the wheel wrapped in his pilot's helmet. Invited into the vehicle for the short outing, Siviter's Aberdeen terriers and the curly-coated retrievers yap-yapped and wriggled and slithered around us. A half-dozen tails wagged like furies in our faces, the owners excited beyond measure in anticipation of scents wafting to their small damp snouts at forty miles an hour.

I looked up to see a hand waving fleetingly from a window. It was the Peasant Madonna of the violet eyes who first greeted us at the porch. Would she eventually marry a young herdsman on the Estate? Would she have to compete with the poultry maid? In a fit of amour fou would she let one of the eminent men who passed through the bedrooms at Crick's End take advantage of her lowly status?

Soon we were back at Etchingham. Just past the great church and fifty yards short of the Ambrose Tavern, we turned left into the small station yard. We said our thanks and goodbyes to Dudeney. I searched my pockets for our return tickets to Charing Cross and a pencil stub. I had earlier spotted an advertisement for Abdulla's cigarettes on a station wall with a piece of doggerel too amusing to let go without noting it down to share with Eddie Marsh at a future date. Our tickets located, I opened my notebook and transcribed the ditty titled 'Desert Drama, the Lady Sheik'.

'When Percy won Third Beauty Prize for figure, face and hair,
He little recked his "Greek god" chin would prove a fatal snare;
He caravanned o'er Desert Sands, a traveller in Oil,
Till Fatma deftly kidnapped him – a coy reluctant spoil.

In vain, the melting Lady Sheik heaped treasures at his feet,
And fattened him on golden dates, and sherbet sickly sweet;
'Twas not until Abdulla's Best had proved too fierce a bribe,
He scuppered his career in Oil to rule her Heart and Tribe.'

As I transcribed the last stanza, a most unexpected intrusion burst upon this mild occupation. The piping voice of the young news-vendor caught my attention. He stood small and keen in front of Holmes, urging him to purchase a copy of the *Evening London Standard*, freshly-delivered off the London-to-Hastings train.

'Late Extra! Dead Body at Scotney Castle,' the boy sang, his face turned upwards, his apron displaying the bold headline black upon yellow on a poster.

'Heavens, Holmes,' I called over, amused. 'Fame indeed. Scotney Castle has found its way into the *Standard*!'

On outward journeys by train or diligence Holmes cat-napped like Napoleon force-marching to Paris from Elba, but on the return he often fell into a much deeper sleep. I anticipated my companion would wave aside the small beseeching vendor. Had he declined to make the purchase, I would have followed suit while offering the boy a ha'penny in compensation. Thereby we may never been hurled into the astonishing matter of the dead Boer at Scotney Castle.

Rather than waving the boy away, my companion stared down at him and demanded 'What did you say?', one hand going swiftly to a pocket. 'Dead Body at Scotney Castle,' the news-vendor sang out once more, pushing a copy into my companion's outstretched hand and taking three-halfpence in return. Holmes unfolded the newspaper and turned to an inside page as directed. He read for a moment and glanced up.

'Watson, listen to this. 'LATE EXTRA. From our local Correspondent by wire'.'

The report commenced with the curiously garbled sub-heading 'Well-Dressed Unclad Body Discovered At Lamberhurst' and continued, 'To-day, at around 4pm near the village of Lamberhurst, on the Kent and Sussex border in the Valley of the River Bewl, in the undertaking of his rounds, James Webster, woodman on the Scotney Castle Estate, came across the unclad body of a man lying mostly submerged in the wagon pond, off the old Carriage Drive at Kilndown Wood, believed drowned. Age is estimated around 50. Gentlemen's clothes of a good quality and condition lay at a short departure from the verge, neatly piled, and topped by a crimson hat like a bowler out of a Mexican sombrero, bearing a hatband made from the skin of a yellow and brown spiny snake. Death is estimated to have taken place within the previous hour as the arms and legs were still supple. It was noticeable the dead man's chest was unusually seared by the sun in a triangle to a point some five inches above the navel, with similar ruddiness of arms right to the armpit, and the legs from above the calf to just below the knee. Exact details are few but no traces of struggle or nearby disturbance have been reported. A man in this garb was seen standing at the edge of the wagon pond in the middle of the afternoon, around three o' clock, by Lord Edward Fusey, owner of the Estate, whose house overlooks the valley from the top of a nearby hill. While suicide is a possibility, the empty pockets of the clothing and weathered condition of the skin incline the Lamberhurst constable to agree with Lord Fusey's suggestion the body is most likely that of a passing tramp, who, having stolen a gentleman's clothing, felt obliged to bathe in the wagon pond and consequently drowned.''

Turning to me with an air of excitement, Holmes demanded, 'Well, Watson, what do you make of it?'

'What do you make of it, Holmes?' I parried, staring at him. He was on a hot scent but as yet I could not in the least imagine in what direction his inferences were leading him. Without responding to my own query, he returned to the *Standard* and continued, ''A pair of shiny dark glasses was discovered between finger and thumb, but identifying papers or other memoranda are lacking. The old smugglers' track is a favoured route of indigents and vagabonds overnighting in the castle ruins on their way to London. No further action is expected'.'

Holmes lowered the newspaper.

''The body is most likely that of a passing tramp?'' he repeated. 'How could this be?'

He raised the paper again and continued reading out loud. 'The probability remains that the deceased has been the victim of an unfortunate accident which should at the very least have the effect of calling the attention of the Estate owner to the parlous condition of the wagon pond verges'.

Once more Holmes lowered the newspaper, frowning. 'Again,

Watson, I ask, what do you make of it?'

'Apart from the sensationalistic prose, Holmes, what should I make of it?' I replied evasively. 'Any self-inflicted death or accident is a sad event.'

He cocked his head. ''Self-inflicted death or accident' you have already decided?' he demanded. 'Is it not obvious to you this matter strikes rather deeper than you think?'

He looked back at the report, his brow still furrowed. He muttered, 'It makes no sense.'

Even now I find it hard to divine what confluence of suspicions in Holmes' keen and penetrating mind drew him so quickly to conclude something sinister lay behind the unfortunate victim's death. It was as though lead had turned to mercury. His eyes positively gleamed with excitement against the startlingly white skin of his face.

'Watson, my instinct tells me there is something here afoot. Surely you agree there are points about the case which promise to make it unique?'

'I am sure I do agree, Holmes,' I responded. 'But we have a train to catch.'

'What was it Siviter told us about the pond at Scotney Castle?'

'That it replicates the wagon pond in Constable's painting?'

'That is its provenance - but what of its condition?'

'As it was dug only the other day to anticipate Pevensey's arrival, I would deduce...'

'Yes, Watson, well done – the *Standard* reports a dangerous condition of the verge. This clearly cannot be. In conversation with this special correspondent why has Lord Fusey failed to exculpate himself by bringing this fact to the man's attention – why so?'

He paused, still maintaining a perplexed expression. Then, 'It seems to have been a very deliberate affair... yet if this is foul play... murdered men are seldom stripped of clothing.'

I was thunderstruck at so sudden a reference to murder. 'Holmes,' I protested, 'you have just read out the constable's conclusion - an indigent may have wanted to bathe...'

Holmes turned to me sharply. 'You look a little bewildered, Watson. I tell you, there is the dark shadow of an unusual crime behind this occurrence which a singular chance has placed in our hands.'

'Holmes!' I returned, unable to hide my incredulity. 'I am inclined to think...'

'I should do so,' my companion retorted, quickly vexed when challenged in an assumption. 'Do you deny the report has given us a set of very suggestive facts?'

I fell back into an unsettled silence. I had had no time to give any thought at all to such facts as we were offered. Were we so quickly deep in some weighty quest, I wondered?

Again Holmes plunged back into the *Standard*.

'Watson, you do not need a double lens or a measuring-tape to examine such simple facts. They are not laid down in faded pencil-writing in this report. There are several most instructive points about it, not less than seven, whose value we can only test by further inquiry. Even four such points should have you reaching for your service revolver.'

I was keen to reach our lodgings as soon as possible. 'Holmes, may I humbly ask for even one of these instructive points which indicates anything other than the suicide or accidental death of an itinerant wanderer, other than a mistaken description of the verges?' I requested, allowing a hint of sarcasm to creep into my tone.

'Answer this, my dear friend, are knee-breeches the summer uniform of England's tramps?'

'Why, no, Holmes,' I responded. 'I would hardly think…'

'Why else would it say his legs were 'unusually seared by the sun… from above the calf to just below the knee'? Surely vagrants are more accustomed to corduroy trousers tied beneath the knee with string!'

There had been more than one occasion where Holmes just as swiftly concluded we were in the starter's blocks of a desperate crime, only to withdraw his claim on a further moment's cogitation. I felt the lack of the service revolver Holmes had mentioned. Our considerable speaker's fee in large bank-notes was tucked in my coat. I would not breathe freely until I climbed our stairs and locked the money in the bureau of my dressing-room.

I glanced up at the station clock. Perhaps upon a moment's

100

consideration Holmes would discover an irredeemable flaw, one which would put the kibosh on his quick conclusion. I hoped we would soon be aboard the evening train whirling back to Charing Cross and thence by brougham to Baker Street and home.

My companion's face stayed buried in the Standard.

''A pair of shiny dark glasses was discovered between finger and thumb, but identifying papers or other memoranda are lacking what do you make of that?' He looked up sharply.   'This further point cannot have escaped your Machiavellian intellect? Watson, there is a thread here which we have not yet grasped, and which might lead us through the tangle.'

I replied brusquely, resentful at the gibe.   'I cannot answer about identifying papers, but perhaps the dark glasses were in a pocket when the clothing was stolen?'

I turned from him, attempting his trick of feigning lack of interest, to no effect.

'If a tramp came across a pair of dark glasses in stolen clothing why would he retain them?' Holmes demanded. 'How likely are they to have been his own purchase or a gift? If it were theft, rightful ownership could speedily be established by the confluence of costly clothing in good condition and these dark glasses. The authorities would lay an unanswerable charge at his door and throw him in prison.'

'Holmes,' I broke in anxiously, 'the train will be here at any moment.'

Ignoring my intervention, Holmes shot a further pensive look at the article. 'What then of the pockets, Watson? The fact they are completely empty?'

'Holmes,' I said impatiently. 'Should they contain a milliner's account for thirty-seven pounds fifteen made out by Madame Lesurier of Bond Street? Or the stolen plans of a revolutionary submarine? What of the pockets, Holmes, beyond the fact they are empty?'

'It is their very emptiness which should engage you. Even vagabonds would transfer two inches of tallow candle and wax-vestas when they shed their former skin.'

He threw me a determined look. 'No! I declare the wit of the fox is here. This is the most finished piece of blackguardism since the days of the Borgias. All the indications seem to me to point in that direction. I repeat, there is the smack of a great crime in the air.'

Dismayed by his hyperbole I stood forlorn at his side at a country railway station. Little did I imagine how Holmes' deduction would eventually be realised, how strange and sinister this new development would be.

''Skin of a yellow and brown spiny snake...'?' he continued, with an incredulous look. 'Watson, how many spiny snakes have you encountered in your travels? Did you trample on them in the Himalayas or the Khyber Pass? Did these same snakes sneak inside your blanket by night and scratch you? I warrant not! Sea urchins, sand dollars, basket stars which make up the Echinodermata have such spines, not snakes, but such creatures are scarcely of utility for a hatband, though...'

After a short reflective pause he added, '… not from Asia or South America but South Africa.'

He swung round to face me. He spoke in a sharp tone. 'Watson, we must waste no time. There are withers to be wrung! An unclad corpse and a pile of clothing topped by this hat is no accident. It is an object-letter as cunning and deadly as any we have had to decipher. I say that in the history of crime, even if we include the Brixton Mystery, there has seldom been a tragedy which presented stranger features.'

Before I could remonstrate further, with a quick gesture he beckoned the newspaper boy, still close, to approach him. 'Is there a jitney or post-chaise in the village?' he asked.

Keen to make a penny, the boy replied, pointing to the yard at a vehicle even smaller than a Governess cart, 'Sir, I have a dog-cart for my papers.'

'So you do,' Holmes responded quite amiably. 'No doubt you are a veritable jehu, but I do not wish for a mettlesome dog. We would rather a four-in-hand.'

'There's a sociable on hire driven by a pair of spanking greys. It stands in the village at the ready.' The boy added, 'though quite a departure from here.'

'See this,' said Holmes, holding up a sixpence. 'Put quicksilver in your shoes and bring us the swift four-seater.'

'And if he's here within the quarter-hour?' the boy responded.

103

'Then ninepence,' Holmes responded with a short laugh.

The young vendor threw the last of his newspapers into the clap-trap conveyance and set off, the dog galloping like a small race-horse sensing the tape not far ahead. Standing at my comrade's side, puzzled and unnerved, it seemed to me Holmes' eyes had scarcely glanced over the paragraphs before we were to spring into a cab and rattle off.

I persisted. 'Look here, Holmes, this is all surmise. You confessed at the time we were engaged in solving the disappearance of Silver Blaze that the provisional theories you formed from the newspaper reports were entirely erroneous. You cannot cry murder at every turn. Why, the constable stated...'

Holmes' quelling expression caused me to falter and fall silent.

'Watson, do you have a more favourable hypothesis? The constable, you say? Was it not a constable in 'the Hound' who sent the good doctor and all others down a blind by his interpretation? Was it not the same Peeler who concluded the deceased tip-toed in the dark rather than running for his very life? 'The constable stated'! Is it not obvious we have a Peeler whose head is more for ornament than utility, a man more accustomed to using his muscles rather than his wits? He will state whatever is put into his brain by the Lord of the Manor, Fusey. I surmise, you say, but at least it covers all the facts. When new facts come to our knowledge which cannot be covered by my assumption, it will be time enough to reconsider. No, Watson, and again no! I say this is at the very least a suspicious death.'

'A suspicious death?' I responded more boldly, a hint of sarcasm returning to my voice. 'And at the hand of anyone in particular, have you already decided?'

Holmes flared at my dogged manner. His pale cheeks began to flush. 'You must take this seriously, Doctor! I am not about to make a joke! There is much that is still obscure though I have quite made up my mind on the principal facts. I say there is a great driving-power at the back of this business.'

For a further moment he stared at me angrily.

'As you ask, Watson, I shall tell you. I believe this man's death points unerringly at the very denizens we have just been instructing in our work.'

'The Kipling League?' I stammered in disbelief, horrified at this unexpected accusation.

'The very ones,' Holmes affirmed. He smiled grimly at my dismay. 'Watson, you must join me in a double-game against a most powerful criminal syndicate.'

'Holmes,' I gasped, 'by habit I trust to your judgment though less often to your discretion. If murder this is – and it is still only a matter of the most extraordinary speculation - it is exceptionally outré and sensational. I have heard your reasons and while I am intrigued, I am quite unconvinced by your deductions. The most repellent man of our acquaintance, even a Professor Moriarty, should not be killed and left naked in a wagon pond. If murder it is, the most grotesque of human minds must lie behind it. Yet you lay the authorship of such a crime upon the Kipling League whose members are pre-eminent in the whole of London!'

I stared at him with grave concern. 'Holmes, have you become unbalanced? The members of the Kipling League are not wax figures of Voltaire at Madame Tussaud's. Has too much Medlar jelly left you demented? Am I mistaken in believing you are the author of a famous saying taught to young detectives at Scotland Yard, that the temptation to form premature theories upon insufficient data is the bane of our profession?'

Even as I uttered these heated words, I knew all argument was folly. The subtle eagerness, the suggestion of tension in the brightened eyes, the briskness of his manner, all showed me the game was in play. My companion's face wore the grim and determined look of Nelson's admirals at Trafalgar on sight of No. 16 battle signal.

Holmes responded, 'Good old Watson! Ever obsequious to the rich and powerful! As you say, it is grotesque, and, yes, they are indeed pre-eminent names, yet I say there is more to this League than a Lodge of the Ancient Order of Freemen. They play a deep game! The very second I adopted the hypothesis everything seems to fit – or at least nothing so far appears to traverse it - otherwise it is as random a death as ever was reported.'

I answered with considerable understatement, 'Holmes, they will be much surprised at our return.'

'I had not realised the faculty of deduction to be so contagious, Watson,' he returned bitingly. Heedless of my concern, he went on, 'It is certain those who killed him have had the co-operation of Lord Fusey. His sighting of a tramp – in mid-afternoon, so he states – has already placed a certainty in the local bobby's mind both to the calling of the soul which once inhabited this corpse and the hour of

106

death - and will no doubt in the coroner's too. At most he will record an open verdict.'

He stared back at the *Standard*. 'Yet,' he went on in a lower voice, 'why invent a tramp?'

He held the newspaper towards me. 'Watson, a further point for you to examine - this hat. What do you make of 'a bowler out of a Mexican sombrero'?'

'I make nothing of it, Holmes.'

'What if we suggest 'bowler' means a high crown, and the *Standard's* use of 'sombrero' denotes the width of brim, what then?'

'Why, it would be a hat crafted for the Tropics!'

'Bravo, my friend. That is the deduction I would draw, which I am about to augment and solidify.'

Dread seeped through my every vein. I was being swept along like a coracle on a choppy sea. I knew from bitter experience my courage to protest against so forceful a person as my comrade-in-arms would be found deeply wanting.

Holmes pushed the newspaper to me, turning away to peer across the station yard for a sight of the sociable, the vehicle favoured by Edward as Prince of Wales.

Returning his glance to me he continued, 'Watson, we are spies in an enemy's country. We must make great haste. You referred to my ability to track the Lanchester by its tyres. I am sure that noble carriage was used to convey the corpse from Crick's End to Scotney Castle. By now Fusey's men will have smoothed every inch of the Kilndown track with Pevensey's Ratel brushes. They will have scumbled madly around the wagon pond. As to my reference to the clay and chalk-dust on our late arrivals' shoes, those shoes will have had the boot boy's fullest attention. Your reference to my small trick of divining the trade of the artisan – or hardships of the tramp – by the callosities of his knees or fore-finger and thumb may cause some consternation. There is no account in the *Standard* of any hard and repetitive work or callouses on the corpse from sleeping rough, despite the visibility of its every joint and palm.'

I glanced around. With the imminent approach of the London train, the long narrow platform bustled with day-trippers carrying baskets filled with the produce and medicines of the fields.

'Holmes,' I scolded, with a coldness born of angst, 'a charge of assassination is furiously indiscreet so openly proclaimed in a public place not a league from Crick's End.'

Holmes swung round abruptly, noting for the first time the growing assembly behind us. Beckoning me to follow in his wake, he strode along the platform towards the far, deserted end. I followed ill at ease. At the very least we must return the handsome stipend if we stood before them on their portico with so extraordinary a charge. Walking at Holmes' back I had time to recall a not-to-be-forgotten moment shortly after we took up quarters on Baker Street. It was at the start of a case which culminated most unexpectedly on Powys Mountain in distant Wales. At first I put my reservations to him quietly, then, as now, in incremental steps more forcibly as he refused to accommodate my argument and concern. Later, I realised I should have recognised in the threatening, deep-lined brow one of

108

Nature's plainest danger-signals. Finally, unwisely, I angrily spoke of his 'overheated intuition'. Holmes' lanky body stiffened. A terrible change came over his face as he heard my words. His features turned perfectly livid. A small spot of crimson flared up on his cheek. It was some seconds before he could get out a single word and when he spoke it emitted in a high unnatural tone. With a coruscating eye, he shouted, 'Watson, keep to the forefront of your mind, I am not Captain of a rusty seven-knot tramp-steamer with thirteen crew, so do not treat me so! I am Nimrod, Son of Cush, a mighty hunter before the Lord!'

I preferred to avoid any repeat of this experience on a railway platform in Sussex crowded with leave-takers and travellers.

As we moved along the platform a searing memory from the earliest days of our association brought an embarrassed flush to my cheeks. A hansom had deposited me at The Guards in time for lunch. Over my meal I read a report in The Speaker which stirred me to a frenzy. Authorities had arrested a titled lady in the East End of London and marched her off to gaol, accusing her of being the leader of a gang shipping Welsh women into sexual slavery, drugging them with an exotic chemical and placing them aboard the S.S. Caledonia heading for a port in Palestine. From there they would be transported overland by camel to Al-Hillah, a town in Mesopotamia near ancient Babylon, thence onward to a jobbing life as daughters of Eve along the incense routes of Arabia Felix, forced nightly to dance from the vagina.

Incensed by this account and certain of the titled lady's innocence I left The Guards and sped to our Baker Street rooms where I read the account aloud to Holmes seated at the fire-place, decanter at his side. He listened with growing agitation at my recital. At the conclusion he half-rose swiftly to his feet, declaring with flashing eyes, 'Watson, this case grows on me. We have a good week's work before us. It quite certainly contains points of national interest! I say there are dark complications here and important State secrets at serious risk. The police may be complicit in a deadly plot. Not one word further! Retrieve your six-shooter from Mrs. Hudson, load it and slip it in your Norfolk jacket. We must at once repair to the Mile End Road and save this woman from a dreadful fate. I fear the worst. She is a pearl of rare variety. Why else do you suppose she would be dressed (Holmes pointed at The Speaker) 'in fine, thick silk material interwoven with gold threads' known as samite? That is the evening wear of the English aristocrat, yet in her bag she hides a yard of shantung and a Muslim shift of coquelicot-coloured silk with white diamond spots like India handkerchiefs, whose true purpose we can only guess at. While you retrieve your revolver and a dozen cartridges – and your stoutest oak cudgel - I must work out which route to take. No, I am already clear on this – we shall take the Euston Road to Pentonville, and then to the Angel, City Road, Eastern Street, Commercial Street to the Aldgate. Watson, I say fly as the very wind, we must leave at once!'

With so urgent an injunction ringing in my ears I rushed into a Norfolk jacket, yanking on my outdoor coat and hat even as I ran into Mrs. Hudson's rooms. I thrust a handful of cartridges into a pocket while I unrolled my Army revolver from its oil-cloth. The same revolver remained my weapon of choice even though on my departure from Afghanistan the Amir took me to his armoury and begged me to select a weapon from a cornucopia – gold-mounted Remington repeating rifles, breech-loading pistols, silver mounted revolvers, Brown-besses, military sniders, even rook rifles and a stick gun.

As it transpired, the woman was a Drury Lane actress, a lady titled only in Oscar Wilde's play, the part requiring a ready change of costly clothes. For a small donation to the Policeman's Pension Fund, the arrest and charge had been induced by a theatrical publicity agent. I was half-way down the stairs en route to Whitechapel before I realised my companion was far from treading on my heels, obliging on me an abject and humiliating return to the sitting-room to Holmes' loudest guffaws.

The episode was a turning point in my relationship with Holmes. Through the cruelty of his laughter whatever confidence I may have had in my ability to become a Consulting Detective like Holmes evaporated like ice under an Indian sun.

On the railway platform at Etchingham I tried again. 'Holmes, I believe I have made it clear I take this death at Scotney Park to be a sad occurrence but not of sinister significance,' adding in an attempt to defuse his ire, 'however, no further cautionary word will proceed from my lips if you will kindly offer me a fuller explanation.'

My companion nodded. 'Watson, read out once more the facts of this discovery. I emphasise, the facts alone will be quite sufficient. From small facts can great inferences be made. The detail can be added when we have wrung them from the withers of Siviter and his gang.'

I winced. It was becoming clear to me I should humour him until despite the black fear now seeping through my veins like the ink of the octopus I could devise some strategy to bundle him aboard the train.

'Well,' I began, attentive to even the smallest discordant clue to counter his charge of murder, 'what of the matter of the neat pile of clothing at the wagon pond's edge?'

'A pile of clothing in good order, yes…meaning what?'

'Someone must have placed them there.'

'Watson, you scintillate. Of course someone placed them there, but someone other than their owner, I suspect, thus giving what impression?'

Seeing my unwillingness to attempt an answer Holmes continued. 'Why, as you imply, that entry into the water was under the wearer's own command, what else? So, Watson, what further point do you elicit from this pile of clothing – what of the consequence for the corpse?'

'It was unclad.'

'Indeed. You have one more specimen of the grotesque and tragic to add to your collection. We must ask why. Why was the body stripped of clothing, but first, another vital matter. On which estate is this wagon pond located? Answer me, Watson, stay with me on this!'

'As it says, Holmes. At Scotney Castle.'

'Which has which other body of water, in addition to the wagon pond?'

'As we have never visited Lord Fusey's estate…'

'Now, Watson, make an effort - throw your mind back! What of Pevensey's second canvas? Do you recall the subject? A ruined castle and...?'

'Ah, yes, a moat.' I stared at him. 'What of that?'

'Good, Watson. A moat. Fed by a small stream as I recall. We have a body of water in each painting on the Fuseys' estate. In the Constable a wagon pond and in the other a moat.' He stopped to peer closely at me. 'Do you not find that a matter of quite extraordinary interest?'

'Of some small interest, Holmes, perhaps,' I responded, frowning, 'but hardly enough to spark a riot among an Old Bailey jury. If Siviter commissioned Pevensey to paint a wagon pond at the Fuseys' estate in homage to a Constable, would it not be natural to ...'

Holmes broke in, 'To pair it with a moat? Indeed, but do not let that convenience detract from its significance. I do not believe it can be so readily explained. It begs a question for which as yet I myself have no answer – why did he commission the second oil? Surely an homage to Constable is an homage to Constable? Why not let it stand alone? Why gild the lily? And why so late – hardly a day or two ago? Now let us proceed to the oils themselves... I recall the lively brilliance of the palette knife but you have a subtler eye. Which colours did he employ for the surface of the wagon pond?'

'Holmes,' I protested,' why on Earth does it matter which colours...'

Holmes' impatience with my obstruction turned to dudgeon.

'Watson,' he returned, his voice rising sharply, 'if you would indulge

113

me the while!'

'The higher and warmer notes,' I hastened in response.

'Please be precise. Which colours? There is a point to my enquiry.'

'Light tones - yellows, oranges and reds.'

'Which means?'

'Very picturesque?' I hazarded.

'Indeed picturesque, Watson. Painterly even. But I mean the use of such a palette - it would indicate what? What of the water's depth?'

'Shallow, Holmes,' I replied, bewildered. 'Those are colours for shallow water,' adding, with a tinge of sarcasm, 'as befits a wagon pond.'

'How shallow, Watson?' Holmes pursued. 'Come, you are a military man! You must have driven many a wagon into a pond to soak the wheels.'

'Eighteen inches at most, less at the edges,' I replied, still mystified, 'though I remember in the Hindu Kush we nearly…'

'And the second oil? What of the surface of the moat, what colours did Pevensey employ?'

'Umber or burnt sienna and dark purple for the reflection of the castle brick…' at which again my companion broke back impatiently. 'Watson! Not the reflection of the ruin – the reflection of the sky!'

'The darker blues, as I recall. Yes, mostly Stone Cobalt blue.'

'Which indicates?'

'Much deeper water.'

At this my companion's voice lost its assured tone. 'Much deeper,' he repeated. He shook his head, muttering 'It makes no sense...' several times.

Then, 'Watson, at which hour do you suppose death occurred?'

'According to the Standard around three o' clock – sometime between Lord Fusey's sighting and the woodman's discovery of the corpse at four.'

'And you have no reason to dispute that?'

'I have no evidence to assume otherwise, no.'

'Nor to oppose outright the constable's presumption?'

'Neither. It seems a perfectly reasonable conclusion.'

'As you say,' Holmes agreed. 'And where were we at that very hour?'

'Holmes!' I cried out in amazement. 'You well know!'

'I insist you tell me, Watson!'

'Why, we were in the parlour at Crick's End.'

'Doing what, precisely?'

'I was on my feet giving my introduction…'

'Precision, Watson. It was I who was on my feet. And who was I addressing?

'Our host Siviter and Viscount Van Beers.'

'Again, Watson, it is time you developed an affection for detail. Were we not joined by Alfred Weit and Sir Julius at three o'clock precisely? If you recall, Siviter told us it was so.'

'Holmes, entirely coincidental, surely?'

'I consider their arrival at that exact hour a matter of great consequence, by no means mere coincidence.'

If the publisher of *The Strand* had not recently told me my readers' taste was changing and I should take heed in the extravagance of my portrayals, I would have described Holmes' eyes as 'glittering like Egypt's deadly Coastal cobra'.

Holmes gestured. 'Please return to the newspaper report. What else does it offer a Consulting Detective?'

''The face, arms and legs, and upper torso burnt by the sun'.' I looked up. 'That is certainly odd, Holmes, I agree – 'burnt' must be an exaggeration.'

116

'Bravo, Watson!' Holmes responded. 'As you say, even though a tramp is painfully exposed to the vagaries of England's weather, this summer has hardly begun.'

He stared thoughtfully at the newspaper in my hand. 'Since when do our tramps take time off to winter in the Tropics? What else could it mean, weathered legs from just above the calf to just below the knee?'

By now the build-up of passengers was encroaching upon us. Holmes ushered me further down the platform. 'Watson, let us return to the pile of clothing. Besides being neatly piled what other detail are we offered?'

With whatever confidence I had gained from the day's commission melting, I ventured, 'The pile was topped by a crimson hat.'

'Topped by a crimson hat, which indicates…?'

Haplessly I offered, 'The owner has a taste for unusual head ware?'

'You are on your very best form, Watson,' Holmes responded tartly. 'Certainly it is not a hat from the Ponting Brothers or Underwood and Sons of the Camberwell Road. I mean what of the placement of this object of attire? Let me offer you a hint, 'topped by a crimson hat'.'

'Placed where it would catch the eye?'

'Yes, not cast upon the ground beside the pile of clothing but placed with deliberation. In addition to the crimson colour and width of

117

brim, distinguished by the owner's choice of...?'

'Snake-skin hatband?'

'Certainly not a hatband from a common viper - and not a snake at all, but a...?'

'Lizard?' I hazarded.

'Excellent! A hatband struck from the majestic spiny lizard, a reptile inhabiting the scrub forest and dry grassland south of the Crocodile River, West of Swaziland and Zululand and the Portuguese possessions, and East of the regions of the Bechwana and Bangwaketsi peoples...' at which he paused to draw breath, looking at me triumphantly, 'which is where precisely, Watson? No, don't worry, you are an India hand, I shall answer for you. The Transvaal!'

Without further ado, my companion commenced to supply me with the most striking illustration of those powers for which he is justly famed, a fine example of the contingent value of the obscure.

'The yellow-to-brown colouration, the distinct whorled scalation and spiny tail evident from the description tell us at once it is the mighty Sungazer lizard! You see, Watson,' he rushed on. 'Southern Africa is rich in reptiles, but like Darwin's finches they are closely confined to their different regions. This hatband is from a giant girdled lizard, the largest of the cordylids, which lives nowhere else but in underground burrows in the boulder fields and rocky outcrops of the highveld of the northern Free-state and southern Transvaal – where the goldmines are.'

118

Holmes stopped abruptly, drawing breath. Then, 'Watson, tell me, you still see no connection to Crick's End?'

'None whatsoever,' I replied stubbornly, growing hot with anxiety. I dreaded the cab's imminent arrival. 'Except the tenuous connection you draw from a hatband - what does it matter if the band is made from a girdled lizard from the Transvaal or Gnathostomata out of time, trawled up from some deep ocean? Surely we have examined this enough! As to murder at the hands of the Kipling League, I fear – I hope - you are pulling my leg.'

'Tut, man, do you not yet agree the man was a victim of murder?'

'I do not, Holmes, but as you so manifestly do, do you have any identity in mind?'

'I am certain it will prove to be the body of a Boer.'

With a choking laugh I exclaimed, 'A Boer? Here in the depths of Sussex? Holmes, this goes too far! It is the most absurd... if this corpse could sit up and scratch his head, he would say 'I have never been in Africa in my life, so you can put that in your pipe and smoke it, Mr. Busybody Holmes!'!'

'Watson,' Holmes broke back angrily, 'I keep begging you to quit the habit of a lifetime, you must try your best to think!'

He paused. In a milder tone he asked, 'I have another question for you. Where have you seen that hat before - is the description not oddly similar to one we have only very recently seen?'

'To the best of my recollection,' I responded, 'the only hats I have

119

seen today except your travelling cap and my topper and Siviter's wideawake and Sir Julius' fedora is Dudeney's leather cap, and that mostly from the rear...'

Even as I spoke these words an image flashed before my eyes, the flamboyant figure in Pevensey's reprise of a Constable.

'By the living Jingo! The figure by the wagon pond,' I exclaimed.

'Watson,' Holmes responded in high delight. 'An Age of Miracles is upon us – well done!'

'But Holmes,' I returned, with sudden exhilaration, sensing a flaw, 'Pevensey was painting at the wagon pond until just after three this afternoon – that I remember Siviter telling us. The inclusion of a figure with such a hat must prove...'

By now my companion was paying me no attention. Yet again his gaze ('eyes sparkling like a Golconda diamond') darted across the railway yard for a first sight of the sociable. Ignoring my words, he pulled out a black clay pipe, filled it from a pouch of seal-skin, and set about firing up the last gasp of Abdulla's Egyptian tobacco provided on an occasional basis from Salmon & Gluckstein of Oxford Street - 'Largest and Cheapest Tobacconists in the World'.

Despite my deepening anxiety, it intrigued me how Holmes could undergo the most extraordinary metamorphosis from torpor to energy, from the pallid and introspective dreamer so often displayed before me at Baker Street where he will lie for hours or days with a vacant look, hardly speaking, to the alert and hyper-active man on the station platform before me. What combination of chemicals, normally dormant but at a ready manufacture in brain or gland,

120

produced this startling result?

With no sight of the sociable, Holmes turned back to me. 'Watson, you are outraged this corpse was left unclothed, yet I say killing someone and leaving his body bereft of clothes in a public place was for a purpose.'

'What would you deduce?'

'It can only be to expose the patterning on the skin.'

I stared at Holmes in bewilderment. 'Holmes, the report makes no mention...' I paused and guffawed. 'Ah, you mean, what of the fish tattooed on the corpse's hand in a peculiar pink pigment which the constable failed so lamentably to spot, the sign of the Hung anti-Manchu secret society?'

'Watson,' came Holmes' immediate response, 'despite your quite admirable attempt at humour, think, I beg you. Among the many foolish customs of the white man in Africa is the way he exposes his body to a drubbing by the celestial orb. He takes scissors and chops the knees off breeches. He rolls up the sleeves of khaki shirts to the armpit. He folds the shirt front inward to expose as much of his chest as possible which, might I bring to your attention, clearly approximates a 'V'. In short, this is the corpse of a migrant bird from Tropical climes.'

'Holmes,' I scorned. 'This is absurd! On what pretext are we to return to Crick's End with a charge of murder! With what evidence shall we confront Siviter and the Kipling League? Some dozen lines contrived by a sub-editor's lurid mind for the Late Edition of the *Evening London Standard*? A naked corpse, quite probably the victim of drowning, lying in a wagon pond at Scotney Castle in Kent? Nearby, clothes neatly folded and topped by a crimson hat perhaps of Tropical origin. Shall I go on – the V-shaped markings on a corpse's chest... the use of reds, oranges and yellow for the wagon pond. Oh, yes, not forgetting a majestic spiny ... cordylid.'

I stared boldly at my companion. 'Can you not see? They will think, as I am myself inclined to, you are demented. At best they'll greet us at the door and conclude you have a pawky sense of humour never before discovered, even by you, despite all your forensic skill, against which both they and I should guard ourselves. Certainly its employment in this enterprise and fashion is extremely untimely.'

Other rail passengers were growing ever more numerous around us. I went on in a lower tone, 'My dear Holmes, by long experience I have learned the wisdom of obeying your injunctions to the letter. Yet I must now inform you I am seriously disinclined to believe your conclusions despite the edifice you erect. You must rally support for any facts you muster. So far, the facts themselves are far from dramatic or remarkable except through the lens of an overblown interpretation. On the contrary. They are so slight and commonplace that I would not feel justified in laying them before our loyal public regardless of the clamour for further chronicles from the Editor of *The Strand.* You may have – will have - ranged against you constable and coroner and Lord Fusey and his woodman too, and if you have your way several illustrious members of the Kipling League. And Pevensey. And further,' I threw in desperately, 'why return to Crick's End? Why not to where the crime took place, at Scotney Castle, if crime it is, which is still so entirely debatable?'

To this last objection, Holmes responded with an impatient cry.

'Watson, for heaven's sake, apply your telescope to your eye not your ear! We do not need to look where the body lay but where its heart ceased beating. Have you not learned in our many years together, where the corpse lies may be the greatest lie of all? Have you not had your fill of sightless eyes? Besides, by now it rests under blocks of ice on some butcher's slab in Lamberhurst or Tunbridge Wells. What do you hope to discover? A pair of ammunition boots? The body on a gun-carriage, his boots reversed in the stirrups of his favourite charger, led by his groom with his dog beside him? This is not an instance where I lie on my face with a pocket-lens to my eye. No, Watson, there is no crop for harvesting at Scotney Castle. Do you not recall the words of Brother Mycroft – 'give me the details and I will give you an expert opinion'? And uttered where? Seated in his arm-chair among the periodicals at the Diogenes Club. This is a case where the art of the reasoner should be used rather for the sifting of details than the acquiring of fresh evidence. We have enough from this newspaper account. Pevensey's oils have told us Scotney Castle contains both wagon pond and moat. The evidence you use to refute my conclusions, namely that this person – shall we call him a passing stranger - was sighted at the wagon pond at three o' clock, the presumption it was a self-inflicted or accidental drowning, the inference the clothes and dark glasses were stolen, all comes from one direction and one alone. As to further clues on offer at Scotney Castle, do you imagine the marks of an assassin's heel would survive the excited tramplings of the local Peeler or the horses' hoofs as they roll the wagon back and forth to soak the wheels?'

CHAPTER NINE
Holmes Insists A Murder Has Taken Place

The light carriage pulled by a fine pair of greys came clip-clopping around the bend from the village, the cabman high astride the raised seat at the rear. He was attired in a blue surtout rather the worse for wear, tipped at the collar with red, and leather breeches and brown top boots. The reins ran through the harness of the collar and up at a steep angle into his hands. At the rear, attached by a slight chain, trotted a carriage-dog, a brown-spotted Dalmatian. The young newspaper vendor clutched anxiously at the cabman's side like a noviciate postilion. We watched the cab's pair of handsome greys begin to turn in a slow circle, the young vendor beckoning us with excited gestures. At that same moment, to my despair, with a snort of its long black nostril, the train for London steamed alongside the platform.

'Holmes,' I cried, 'I implore you. Let me pay the boy his ninepence and give the cabman a florin and send him home, and we shall be on our way to London.'

My companion paid no attention to my urgent appeal. Beckoning me to follow, he strode across to the carriage, looked up at the coachman and demanded, 'Do you know Crick's End?'

'Everyone do, Mr. Sherlock Holmes,' came the response.

'So you know me, my good man?'

'Everyone do, Sir,' the coachman replied. 'We heard you was at the manor.'

'Then hasten there at your fastest pace,' Holmes ordered. 'How long do you estimate?'

'Half an hour should do it.'

'Half a sovereign if you do it in twenty minutes.'

Holmes clambered in the cab before me and looked back through the open door with a quelling expression. 'Come in and seat yourself comfortably, Watson, we still have some time before we confront them at their door. Now,' he added, once I had joined him with a hang-dog look, 'bring out the gazetteer. Let us have the facts. Take up where you ended on our downward journey. Please select the most important elements concerning the Transvaal from events preceding the South African War.'

Not since *The Five Orange Pips* had I seen Holmes riven by such barely-contained excitement. Soon we should be grotesquely insulting four of the first brains of the greatest, wealthiest, and most powerful empire the world has ever seen. My spirits drifted ever-downward. I retrieved the gazetteer, and began, 'The Transvaal is central to the strategic map of Africa.'

'Yes!' Holmes breathed. 'Go on! Do go on!'

Main towns: Potchefstroom and Pretoria.
Republic founded in 1840 by dissident descendants of the Dutch settlers in Cape Colony and Natal.
Annexed in 1877 by Cape government on spurious grounds of 'disorder'.'

'Once Bismarck made his unexpected lunge at Angra Pequena, the

Cape had a new German colony on its north-western border. If the Transvaal, at a second attempt, could take Bechuanaland, it would join hands with Germany and snap its fingers at British paramountcy.'

I looked up. 'Holmes here is a mention of Viscount Van Beers.'

'Good! Excellent, in fact!' Holmes cried. 'Read on.'

'1897 Van Beers sent to Cape Town to pick up the pieces after the Jameson Raid. He returned to London in 1897 'to stamp on Chamberlain's 'rose-coloured illusions' about South Africa. Kruger re-elected for a fourth term as President of the Transvaal. Kruger believed Van Beers' aim was to humiliate the Volk, divide them from their fellow Boers of the Orange Free State and the Afrikaners of Cape Colony. Kruger purchasing large quantities of guns from Germany. The gold-rush to the Transvaal turned South Africa on its head: the new political centre was Johannesburg, not Cape Town. The Transvaal Boers could unite the whole of South Africa in a republic and Britain would lose both Natal and the Cape.'

On I read. ''If war was to ensue, it needed a crisis. It is now known Van Beers forged a secret alliance with the two richest 'gold bugs' of the Rand, Alfred Weit and Sir Julius Wernher. In 1899 they and Van Beers paid for an anti-Kruger press campaign in Johannesburg, a significant destabilising factor in the path to the outbreak of war. Weit and Wernher among other of the Randlords believed to have joined with Van Beers in a secret plan to settle the newly-annexed Transvaal and Orange River Colony with Anglo-Saxon emigrants.'

Holmes muttered, 'Secret alliances... the Jameson Raid... why, the unscrupulous, unprincipled adventurers!'

My heart was turning leaden. 'Holmes,' I protested, putting the gazetteer to one side, my eyes on the paved road unravelling beneath us, 'these leaps of yours are most entertaining but they remain mere will-o'-the wisps of your imagination. I can hardly bear the thought of standing at your side as you confront the members of the Kipling League. I do not judge Van Beers to be of a particularly forgiving disposition. We are recklessly to accuse four – throw in Lord Fusey, five - of the richest, most masterful men in England - six if we add the President of the Royal Academy – with the murder of a stranger, perhaps a Boer, more likely a tramp in stolen attire, with not a jot or tittle of proof! One does not need to be a toady or a sycophant to recognise the power and eminence of the Kipling League. They are men of the utmost wealth and consideration. Why, Holmes, the four in the parlour were in King Edward's grouse-shooting parties when he was heir to the throne!'

Despite my heated protestations, Holmes' demeanour remained as resolute and collected as ever I had seen.

'For fear of being overheard, Watson,' he replied, pointing upwards to the cabman's perch, 'let us henceforth refer to these members of the Kipling League as the Sungazer Gang. I tell you, notwithstanding you deem them the greatest subjects of the Crown, they have the edge over all the crooks and loafers we have ever encountered in all the underworlds of Liverpool or London.'

'By the by,' I returned, 'though I do not suppose it to be of the slightest importance - certainly you appear to consider it entirely inconsequential to your case - you have not yet answered how you intend to attribute opportunity to the Kipling League when, as you admit, all four were in our presence in the parlour at three this afternoon, the very hour this crime, if crime it is, is purported to have happened quite some miles away.'

Mistaking my companion's failure to retort at once as discomfit at my reminder, I took a risky step and added a provocation. 'Surely that is fatal to your theory?'

Rather than answering with the angry words I anticipated, Holmes responded with a heightened amiability which served only to increase my agitation. 'Watson, of course that is fatal to my theory – of course we were with them at that time.'

'But Holmes,' I floundered, 'if we were with them ... how can they be...?'

'Perhaps I should put it another way,' Holmes went on. 'Of course we were with them at three o' clock, the very time the coroner will rule the time of death. That was their intention. Watson, don't you see, that's the infernal genius of this ... this Sungazer Gang. They will call us – you and me - as principal witnesses before a jury of honest foremen and clerks from the stores. I contend you and I are the planet-wheel in a most cunning scheme. Do you not see,' he repeated, voice dropping low, 'that is why we received their urgent summons. We are to be their alibi if needed.'

'Alibi!' I exclaimed. I gave an incredulous laugh. 'My dear fellow, surely...'

'Surely you say! I say surely you see the similarity to the Foxy Ferdinand matter?' Holmes retorted.

This was a reference to the case of the Prince Regnant of Bulgaria four years earlier, a matter of the most profound international importance. My account in manuscript form lies in the tin box under our landlady's supervision, never to see the light of day until the Prince's death or exile.

Holmes shook his head.

'Vanity, Watson! Vanity as vast as their power and wealth. I say they retained this Boer as their guest behind those high Yew hedges until this morning, kept alive like a chicken for a voodoo ceremony in Port-au-Prince - until they were assured I was back at Baker Street fresh from my peregrinations around the docks. Hence the watchman with the amber eyes who never sold a hare. Once they were assured their telegram had found its mark, they killed the Boer and cast him in the moat.'

'Moat, Holmes?' I exclaimed in great surprise. 'You are mistaken. The body was discovered in the wagon pond.'

'Indeed – an inexplicable fact for which I do not as yet have an answer.'

My heart leapt with disloyal hope as he went on.

'Watson, I agree I must do some pondering on that inconvenient matter. We are lost if an answer to the conundrum is not soon forthcoming. As to motive... it is surely connected to the recent South African War. There remain many unresolved hatreds. Boers' wives and children by the thousand died from enteric fever in our concentration camps. Or a more venal reason. You yourself have recounted tales of the maelstroms that lay around the reefs of gold in Australia – why not around South Africa's Rand?'

'Holmes,' I argued, 'Weit and Van Beers and Sir Julius comprise Randlord and Gold Bugs, but what about our host? Siviter's life is the sub-Continent, not South Africa. I estimate he possesses more than five hundred volumes on India.'

'What drives Siviter is more than India. He is a true adherent of his literary Master. Recall, Watson, Kipling's poem The Mary Gloster - hard work, duty, self-sacrifice and resilience. These Sungazers are hardly red republicans. They are men of Empire and the White Man's burden.'

He was silent for a moment, followed by, 'But what of India?'

'Populous?' I ventured, edging towards firmer ground.

'Very populous.'

'Colourful?'

'Yes, colourful.'

'Large?'

Holmes frowned impatiently.

'Yes, Watson, yes, it is a sub-continent, very large, very populous, but politically?'

'Why, in ferment,' I replied.

'Indeed, Watson, there you have it. To a medical man like you, India is the geographic expression of mosquitoes and fevers. India and Afghanistan left you with a shattered leg and shoulder, a half-pay surgeon on a pension of eleven shillings and sixpence a day. But what of salted Anglo-Indians like Siviter? For him it is the great pilgrimage to Hurdwar on the holy Ganges. The 'wind of March against the lattice blowing'.'

Stirred at this unexpected poetry coming from my friend. I joined in, a chorus to his verse. ''Tamarisk-trees white with the dust of rainless days'.'

'The road from Jugdullack to Butkhak! What of the festival of lights at Chiragan? The Levées at Government House. The Carabiniers... the drink called peg. The Squadrons – think, old warrior that you are, of the Punjab Cavalry!'

Tears sprang to my eyes for the second time that day. 'The day-long rolling thunder among the Khyber hills. The 14th Bengal Lancers,' I added.

Holmes leaned forward. He continued in a low and serious voice, 'To them it is love and longing of a mystical kind. Yes, Watson, you are right. Rail as he might against the tide of unclean humanity amid the seething, stinking bustees of the presidency cities, when Siviter dies we will not discover 'Crick's End' lying on his heart but Lahore or Simla, the Abode of the Little Tin Gods. In short, he adores being Heaven-born, white stranger within the gates of Hindoos, Mohammedans and the Sikh, set apart in a vast, anonymous multitude, scion of an empire which contains only Milords Anglais, soldiers, shipowners, magnates, famous barristers and explorers.'

He paused dramatically. 'Now, however, England's rule is being ripped asunder by agitating natives. You heard his references to lascars – 'caste-ridden, venal and incompetent', and 'hybrid, University-trained mules'. Even if Siviter has not yet cast his topee into the waters of Port Said en route to Blighty, India is saying good-bye and he must turn with urgency elsewhere.'

As he spoke, the coachman called out 'whoa!'. The horses halted. The tinkle of a thin chain from the rear told us the brown-spotted carriage-dog was being released and led away.

Holmes continued insistently. 'As India loosens from Siviter's grasp, what then? You read his words in the gazetteer. England is 'slipping down the broad, easy decline to our extinction as a Great Power with an influence to exert on the side of the angels, with a civilising tradition to plant all the world over'. Where better to cast the fly of the White Man's burden next than on the sweated backs of Zulus and poor devils in Matabeleland?'

With a jerk our journey recommenced. The promise of a half-sovereign in mind, our driver whipped up the greys. We sped at a flat run, the vehicle whirling along the ridge. Holmes resumed his discourse. 'I have enough to beard them in their lair, though mark my words, before we pass this to Scotland Yard it might take seclusion and a seven-percent solution, or an ounce of shag from Bradley's before we meet them in a Court of Law.'

He wiped the condensation from the cab window and continued, 'Take the corpse. It is clear the local constabulary has no thought of suspicious death, itself no small achievement by the Kipling League.'

'Holmes,' I broke in, 'if death was not by drowning, what then?'

'As yet that too I cannot tell you. Certainly death was not by poison *à l'anglais.* The muscular contortions strychnine causes would leap out even to a local bobby's untutored eye.'

Holmes fell silent. I stared at him most dismally. After a pause I ventured, 'Why naked, Holmes? Can you explain that to my satisfaction? Was this perverted and insulting act solely to expose the weathering of the skin, and if so, why?'

'The matter of disrobing is extremely clever. Without doubt one aim was to open up the body to reveal the sun-scorched skin. While possibly it was to insult – we shall return to that - I do not believe it was with a perverted intent.'

'You say 'one aim' was to open up the body, Holmes. And what of another?'

'If I am right in my deduction, it was a signal.'

'A signal?' I exclaimed.

'A signal,' Holmes confirmed. 'Through the fact a sun so violent is clearly indicative of a Tropical clime.'

'And at whom is this signal aimed, I pray?'

'At whom, indeed. It behoves us to discover.'

Holmes paused again.

'Then, the perfect crime in their grasp, the assassins' luck ran out,'

Holmes went on, his words jerking with the jolting of the carriage, 'by sheer chance – an uncalculated delay resulting from your intense satisfaction in consuming Imam Bayildi – we were caught by the clamour of the newspaper boy. A half-hour sooner we might have concluded our journey to London by the earlier train. We would never have heard him singing his song 'Late Extra! Dead body at Scotney Castle'.'

'Holmes,' I expostulated. 'You try to insult and divert me all at once but I see why. I know we share a love of all that is bizarre and outside the conventions and humdrum routine of everyday life but are facts not of some importance if this is a case of murder as you assert? As yet I cannot see anything save vague indications.' I added cuttingly, 'So far you are able to deduce neither opportunity nor motive! It seems quite feasible the victim died sometime this afternoon when we were in camera with Siviter and his companions, a matter you refuse to address despite my persistent questioning. You assert the body was thrown in the moat. How you come to that conclusion mystifies me completely. The corpse was discovered in the wagon pond. As to its nakedness, that was, you say, a semaphore, but you have not the faintest idea at whom the signal is directed.' I added, smiling grimly, 'Otherwise, Holmes, you are as right as you have ever been. We have most truly got these murderous Sungazers on the run. As it is so critical to your case against the Kipling League, I repeat, what of the timing? Were they seated in front of us at Crick End at three o' clock or not? You impute contrivance and precision to these events. It is incumbent on you to enlighten me. Otherwise, turn this carriage around and let us emulate the Grand Old Duke Of York and beat a path back down the hill to Etchingham and let the Pullman car carry us home to Baker Street.'

To my intense frustration, rather than answer my query, he continued as though speaking to himself. 'Yet what am I to make of...?', though to which point he was referring he did not elaborate.

He continued to stare out through the cab window, repeating over and over, 'It makes no sense.'

Unwisely, I determined to force my opinion on him. I took a firm grip on his arm, as with an errant schoolchild's ear. He wrenched his arm away. In a savage voice shouted, 'Watson! You fidget me beyond endurance. I beg you, cease all questioning – and at this instant! I must ask you to remain completely silent. Keep your concerns to yourself. Do not inflict them on me any longer or we are utterly lost.'

Astonished by his ferocity I did as I was bid. He slumped back with a disconsolate look.

'Watson, this Kipling League has set me an equation of the utmost complexity. There are no clues hidden in a tobacco jar. Each one seems to slip through my fingers. Except the matter is beyond humanity – which like Siviter's tale of his ghostly monks I do not believe it to be - there should be no combination of events for which the wit of man cannot conceive the explanation, yet I admit I am stretched beyond anything we have so far confronted. If I cannot solve it, they will defeat us.'

He reflected gloomily for a while, then, 'Watson, remind me of the words carved on the Hung League's north temple gate. I believe you committed them to memory at the time?'

'At the sign of Yin-kui the water is deep and difficult to cross, but in Yun-nan and Sze-Chuen there is a road by which you can travel'.'

135

After a short pause my companion continued in a sombre voice, 'We must find the road to Yun-nan and Sze-Chuen. If this Kipling League defeats us, such would be my humiliation I assure you I would have no choice but to consider immediate retirement to farm my bees. In short, your chronicles will draw to an end.'

So alarmed was I by this threatening proclamation I ceased all speaking. Moments passed. My comrade-in-arms turned his head towards me with a most quizzical look.

'Watson, I admit we build on quicksand. When I hear you put the pieces together - and with such a dubious expression - they point to the constable's conclusion, a suicide or an accidental drowning in a wagon pond, perhaps of a tramp who stole a gentleman's clothing and unwisely retained the pair of shiny dark glasses.'

He followed this with a shake of his head. 'No, Watson, my every bone and instinct tells me it is foul play. When I listen to your objections, they do not hang together. If you will believe me, these Sungazers… I am certain they have committed a heinous crime yet I cannot give an answer to the two most puzzling riddles they have set us.'

'Why the corpse lay in the wagon pond and not the moat?'

'That is the one,' Holmes nodded.

And why the pair of paintings?'

'I see at least you follow, Watson, despite your trepidation, well done.'

136

He lapsed into a deep silence.

'Holmes,' I began, keenly aware the distance between us and Crick's End was narrowing like the shadow of a great Himalayan mountain rushing towards us at the setting of the sun behind it, 'you must follow your famed dictum, 'no matter what....'.'

As if he had no inkling I had spoken, my companion continued juggling with an equation, his words low and troubled. 'Surely the moat is where a drowning purporting to be a suicide or an accident would best take place...? This was followed by, 'A second canvas so recently ordered... why? Why would Siviter gild the lily?'

Perhaps it was a trick of the light but I was sure I discerned a shade of anxiety starting in my companion's heavy-lidded eyes which was spreading out to his expressive face. His head had dropped, like a bull's awaiting the torero's estocada.

Finally Holmes spoke. 'Watson, you may be right. Perhaps I have leapt to the wrong conclusion. Nevertheless we must risk bearding them in their den, and soon, while the traces of crime might still be there.'

We had covered the length of the Straight Mile. Scarcely fifteen minutes remained before we would reach our destination. My companion's fingers drummed on his knees.

He spoke again. 'If I am right and the corpse was first dropped in the moat, why did Sir Julius and Weit hurry back to Scotney Castle to haul it from such deep water and place it in a pond not more than eighteen inches deep? What triggered this urgent and inexplicable act? It cannot be beyond the limits of human ingenuity to furnish an explanation.'

'Sir Julius and Weit?' I gasped in the greatest disbelief. 'Holmes, I beg of you most sincerely, furnish such an explanation in the next few minutes. We shall soon be at their portico.'

More moments passed. He turned back to me. 'Watson, you recall the lesson from *A Study in Scarlet* and *The Sign of Four*. We were compelled to reason backward from effects to causes. We must start with the unequivocal, such matters which even you in your disputatious mood cannot challenge. At three o' clock exactly Sir Julius and Weit made their hasty entrance to the parlour...'

I interrupted, frowning. 'Holmes, why do you impute haste in the pair's arrival? They seemed quite calm and orderly. Weit even asked me...'

'...about his health? Yes, he did, and you promised him the span, but how do you explain their shoes and spats splattered with chalk and clay? It would have taken a mere moment to get the servants to wipe them clean. And why would Sir Julius arrive among us in a parlour still clutching a hat? He must have pushed into the house before your Botticelli house-maid could meet him at the door to wrest it from him. No, Watson. They had an urgent need to be seated before us at three this afternoon precisely.'

His fingers continued drumming.

Suddenly he asked, 'How far did Siviter say it was to Scotney Castle?'

'Some twelve miles – as the crow flies,' I responded.

'By Dudeney's conveyance, what time would it take to get there by road, do you suppose?'

'Not more than half an hour each way.'

'Then to fish up the corpse from the moat and take it with its pile of clothing to the wagon pond...' Holmes mused. 'They would want to hurry such an assignment. Ten minutes at most ...'

He darted a look at me. 'Watson, the telegram we sent from Tunbridge Wells to announce our arrival, at what o' clock did you hand it to the station porter?'

'Your gold watch showed 1.15.'

'And the telegram would have reached its destination at Crick's End when, do you suppose?'

'I would say some twenty minutes later.'

'Hum! Let's say not much after half past the hour...'

Again his voice fell to a murmur. 'But if Dudeney was at the Etchingham Railway Station to meet us... I am certain when we arrived at Crick's End both Weit and Sir Julius were there, but hidden. Transport by motor-car would be the only method. Only so could they have reached Scotney Castle and returned to Crick's End by three. But why....'

His eyebrows lifted in triumph. 'Watson, I have it!'

'Namely?'

'The unexpected arrival of our telegram, what else? The moment they heard we would be at Crick's End three hours earlier than expected, a rush ensued to remove the body from the moat and take it to the wagon pond.'

His face took on a most perplexed look. 'But, Watson, why?' And again, 'It makes no sense!'

Holmes gestured at the newspaper jutting from my coat.

'Watson, please take the newspaper and pass it to me.'

He reached forward and took the *Standard* from my outstretched hand, flattening it out upon his knee.

''A body lying mostly submerged ...' Watson, 'Mostly submerged', what would that mean?'

'That it would be largely under the water, surely, Holmes?'

'Indeed it would mean that exactly, Watson. And therefore...?'

'Mostly wet?' I answered, bewildered.

'Mostly wet, yes, Watson, you improve all the time – and as a consequence, what of its temperature?'

'Why, the part above the surface would be affected by the temperature of the air, and similarly...'

'... the greater part of the body, lying mostly submerged,' Holmes broke in, 'would be affected by the temperature of the pond. Precisely, Watson, well deduced - as befits a medical man.'

As from nowhere my companion asked with a slight smile, 'Watson, I am struggling to remember... for some reason it has sprung to mind. If my memory still serves me, are you not the author of the Watson Codex? A monograph upon obscure nervous lesions – the pathology of catalepsy, I believe?'

I frowned. 'I am, Holmes, the author of the Watson Codex, but as to nervous lesions you believe wrongly. That is Dr. Percy Trevelyan.'

'Ah, yes,' Holmes replied unapologetically. 'Then, my dear fellow, what?'

Before I could elucidate, his grey eyes turned to slits. Unaccountably a scowl began to cross his face. 'No! Now I do recall. Your Codex is an acclaimed work on stiffening of the limbs upon death, is it not? From the great expertise you gained by examining many a corpse in the cholera epidemics of the 1870s?'

'I am the author of such a report, Holmes, yes,' I plumed, though uncertain why such medical experience should merit his accusatory tone. As a young and impoverished medical student I had fought hard to obtain fresh corpses against the larger pockets of the Burkers and their dissector clients. 'I began my examinations in the cholera epidemics you describe, and brought my Codex to a conclusion in Afghanistan and the Forgone Valley. Those regions possess a treacherous clime, full of fever, and a population of hostile... '

In addition to almost daily random deaths from disease and general hardship, I had added to my store of knowledge of rigor mortis from certain military events. After my release in 1880 from attachment as Assistant Surgeon to the Fifth Northumberland Fusiliers on account of wounds to leg and shoulder, I spent seven weeks recuperating in the Russian Hospital for Officers, near London's Grosvenor Square. It was here I was recruited for secondment to a Russian regiment fighting Sufi rebels. I took the opportunity to conduct measured tests in the field on how quickly muscle lengthens or shortens after death. From such reports I later published my work *Estimation Of The Time Of Death By Examination of Rigor Mortis In Subjects In The Forgone Valley.*

Holmes' expression had turned ugly as though his rediscovery of my expertise in rigor mortis was inflicting on him some significant harm. This was confirmed when, to my astonishment, he said, 'So, Watson, you will be my Nemesis, not theirs.'

At this caustic rejoinder he thrust the newspaper back at me and fell into an icy silence. I stared back at him reproachfully. A furlong passed while Holmes continued to consider me without uttering a word. Seldom had my fellow lodger examined me for more than five seconds and even fewer the occasions accompanied by such a discomfiting look.

'How do you mean, Holmes?' I spluttered.

'It is you the Sungazers will call to the witness stand on their behalf. The Watson Codex will be the principal weapon in their armoury. It is you who shall defeat me.'

Before I could protest my undying loyalty, he went on, 'Remind me, what was the question which most vexed you – the fatal flaw in my supposition, I believe you called it?

'The time of the death, Holmes. If it took place around three o' clock today, between Lord Fusey's sighting - corroborated by Pevensey's painting - and the woodman finding the corpse one hour later, all four Sungazers...'

'... were seated in rapt attention before us?'

'Quite so,' I responded.

He continued with his injured expression. 'And you are prepared to state that in open Court as evidence in their favour?'

'Under oath?' I enquired.

'Under oath,' Holmes confirmed, eying me keenly.

'I would have to.'

'Even if it destroys our case against them?'

'Even if, Holmes, though I wish...'

'Do you not see it as the blackest treachery?'

'Holmes,' I cried, 'I am a member of the medical profession!'

'As you say, Watson,' Holmes retorted with a further sullen glance, 'I understand completely. You must do so. You might save them from the gallows on that fact alone. You shall be their hero.'

He went on, 'Remind me, Watson, what was it your Codex contributed to the study of rigor mortis?'

'The precise effect of the prevailing conditions on the body when death occurs.'

'In brief?'

'That rigor mortis does not set in at a standard rate…'

'But varies according to…?'

'The ambient temperature.'

Holmes threw me a puzzled look. 'Watson, it comes back to me. I now recall your Codex won the Order of Merit for Comparative Pathology from the Karolinska Institute and a thousand kroner. Why would so unexceptional a conclusion gain you so prestigious an award? Surely you state the obvious? Even with little knowledge of the stiffening process, would not everyone anticipate a variation in onset according to the heat or cold?'

'It would be so expected,' I responded calmly, 'but clearly you did not subject the tables containing my conclusions to a detailed examination.'

'These conclusions being… ?'

It was not often I could lecture Holmes with my greater knowledge of a subject.

'Even in the dead one might suppose the colder the surroundings the quicker muscle contraction would occur, as when we shiver....'

'One might indeed so suppose, Watson – indeed I myself so suppose.' A keen look had now appeared on my companion's face. The ugly expression was dissipating with each passing second. 'Watson, I repeat, indeed one would, whereas...?'

'My findings showed results quite contrary to intuition.'

'Which are?'

The opposite is true. Cold slows the onset of rigor mortis...'

'And therefore warmth...?'

'... causes the body to stiffen faster.'

The very instant he absorbed these words, my companion's sullen mood was lifted.

With a loud cry he shouted, 'Worshipper of Minerva! Watson, I rank you among the demi-gods of medicine! Of course! That's it!' He clapped his hand in delight. 'That's why they fished him from the moat and plopped him in the wagon pond!'

He leaned back with a series of loud ejaculations of interest and excitement. It was as if a set of clues was falling into place like the wafers of a Bramah lock. I started to enquire what all this meant but he clapped his hands together and exclaimed in an excited tone, 'Watson, you have done it!' This was followed by 'By Jove we have them in the dock!'

Like a dashing foxhound drawing a cover, he sped on. 'This murder is not the work of a tinder-box imagination. It has been most cleverly designed. Thanks to your Codex, we most definitely have them! I reverse my recent charge - it will be you who places the hangman's noose around their necks. I took you and your Codex to be a most powerful ally in their favour but it has now turned King's Evidence. It will be you, not I, who will be their Nemesis.'

With an eager look he questioned, 'Your Codex provides proof of this, from taking the most exacting measurements on bodies in both the warm and cold?'

'I assure you it does, Holmes,' I responded, my dread returning.

'Based on...?'

'Based on my scientific study on many tens of Timurid warriors' corpses.'

'Then if you please, give me further instruction. There is some haste - as you remind me, we shall be at Crick's End soon!'

I began, 'For many months I recorded the times of onset in great detail. You say 'on bodies' but my investigation was not conducted on Timurids' bodies in the sense you would assume.'

'On what, then?' my companion demanded.

'On their toes,' I replied.

Holmes' eyes opened wide. My friend has so often astonished me in the course of our adventures that it was with a sense of exultation that I realised how completely the situation was reversed. Except for the intense but fleeting look he gave me at the very start of our acquaintance a quarter-century before, when young Stamford brought us together so fatefully, I do not believe Holmes had ever stared at me so hard, and never in such wonderment or grave suspicion as at that moment.

'Watson,' he exclaimed, 'on Timurids' toes? You surpass my own experiment beating corpses with blackthorn cudgels to ascertain if bruising can occur post-mortem! Surely you tease? If you are entirely serious I am more astonished by your words than if a Barbary ape clad in morning coat, waistcoat, and striped trousers forced his way through the windows of this carriage, settling on your knee and speaking in good English! On Timurids' toes? Rather tell me you concerned yourself with the major limbs – the legs and arms?'

'For many years that was the practice of my profession,' I acknowledged, 'but after many close and careful calculations during several engagements in the Khyber Pass I realised development of rigor mortis in the larger muscles can be dangerously unreliable.'

'Compared to toes?'

'Compared to toes.'

Holmes clapped his hands in admiration. 'Watson, Watson!' he exclaimed, 'instruct me further. What were your results? I might tell you, my dear, dear friend, I do not recall another instance where so much depends on your medical knowledge,' adding, 'Would your measurements remain the same in England's clime as those taken from corpses in tongas in the far-off reaches of South Asia?'

'They would,' I acknowledged. 'Temperature is temperature.'

'And the human body is the human body, well said! Come, Watson, I rely completely on your expertise. In your hands alone lies our entire case.'

Despite the deepest worry over Holmes' accusations against the Kipling League, a surge of pleasure rose within me. It is a rare occasion when he expresses such a need of me.

'In cooler temperatures, onset of rigor mortis can be more than two hours longer whereas...'

'More than two hours longer?' Holmes broke in. 'As you say, how that flies in the face of intuition!'

He fell silent as though engaged in some calculation and then resumed, 'Two hours longer in the cold...my heavens, and you sat all the while with dead Timurid warriors, tweaking their toes? Presumably the toes were still attached to their former owners? Bravo, Watson!'
After a pause he added, 'Think of all those flies!' Then, mysteriously, 'Had we caught the three-ten train they would have left him in the moat.'

Clearly restored in spirit (the complete reversal of mine), my companion sat grinning at me. Fields of dark Sussex Reds passed us by.

Holmes leaned over to pinch my arm with affection. 'Watson, do you by chance have your Codex with you in your medical collection? So precise is the timing of these events…'

'It has become a talisman, I go nowhere without it,' I replied.

Holmes seized the leather-bound tome almost before it cleared the Gladstone bag. After a brief scrutiny he looked up, remarking with some admiration, 'These are pages of the most complex and impressive calculations!' A further period of examination ensued. He looked up. 'Watson, I failed in my duty as a Consulting Detective - I should have read this magnum opus most thoroughly when you offered it to me more than twenty years ago.'

A moment later a frown flickered across his face. 'These summer temperatures, they seem remarkably low. How can that be?'

'Holmes, you must surely recall from your Great Hiatus in the East,' I replied, smiling at his bewilderment. 'This Codex was commissioned by the Russians. Muscovites calculate temperature in Centigrade. '

Holmes looked back at a table. 'So if I want to turn 50 degrees in our language into Russian, what then?'

'You must subtract 32 and multiply the result by 5 and divide by 9.'

'So I must… which would be?'

'In Centigrade, 10 degrees.'

His forefinger slid down the page and came again to a stop.

'10 Centigrade,' he murmured. 'Onset 10 hours 23 minutes.'

He stared at me across the jolting cab in great surprise. 'Ten hours 23 minutes, Watson,' he repeated. 'You surprise me.'

At this, he returned to the Codex tables. 'And for a warmer temperature, shall we say at 70 degrees in English? Come, Watson, I rely on your addition and subtraction. What is 70 in this foreign tongue?'

'Around 21,' I responded.

Again his finger travelled down the columns.

'Eight hours 32 minutes.' He looked up. 'Almost two hours shorter. There is clearly much chemistry in rigor mortis. One day we must pursue it together.' He paused, looking hard at me. 'Watson, I admit I am amazed. I shared the constable's perception that stiffening takes place far faster.'

'There is the common view that if you come across a body where the arms still flop, its heart must have stopped beating within the hour – even doctors cling to that assumption.'

'But the reality...?'

'I can assure you, Holmes, the truth is very different – as you see from my experiments.'

'Then I must rely entirely on this rarest of expertise. If we had caught the three-ten as they expected, our talk would have taken place at six this evening...and the corpse discovered by seven. Take away ten hours twenty-three minutes...' His fingers fell one by one on his knees as he subtracted. 'According to your tables they must have killed the Boer shortly after breakfast and dropped him in the moat soon after.'

'Holmes,' I began, 'I watch you engage in such calculations with a mixture of concern and mirth. Perhaps before we arrive at their door and end our careers in detection...'

'... why yes, you should be enlightened – but first let me ask you, in the mill-attic...the canvas on the easel, the copy of the Constable. Did nothing about it disturb you?'

'Nothing, Holmes,' I responded, puzzled at this switch. 'What was there to disturb me? It portrayed a rustic scene, no more.'

'A very rustic scene, and cleverly done. A set-piece for Lady Fusey, a reminder of her early years on the Stour. Of the pair, would you say it was the principal commission?'

'Certainly it is the larger and more impressive.'

'Then we agree. Tell me, why did Pevensey rush to complete it? Why the sudden acceleration this afternoon? What was it that made him put on such a burst of speed?'

'I was not aware that he had.'

'Well, I can answer for it, Watson, that it was so.'

'Then perhaps you will tell me how you make that judgment?' I requested with a distinct edge of panic.

'Think back to our encounter with Pevensey in the mill-attic. At my questioning, did he not agree most artists in oil first sketch the outlines on a grid?

I nodded, unsure to which far and dangerous territory the pied piper in the carriage was leading me, while certain it was in a direction I had no wish to go.

'... and after completing the background items - hills and distant farmsteads, shall we say - he would return to the central elements and with the finest brush, in the most careful detail, paint the very essence of the commission?'

'He did, yes.'

'In Constable's Flatford Mill those elements were...?' Holmes pursued.

'The wagoner and cart - and the dog, though as Siviter explained, where Constable painted a dog, he asked Pevensey to staff the painting with a figure....'

'A figure in a flamboyant hat. So he did, my friend. And added very late in the painting's construction. It was that figure he painted in last of all.'

'What makes you so certain, Holmes?' I demanded.

'Because the sheen was on that figure and on that figure alone. Do you not consider that quite peculiar?'

'I might, Holmes, if I had any idea what you are talking about,' I replied. 'What of the sheen?'

Holmes pointed at the valise clutched by my side.

'Retrieve the Gazetteer and turn to the page on Pevensey. Read it to me.'

I seized the Gazetteer and flicked speedily through the pages.

'Is this what you mean, Holmes?' I demanded. "Pevensey prides himself on his acquaintance with the qualities and hues of different pigments in their dry state, to judge the 'goodness or deficiency' of them when ground in oil'?'

'Exactly that, Watson. Note how he 'prides himself on his acquaintance...' Yet Pevensey used boiled linseed as the medium for the passing stranger. We know from his admission the glazing was not achieved by scumbling, a fact I had already noted. He would need a hog-hair brush. He did not have a brush of that description with him. I ask you once more, does this not strike you as peculiar when he agreed the important details are left to last precisely to be completed with the greater care? Why did Pevensey turn to boiled linseed oil for the final touch – the figure of a man in pride of place? It is completely out of character.'

He cocked his eye at me to see if I had followed his reasoning.

I had not. 'You have lost me, Holmes,' I answered. 'However great my reluctance – and great it is - if I am to play any part in your charge against the Kipling League, I insist you enlighten me while there is still time. What does it mean, using boiled rather than any other state of linseed oil?'

'Boiled linseed leaves a tell-tale sheen. Worse, it has a tendency to crack.'

'Then why...?'

'Because Pevensey needed the paint to dry much faster. With boiled linseed oil you do not tip-toe across the canvas, you race.'

He continued with a most enquiring look, 'I ask you again, Watson, what was it this very day which drove Pevensey to complete the canvas by over-painting the dog with that figure at such break-neck speed? He is not an artist who turns readily to boiled linseed oil – certainly not for such a commission. It could only have been from the most unconscionable constraint.'

I stared in astonishment at my companion. 'Holmes, on so flimsy an edifice of chemistry you believe you can build a case for murder against the Kipling League?'

'Not of itself, my good friend, we need more, yet why did boiled linseed oil spring to mind when I heard the cry 'Dead body at Scotney Castle'? Such oddities are as telling as the curried mutton in *Silver Blaze*.'

By now his face had regained a determined expression. 'Watson, there are matters to be pursued. Please obey my injunctions to the letter. Immediately on our arrival you must push through their door and sweep the staircase to the parlour – that would be a servant's task early on the morrow so we are in good time.'

I digested his words. I was to push past Siviter, offer the household servants my greetings, and with a little delicacy and finesse begin to brush the stairs? And with what? Or should I force a side-window and throw in a plumber's smoke-rocket to create an alarm of fire? If so, did Holmes have such rockets in the Poshteen Long Coat's capacious pockets?

'I must tell you, Holmes,' I gasped in reply. 'I am starting to find this lightly comic. Brush the stairs for what?'

'You remember when Sir Julius and Weit arrived – the condition of their shoes? We would want to examine such particles as fell when they hurried up the stairs. I wager this coat against a light breakfast at the Kit-Kat Café that an examination of those geological particles by the trained and forensic eye will point straight to Scotney Castle. The particles will prove to be the off-spring of the soil of Kent and not the Jurassic clay of the Dudwell Valley.'

CHAPTER TEN
The Return Journey To Crick's End Continues

I sat in uneasy and perplexed disquiet, keen beyond all measure to discover a flaw in my companion's argument before we got to Crick's End. It seemed we were about to fling ourselves into a shark-infested ocean.

Holmes' passing reference to the Kit-Kat Café revived a memory. One Christmas he and I sat for an unconscionable time on the café's stoop with its fine views of Camber Sands, waiting to pounce on the evil Gustav von Seyffertitz. We had reason to believe he was staying at the Green Owl nearby, awaiting the arrival of a boat from Honfleur packed to the gunnels with his men. We ate oyster soufflé prepared in a Charlotte mould at 3d. a serving. Late that moonlit night we hired a horse-drawn bathing machine and rattled into the shallows in the leaky contraption as though setting sail for the open sea, fully-clothed, revolvers and heavy sticks to hand, ready to leap out on unsuspecting myrmidons who never came.

Our carriage slowed as it took a leftward curve up the incline to Burrish's ancient church. We were on the final stretch. Holmes tapped on the wood. The coachman's head appeared.

'If there is a quieter route to our destination, please take it.'

My spirits sank further. Not far ahead loomed the prospect of a confrontation with Van Beers and Siviter and two astute and well-placed Gold Bugs and their millions was looming. Despite his appearance of a completely collected mind, Holmes' assumptions seemed so absurd I wondered if I should make some desperate effort to forestall a most terrible public humiliation. Should I should fling my comrade from the carriage and bind him like a common footpad hand and foot with the agricultural twine I always kept to hand? If so, would the cabman help me in this endeavour – or, given my comrade's fame among workmen and millionaire alike, attack me from behind?

With little hope of reprieve, pushed near to madness by my unwillingness to confront our recent hosts with a pocketful of nonsense, I yelped, 'Holmes, enough! We are nearly there. I beg you, consider where we are with this matter! You have failed to convince me this death is the result of murder rather than accidental or self-inflicted, or if murder whether committed by proxy and by whom its planning was effected, Siviter in a criminal conspiracy with Van Beers, Sir Julius and Weit. Or was it Dudeney acting alone, or under instruction? Or Lord and Lady Fusey - or woodman Webster fed up with tramps rampaging through his master's property? And if not by stabbing or bludgeoning or soft-nosed bullets or poison, then what?'

I paused, struggling awkwardly to get to my feet in the jolting carriage.

'Imagine,' I began, half-bent over my companion, 'this carriage is the Old Bailey, you the chief and only witness for the prosecution, I in frock coat as King's Counsel for the defence. 'Mr. Sherlock Holmes,' I ask, 'Murder, you proclaim? You must show the court Means, Motivation and Opportunity. Let us quickly dispense with the matter of means. There is no question the men you accuse of dastardly murder have the means – they enjoy great privilege, power and position. Gentlemen of the jury, that I accept. One among the accused can command a thousand well-armed men. Mr. Sherlock Holmes, what method do you say they employed for such

misadventure as took place at Scotney Castle?   Stabbing or
garrotting? Blunderbuss or cosh? Titters from onlookers at the back
of the Court.   Neither constable nor Coroner reports a single mark
upon the body, is it not so – just the bronzing of the skin? Gentlemen
of the jury, did my clients murder him by too much English sun?
Mr. Sherlock Holmes, take time to reflect upon your answer to that
question and allow me to proceed to the second of the holy trinity –
what of motive?   Who has most to gain from the victim's death?   Did
this vagrant leave sacks of diamonds or bars of bullion buried at
Scotney Castle whose whereabouts are exposed in a Last Will and
Testament jutting from a pocket – or are dark glasses a great deal
more costly than I had supposed? Loud laughter from the back of the
Court.   You suggest my clients wished to foment a Third South
African War...sprinkle of incredulous laughter... by murdering a
tramp... laughter... in Kent? Roar of laughter.

Finally to opportunity - Gentlemen of the jury, as the Court has
heard, my clients express themselves whole-souled in one desire, that
England should remain prosperous, happy and committed to our
Empire, an Empire larger than the Roman, built peace-meal across
the Centuries by the valour and intellect of such men as have
appeared before you all this week. The Lord Fusey and the President
of the Royal Academy have sworn on oath the victim of drowning
was alive at the approach of three o' clock. Why must we disbelieve
them?   At three o'clock Mr. Sherlock Holmes was lecturing my
clients on the life of an unofficial Consulting Detective more than
fifteen miles away. You have heard Dr. Watson affirm that is so -
under oath.   Where, I ask, is the trail of bloody footprints?
Gentlemen of the Jury, I beg you, let this unfortunate soul rest in
peace. Why not the simple drowning the constable presumed? What
possible reason would cause these eminent men to conspire at so
heinous and contrived a crime as the murder they are accused of by

158

Mr. Sherlock Holmes and he alone? Why can we not assume this corpse found naked in a pond, clothes and hat piled neatly nearby, is simply the tragic victim of an accidental drowning or a hapless suicide? I raise my arms to Heaven and ask - where is the evidence to the contrary?'

I fell back on to the cab bench and reached over to lay my hand hard upon my friend's sleeve. 'Holmes, I speak as your friend and ally. Think what you told the Kipling League today – 'Never do I spring to a conclusion without possession of a sufficiency of necessary and credible facts'. It embarrasses me beyond compare that I myself told them – let me quote myself - 'Not for Holmes the fanciful weaving of ingenious theories miscalled 'intuition' nor the blind acceptance of circumstantial evidence untested by the searching light of cross-examination'! Here you are, scarcely three hours later, babbling on about moats and wagon ponds and the eleven-fifty rather than the three-ten train, the assassination of a Boer, the effect of temperature on rigor mortis, boiled linseed oil and scumbling... and ' I added wildly, 'pairs of paintings – what in Hades does it matter if Siviter commissioned one work or ten?'

My near-incoherent agitation had no effect.

'I simply build the foundations of a case,' Holmes responded, imperturbably. 'I build it as the mason builds the house. You speak of circumstantial evidence as though it were inconsequential yet all the while it accumulates into a collection whose pieces become corroborating evidence. Together, they may more strongly support one particular inference over another, the more valid as proof of a fact when we have ruled out all the alternative explanations. As to the theory you propose, that such magnates have no motivation for murder, why, you are not the student of history I had supposed!

159

Remember,' he added inscrutably, a characteristic further honed by his lengthy stay with the Tibetan Grand Lama, 'the Chinese character for knife is one of the simplest of two hundred and fourteen radicals. Do not be taken in by the meekness of today's assembly – even Red Riding Hood's wolf would look the less farouche seated on a Knole in Siviter's parlour.'

He sat back.

'Nevertheless, Watson, I accept you are finding the meaning of all this is very dark. Do I follow a fixed star, you wonder, or a will-o'-the-wisp? Yet you it is who helped me solve the second of the riddles. You ask, why the second canvas? Why the pair?'

'Given you kindly say I was instrumental in the answer, Holmes,' I replied with growing acerbity, 'I should be eternally grateful if you can enlighten me on my solution.'

'From the start I was certain it is a big fact. What it told us lay beyond my reach until you showed me the Watson Codex.' To my intense irritation he continued, 'But let me digress a short while. If we were to be their alibi, as I am certain was their plan, the very essence of their success depended on the most precise and calculated timing. I repeat, I am sure it was their watchman who stood outside our door purporting to offer hares for sale. He it was this morning who would have sent Siviter successive communications, the first to announce my return from Rotherhithe some fifteen minutes before the hour of eight, the second to say their telegram had reached our door.'

Rather than assisting my understanding, these utterances bolstered my confusion and agitation. I feared I was at breaking-point.

160

'Holmes,' I stuttered, staring at him aghast, 'this is all … quite the most ludicrous thing I have ever heard. Have you taken leave of your senses? How often do you remind me you need clay to make bricks? When you confront Siviter at his door with your accusations he will in his most literary way utter Ophelia's words - 'O, what a noble mind is here o'erthrown'!'

As I spoke, our carriage swung sharp left between the church and a Crimea war memorial, plunging into the Dudwell Valley, the two greys straining to hold the sociable's weight from running loose down the one-in-ten gradient. On the left stood the village school. Settled on the roof facing west, six ring-doves sat in line, pouting chests etched by the yellow-gold rays of the setting sun.

I looked at Holmes in desperation. 'Why take a corpse to Scotney Castle at all? Why not the confines of the Crick's End estate? If they wished to make a murder look like drowning, they have the mill-pond to hand!''

'A corpse on the doorstep of the Kipling League would be a grave embarrassment. These are not claqueurs out to gain the public's attention. They chose Scotney Castle for three good reasons. It is at a departure from Crick's End, it contains a moat, and most of all they can place reliance on their accomplice Lord Fusey. Left at that it would have been simple - but these rich and powerful men took delight in constructing a daring game to occupy a rainy day, far more entertaining than the hunt for elephants and tigers from the safety of a machan. In a word, they aimed to ensnare Holmes in their deadly plot.'

Holmes dropped his voice. 'Watson, not by any stretch of my

161

imagination was I invited as entertainment on an idle afternoon. From my calculations based on your Codex their victim was killed this morning, his corpse taken immediately to the moat. No doubt it was submerged under overhanging branches until discovery timed precisely to accommodate my lecture – your Codex proves the coolness of a moat fed by a stream would prolong the onset of rigor mortis until at least an hour past six, six being the time I should have been on my feet if we had come on the three-ten train. Seven would be the time they scheduled for the corpse's discovery.'

'Holmes,' I broke in desperately. 'The second canvas – you say I helped...'

'...provide the solution to this vexing riddle, indeed you did, and I shall now tell it to you. There was one reason and one alone for Siviter to order the second commission. It was to provide evidence the victim was standing beside the moat at six this evening. The painting would become the set-piece in their defence if needed. They summoned me by telegram to take the three-ten train, enticing me with the prospect of a hamper and a considerable fee. At most I thought this invitation a minor flattery. I see now it was a most ingenious and brilliant conceit. I repeat, the famed consulting detective was invited to Crick End to be witness at a Court of Law, witness for the defence of famous poet, Randlord and two Gold Bugs against a charge of assassination!'

To this day I cannot recollect another instance where Holmes engaged in such extraordinary calculations. His adamant adherence to so preposterous a theory stirred me to the point of insanity.

As though taking my silence to mean I awaited further explanation, Holmes pressed on. 'Yes, Watson, should Scotland Yard by chance

162

adopt an interest, it was essential to the League's original plan I and they together should be assembled at Crick's End at six o' clock. The local constable would be summoned from his cottage to inspect a body found in the moat by a woodman 'in the undertaking of his rounds' at seven, its limbs still short of stiffening, claimed by Fusey to have been alive only an hour before, corroborated by Pevensey's painting. Instead, to the plotters' consternation, we caught the earlier train and I would be on my feet much sooner. According to the Watson Codex, far from a need to delay rigor mortis by keeping the body cool, now they needed to speed the process up, otherwise they might lose me as their witness. Leaving the body in the cool water of the moat would have maintained the suppleness of its limbs far too long. Even the local bobby would have found it feasible the victim died well past the time of my presentation at three. We might easily have been whirling back to London. My value to the League would be placed in serious jeopardy. Hence they hastened to take the body from the moat and place it in the warmer water of the wagon pond. Thus the sheen on the figure in the Constable.'

'Again, Holmes, what of the sheen?' I repeated haplessly. 'Please explain.'

'I asked myself even while we were at the easel in the mill-attic, why did Pevensey suddenly resort to boiled linseed oil? What was the urgent need? Why commit a sin against his own profession? There could be only one answer – *force majeure*. Why else? Imagine him at the wagon pond not long after lunch-time today, completing at leisure the last few brush-strokes in the Constable painting, namely the dog. It is possible up to then he was unaware of the murderous activity taking place around him. He was simply finishing the Constable before returning to the moat by six o' clock to staff the second canvas - at Siviter's behest - with a figure wearing Sir Julius' flamboyant hat. From *The Musgrave Ritual* we know in the early evening a rod of six feet would throw a shadow approaching nine. The shadow and the spectre's reflection would indicate the hour. Pevensey would be driven direct to a railway station to catch the train. After his departure, the body hidden in the waters of the moat among the carp and bream was to be discovered by the woodman at seven. Instead, what happens? Just after lunch, Pevensey was at the wagon pond completing the Constable by painting in the dog. Dudeney drives up, accompanied by Weit and Sir Julius. With at most a hurried explanation, Dudeney lifts a corpse from the back seat or boot and drags it into the shallow water before Pevensey's bulging eyes. Weit or Sir Julius order the artist to overpaint the dog with a living stranger wearing the flamboyant hat, the shadow and reflection to indicate three this afternoon, precisely the time I would be on my feet, the Kipling League before me.'

'Holmes,' I demanded hotly, fearful of the reckoning drawing nigh, 'this is all quite exceptionally ingenious though as near impossible a supposition as you have ever uttered. What of motive? How else can you convince Scotland Yard let alone a jury? This is a case as different from the Abergavenny murder as the moon is from Earth.'

'For the moment it is not motive which concerns me, Watson, it's the proof! As of yet I have not grasped the motive - we must leave it in gold and diamonds and the Rand. Emanations from the recent war in Africa are far from settled. Across the Continent the great scramble goes on. Nyasaland and the Congo are up for grabbing.'

A 'Whoaa' to the horses reminded us of the presence of the cabman hidden from sight above and to the back of us.

'Holmes,' I said, lowering my voice but unable to withhold my urgent tone. 'Please answer me, have I been your true friend and loyal companion through a multitude of almost intractable cases...?'

'You have, Watson, and I am most...'

'And have we not together been confronted several times with death itself – in *The Adventure of the Empty House*, when we faced the threat of Colonel Sebastian Moran, for example? And when we infiltrated the Hermetic Order of the Golden Dawn?'

'Indeed, my friend, we have,' Holmes replied imperturbably. 'I remember clearly.'

'And in *The Adventure of The Speckled Band*?' I pursued.

'As you say,' came the reply.

'Did I not save your life on one never-to-be-forgotten occasion when we were hunting Sir Grimesby Roylott?'

'...in the Dinaric Arc, yes.'

The Dinaric Arc was a vast network of underground caves, lakes and rivers running under the Balkan Mountains in labyrinthine fashion, dark and largely devoid of light.

'And must I remind you Sir Grimesby was reputed to be the third most dangerous man in London?'

'Indisputably you saved me from destruction at his hands, yes, my good friend Watson.'

165

'And what of *The Threadneedle*...?' I clamoured, at which Holmes interrupted with a slight smile.

'Watson, I find your reference to several of our adventures most enjoyable but in turn I remind you we are short of time. Can we follow my maxim, 'If 'p', then 'q''? You have made one point well – which is, unless I have misunderstood you completely, you are a most loyal and brave companion. Is there another point of equal merit to follow from the first? Surely you are now not going to whisper your old school number in my ear, which, unless I am mistaken, was thirty- ...?'

'Holmes, in short, am I not a true comrade upon whose nerve you can place some reliance?'

'I repeat, most certainly you are.'

'A whetstone for your mind...'

'Again, indeed.'

'And if I irritate you by a certain methodical slowness in my mentality, does that irritation make your own flame-like intuitions and impressions flash up the more vividly and swiftly...?'

'Watson, my dear old friend....' Holmes interrupted, a wry look replacing the smile. 'Please, I beg you, cut out the poetry.'

'Holmes, I follow your words closely. I am aware at other times you have deduced from signs so subtle and minute that even when you have pointed them out to me I could scarcely follow you in your reasoning. On this occasion - you must forgive me for putting it so plainly - I would rather follow you into battle against Professor Moriarty and Colonel Moran together, armed only with one of Mrs. Hudson's feather dusters, than confront these Sungazers with what you have in mind.'

My knees trembled with anxiety but I forced myself to continue. 'Tut, man, the facts so far presented are not the slightest bit convincing. Familiar as I am with your methods, it is impossible for me to go along with your deductions.'

'Not for the first time in living memory, surely, Doctor?' Holmes responded with an edge. 'None the less, if you insist, I shall keep on piling fact upon fact until your reason breaks down under them and acknowledges me to be right. I hope by that process to have cleared up any little obscurity which the case may still present.'

In a more conciliatory tone he continued, 'You have my word, Watson, once we confront them at Crick's End, the facts will evolve before your eyes. I have no doubt that we shall have all our details filled in. The mystery will clear gradually away as each new element uncovered furnishes a step which will lead us on to the complete truth.'

'We shall see, Holmes,' I replied, giving him a dubious look. 'I had no idea of the lengths to which your curiosity would carry you. This is not a puny plot in a yellow-backed novel or a sevenpenny by Rider Haggard. Gold Bugs and Randlord – and Siviter himself - these are hardly people who hang around in Tower Hill. To promote the charge of murder against men of such standing – of such wealth, such raw power – on what you speculate seems neither legally plausible nor politically palatable.'

His words were coming to me muffled as though through wool. I bent my head to look out of the carriage. My voice rose to a shriek. 'Holmes, we are approaching the final furlong before we meet them face to face. I simply cannot let you...'

This adamant refusal to accept his deductions overstretched my companion's patience. He ceased his attempts at reason or conciliation. With a violent movement of his forearm he fixed me with a synthetically enraged eye and in a high and strident tone shouted, 'Watson, you dare to say you simply cannot let me? You question both my actions and my motives? You, a doctor — you are enough to drive a patient into an asylum. Do not make me regret I spoke of you with warmth and sympathy! Don't harry me like a badger-baiter! This is not your novel. I am reconciled to the fact you are Ruth to my Naomi but you stretch my good-will and patience to the point of breaking. Pay attention, Watson, I demand you take my assumptions seriously. Throwing down that Tropical hat was a challenge worthy of a Professor Moriarty. From it they knew I would infer their deadly hand. Their dare to me is – 'Great Consulting Detective, put together proof!'

Panic seeped through my brain like fungus through dead wood. Even as Holmes' heated words fled from the carriage, a most remarkable thing took place. Both of us watched in the greatest astonishment. Like a ouija board in motion, summoning up the spirits, a hand was rising of its own accord before our eyes. It proceeded upwards whilst we stared, mesmerised, then arched backward over our heads and rapped against the carriage wall like a spirit from the other side. A commanding voice which, like the hand, turned out to be mine, though I did not recognise either, so feverish had I grown from trepidation, yelled 'Cabman, halt the horses - at once!'

168

With a sharp pull of the reins and a musical jangling sound, the greys halted, their heads turning back like pointers on the leash, looking upward at the driver. The cabman leant forward, his face half upside-down, and stared in at us expectantly.

'Holmes,' I said, dropping my voice to an urgent whisper, my words coming in sharp, jerky outbursts, 'If this carriage contained a bell-pull to a psychiatric unit I would use it to summon six strong men in white apparel. In our time together we have had the good fortune to bring peace to many troubled souls. Now I beg you to bring some to mine. Let the cabman await a while. You have issued a farrago of unconnected facts guised as proof. We must talk in confidence – and now!'

Holmes sat in startled silence, staring at me with amazement.

CHAPTER ELEVEN
A Rabbit's Tail

Taken aback by such vehemence from a usually diffident companion, Holmes waved the cabman to a triangle of grass at the intersection of two lanes some thirty yards ahead. The coach moved forward and we came to a halt by a stream. Head whirling, the setting sun a blur, I sprang out and walked to the bridge. In the twilight of the early-summer evening, the Sussex landscape glowed golden and wonderful in the slanting rays of the setting sun. The shadow of a white signpost moved across an open field, one finger pointed southward to Wood's Corner on a ridge three miles beyond, another westward to Crick's End, less than a quarter-mile down the lane.

I threw a backward glance at Holmes. He bore the angry, aspersive look of a disturbed cock-pheasant. Like a quarry cornered, I turned to confront his glowering countenance. 'My dear and singular friend,' I began, keen to pre-empt his wrath, 'I speak with the deepest trepidation. You know it is my greatest joy and privilege to serve you. I am look-out, decoy, accomplice, messenger and whetstone for your mind and willingly accept my drummer-boy status. It has always been my habit to go along with you, clinging on if only to your little finger or large toe while you leap the yawning crevice. It is my custom to take up distant ground, to be disposed to avoid all pretext for collision. I realise full well I am at my highest value in the role of an interested student observing a surgeon at work or seated quietly in a corner while you think aloud. Even to hardened members of Scotland Yard or the Paris Sûreté the sight of Sherlock Holmes in majestic action has an especially vivid appeal, like the trill of a pipe to a cobra.' I paused. With as much emphasis as I could muster, I added, 'but in this instance I feel the stakes are much too high.'

At this unfamiliar show of defiance, my comrade opened his mouth to start his response. I held up a peremptory finger. 'Holmes, I will not offer subjection to your commands, however righteous. Do you not recall on our way to the Brixton Road during A Study In Scarlet you convinced me it is a capital mistake to theorise before all the evidence is in, because it biases the judgment? I have a vivid recollection of that instance. Bitterly hard as I find it, I must therefore alter my long-held habit of withholding my opinion for fear of needless interruption of your thought. Here, and now, I say there is such a need.'

I ceased speaking and waited with extreme disquiet for his reply. In the stillness I heard little but the thumping of my heart.

My companion cocked a puckered eye at me from a near distance with great curiosity, as though in need of a monocle. It was clear my words had failed to assuage him. When he took his turn to speak, he showed every sign of acute impatience. Umbrage permeated every word.

'Watson, it has been your custom to express incredulity with your eyebrows – now I see you have switched to your tongue! This is a brilliant departure! Am I to understand you have deserted my faction and crossed to the enemy line?' His voice sharpened. 'Are you the Sorcerer's Apprentice - having memorised what to do and say, you wish to do your own witching? Do we have the elements of a Promethean tale the equal of Mary Shelley's? Or like the Pankhursts, are you going to march behind me with a banner demanding the right to vote?'

He stopped. His face more purple than I had ever noted. In a visible effort to regain my cooperation he asked, 'Which part of my reasoning strikes you as faulty? I tell you, Watson, and I beg you to listen, this is no pretty puzzle of the police-court. Large issues will prove to be at stake, I am certain of it. I fear it is a serious international complication, a diplomatic coup d'état.'

His thin fingers twitched. He continued, 'My dear friend, if in the detail you reject my supposition, do you not consider the cumulative effects of what I say to be considerable? Do you not recall my words in The Book of Life – from an observation of a drop of water, a logician could infer the possibility of a Niagara or the Pacific Ocean? I speculate this may not merely be the murder of a Boer but – and I repeat - the promise of an international incident or worse.'

At this my companion ceased speaking, awaiting my reaction to his words, a singular expression of interest on his hawkish features. I felt unwilling to respond. At my silence, he resumed his old manner and demanded sardonically. 'Or is it possible that without my knowing, you are in hot pursuit of the real assassin, a hirsute man wearing Russian Army boots, both left-footed? Someone whose presence in our shadow I have completely failed to spot?'

The sneer in his voice obliged me to retort. 'Holmes, I am not in hot pursuit of a hirsute man wearing two left-footed Russian Army boots. I realise you regard me simply as a minor confederate, one to whom each development comes as a perpetual surprise, but in this instance if you believe I follow you willingly back to their portico, you labour under a grave misapprehension. As to a logician inferring the Niagara Falls from a single drop of water, may I refer you to the tale of the six blind men clustered around an elephant, each asked to guess the whole beast from touching just a single part – trunk, ear, side, tusk, leg, tail. I say we are two of those blind men. I repeat, despite your every effort to brow-beat me into submission, from the insubstantial wares you have laid out at our table you have not for a moment convinced me there is a case of murder to be made, and certainly no case to prove the members of the Kipling League perpetrated a hideous crime.'

'Confound it, Holmes,' I hastened on. 'Surely the game is hardly worth the candle? My trust in your intuition has gone as far as it will. Leave well alone. Nothing about the description of the body seems alarming. It might well be just a drowning and a corpse like any other, except for being seared by a sun fiercer than one we are accustomed to in an English spring. Do you not see that we are plunging at a furious pace to professional extinction? I have long feared that at some point a horrible misfortune would come suddenly to blast your career. Has that time come, I ask? You put forward an unsubstantiated hypothesis, you speak of wagon ponds and moats, spiny lizards, Tropical hats - and Randlords and Gold Bugs howling out like wolves of war. Until now I have been quite unacquainted with your gift for improvisation, other than when you play the Stradivarius. I swear you totter on the very edge of self-deception.'

I held up a hand to prevent him retorting while I gasped in a breath. 'Holmes,' I resumed, words leaving my mouth in short bursts, like a Maxim gun gone berserk, 'your love of the complex and the unusual combined with our recent period of boredom has led you to depend prodigiously on the power of bluff. Let me return a favourite phrase of yours - I beg you to consider the problem in the light of pure reason. Consider too the effect on others of the evidence you have placed before me − a raised eyebrow or a guffaw or chortle from Inspector Lestrade at Scotland Yard is the least of our concerns. And please remember, this comes from your closest ally, not a deadly

173

foe.'

I had shot my musket-ball. Tremulously I added, 'Did you not once say that if it should ever strike me you grow too-confident in your powers, I should whisper 'Norbury' in your ear and you shall be infinitely obliged?'

So entranced was he by this sudden and despairing reference to Norbury, my companion's mouth, at the ready to respond in a most heated and scornful way, snapped shut. He stood looking at me without a word. Seconds passed. I looked away across the fields. From the corner of an eye I saw Holmes biting at a nail, now staring towards Crick's End, now turning to stare at me once more. Finally, he bent on me a wonderfully penetrating and questioning look. 'Watson, you are quite white with passionate earnestness. You impress me with your frantic look.'

He paused, continuing to consider me carefully. 'Your words have a stinging and salutary effect upon me, like mustard in a bath of water. I had quite put Norbury out of my thoughts. By this reference you oblige me to reconsider my ideas.'

A short pause followed, then, 'It is quite a three pipe problem. I beg that you won't speak to me for a good while yet.'

A lengthy silence ensued. Swiftly and methodically he was turning over the facts as though turning over the contents of drawer after drawer and cupboard after cupboard, but as yet I could see no gleam of success brightening his austere face.

At last, in a questing voice he resumed. 'Has my ability to follow the scent faded so quickly?' Turning his back to our carriage as though

174

fearing the cabman could read his lips, he continued, 'I admit our difficulties still lie before us. Like the Sussex hills which surround us, every fresh advance reveals a fresh ridge beyond. It is true that in my deep interest in the criminal mind I might conflate cause and coincidence, though that is usually self-correcting. Blind alleys soon lead to dead-ends and we hurry back to our earlier tracks. Watson, perhaps you have scored a palpable touch, the second in our long career together. I beg of you, do not imagine that I depend on bluff for my though bluff is a powerful ingredient in our panoply of tricks. I must admit the key to jiggling the tumblers into place to force Siviter and a Randlord and his Gold Bug allies into an admission has not yet come to light.'

He waggled a finger at me.

'Watson, I shall accede to your earnestness and listen to what you have to say.' Glancing in the waiting coachman's direction, he added, 'Your reproof is no less formidable for being so temperate in expression. Do proceed.'

Thus encouraged and despite the possibility I was being lured into waters awash with barracuda (there was no end to Holmes' Celtic cunning) I launched myself at him.

'Holmes, you have given me a plenitude of quite extraordinary speculation, more entertaining than any I recall. What you propose is sufficient to speed the most sluggish pulse. The grasp you displayed of pictorial art befits your descent from a French grand-uncle artist. Where I would have sworn on oath there would be a lacuna, your understanding of the chemistry of artists' paint, is new to me and beyond compare. I am sincerely flattered you place such importance on the Watson Codex. As to your great knowledge of

Reptilia, that is known to all. However, despite the presence of a disrobed corpse, male, age around fifty, which might of late have worn a pair of breeches under a Tropical sun, possibly in the Transvaal, a crimson hat like a bowler out of a Mexican sombrero bearing a strip of snake or lizard probably obtained from the Zoo in Regent's Park, and a wagon pond rather than a moat – and paintings of both wagon pond and moat by Pevensey - precisely what do we have?'

I moved in headlong for the kill.

'Absolutely nothing, Holmes, but the misguided and dangerous conflation you fear!'

The dregs of my courage draining, I determined it was now time to maintain a stout and challenging quietude. Holmes gazed at me as though expecting me to continue. At my persistent silence he took up the exchange.

'My dear friend Watson, let me commence with a digression. How often do I tell you and your fine friends like Edward Marsh (though I believe the latter knows), that knowledge is the peacock's tail, one element in an armoury designed mostly to impress. It is linen strung in sequence on a line, as simple to unpeg or drop as pigwash or a golden crown. I warrant overnight I could study and absorb the greater part of Euclid's Elements - and remove them from my brain's lumber-room one hour later if I chose. By my disquisition on painting I prove only that mastering information is the easiest of the black arts and much over-rated. You speak of my understanding of the chemistry of paint. Knowing we would make the acquaintance of the President of the Royal Academy, I prepared by learning all I ever want or need to know from the Picture Encyclopaedia of Art while

176

you assumed I was searching the attic for the Poshteen Long Coat and my gold watch. The Poshteen Long Coat awaited me in Mrs. Hudson's kitchen, drying at her stove. It was damp from my visit to the Rotherhithe docks this morning while you slept. I was reading from the Picture Encyclopaedia in our attic even as I clattered and crumbled before an Everest of your paraphernalia from the Afghan wars, those battered tin-trunks – do move them to your Bank - bullet-pocked pith-helmets – sell them to the Alhambra – studded wardrobe-trunks, shoe-boxes, and a whole assembly of travelling-cushions – surely destined for Mrs. Hudson - plus the greatcoat of green camlet lined with fox-skin fur sold to you at an exorbitant price on the unlikely grounds it was purchased by James Boswell during his Grand Tour. Tell me, Watson, where did you get the lavender-grey frock coat and white top-hat? Was it a loan from the Grand Duke Dmitri for lunch at Skindles after Ascot? Or donated to you together with a bronze medal by an ex-serviceman's charity for long and meritorious service? '

Wounded by these rapier-thrusts I broke back in. My sustained effrontery obliged me to gulp great balloons of air like the giant cat-fish of the desiccating Pusta-i-Telpun swamp. I burst out, 'Holmes, am I to assume this capricious tone is serious? Though seldom have we ever had a difference in thought or word or deed, this time I am not prepared to let you off so lightly. You know full well the lavender-grey frock coat and white top hat are yours, not mine, awarded to you by the Grand Duke Dmitri – though whether for lunch at Skindles after Ascot I am not privy. Your humour over the acquisition of pigwash knowledge aims to disarm. It is a new and clever weapon in your armoury, much to be encouraged. I have been totting up as you speak and to be frank – and please take this as well-intended - nothing you have presented to me as proof of murder is a call to arms, certainly not – if I may split an infinitive – to boldly

177

hammer on the doors of sublimely rich and influential men. Far from a dénouement, it would be a rout! You pant to throw them in the clink and see them hang. You cast all reserve to the winds – and for why? Surely not because for their sins and appetite they control the fate of millions! Did you not tell them this very afternoon you make a point of never harbouring any prejudices and of following docilely wherever fact may lead you? Are you not forever instructing me it is of the highest importance in the art of detection to be able to distinguish from a number of facts those which are vital from the ones which are incidental? Yet here you mix them like salt and pepper. I repeat, none of the facts you present as evidence tot up to anything more than a hill of beans.'

At my words he looked away. His expression changed from one of humouring a child-like companion to stern and pensive. He stared at the river flowing dark-grey below us. White of face he exclaimed harshly, 'Damnation! Perhaps through your superb normality you have come up with a valid point. Do I drown in an excess of ingenuity?'

He paused so long that had he been seated I would, under other circumstances, assumed his narcolepsy had struck him into a momentary asleep. With a sudden determined shake of his head, like a bull staggering under the blood-letting of a picador's darts, he turned back to view me.

'Watson, these many years in my profession have given me a nose for a crime as keen as a vintner's for a fine claret. Were Moriarty not definitively dead, I would say he is alive and well among these Sussex hills. Certainly he must be mocking our disunity from his watery grave in Hell.'
He continued in a low, disturbed voice, 'I assure you, Watson,

178

something vast and evil is taking place around us, though right now it lies a yard or more beyond my outstretched hand.'

He stared once more along the long straight stretch of the River Dudwell to the distant outline of Crick's End. In the crepuscular light, it appeared a sombre edifice, saved only by the jaunty set of the Tudor chimneys etched against the still-lit westerly horizon. To my troubled eye, though at first picturesque in the happier time of our arrival earlier in the day, Holmes' accusations now caused it to take on the grim and menacing visage of the sinister Crooksbury Hall, we encountered in The Adventure Of The Solitary Cyclist.

My companion resumed. 'I can see you are not yet at my shoulder. We shall discuss the matter further before we resume our journey to their lair.'

Although impressed and disconcerted by his serious tone, his words calmed me. I was relieved at the prospect of a hiatus before we clamoured at their door.

'Where do we start?' I asked.

Holmes leaned on the bridge rail, looking down at the river.

'As you point out, the evidence I have offered you is slight – not one witness for the prosecution or a scribbled note - yet we know from our other cases small pickings are to deduction as wick to candle.'

He threw me a swift glance.

'Think on these things once more, try to view them as from afar. The watchman keeping an eye on our Baker Street door. The urgent nature of the invitation. The arrival of Weit and Sir Julius to hear my talk at three o' clock precisely – delayed by what? The indent of a hat too small on Sir Julius' brow. A disrobed body in a shallow wagon pond exposing the effects of a burning sun. A Tropical hat with a band sourced in the Transvaal lying a-top the victim's clothes. The dark glasses clutched between finger and thumb on a jutting arm. Why hold up dark glasses as you sink beneath the surface of a wagon pond – to save them from drowning? The empty pockets. Not far away a moat eight feet deep or more. Pevensey at work on two canvases on the same Estate, the second painting commissioned only two or three days ago. The use of boiled linseed oil for the figure of the stranger replacing Constable's dog.... do you say there is no fusion in all this?'

'Holmes...' I started, trying to break in.

He stilled me with the wave of an imperious hand. 'Let me continue, Watson. I believe you have given me the gist of your argument. I need your ear more than your tongue. Let us cast the net wider to see if further clues cry out for our attention. Siviter's study would be the poison gland of the nettle, the engine through which this plot was hatched. Does an important clue lie there? I recall only an old photograph of his mother wearing black patches on her face to enhance the delicacy of her complexion.'

My recollection of the study was of a well-lit room, an outsize desk sparsely adorned with the silver-framed photograph of Siviter's mother, two fine inkwells, a little silver comfit box, a delicate Ming dynasty saucer of the most beautiful deep-blue colour, an unusual emerald snake ring presented to Siviter by the Grand Duke of Cassel-Felstein, a dish of oranges beside a carafe of water, and a Berliner Gram-o-phone. To each side was a papier mâché mother-of-pearl chair surrounded by a litter of dog-baskets filled with the eager attractive faces of the Aberdeen terriers. One basket was formerly a nursery-bath, with the lid still on it.

'And some 2000 books around the walls,' I ventured.

'Among which ..?'

'Many for the eyes of sailors: Superstitions of the Sea, Knots and Splices, Typee, Know Your Own Ship, South Pacific Directory, Castaway on the Auckland Islands, Stevens' Stowage. Oh, yes, and Nimrod's Conditioning Of Hunters. And books on bees.'

'I too observed his fine collection on bee-farming, twenty-one in all. He has some good in him. But was there anything … absent?'

Among all Siviter's literary treasures on the layers of shelves in his study, there was not so much as a copy of *The Strand* to catch my attention, not even the best-known of our cases – *The Hound of the Baskervilles*, *The Speckled Band*, *A Study In Scarlet*, or *The Empty House*. Instead, on a shelf set aside for three-decker novels and other light reading sat works by J. M. Barrie, Conrad, Olive Schreiner, James Fenimore Cooper, Galsworthy, an Emily and a Charlotte Brontë and a half dozen works of Rudyard Kipling.

'Not one of your chronicles, Watson? Surely not… Not one, you say?'

'Not one.'

Holmes' amour de soi had been stung.

'Aquila non captat muscas,' he said dryly. 'The Eagle does not catch flies.'

We fell silent. Although the sun had yet to set behind the wooded hills, the air above the stream was beginning to dampen and cool.

Still staring along the Dudwell towards Crick's End, brow furrowed, Holmes resumed. 'Something I cannot identify disturbs me, something in the paintings, a clue as important to the prosecution of this case as the tip-toe marks at the Baskerville Estate. We must pass through these oils by Pevensey and step out the other side, or like a palimpsest rub hard at them with oat bran and milk. I say the reason he used boiled linseed oil was to cover up their tracks. Up to then, neither canvas showed any signs of hurry. Its use serves Pevensey well. It speaks loud in his defence. It proves to me he knew nothing of the murder until after lunch today. A President of the Royal Academy does not live in a Daguerreotype world, summoned hither-and-thither to paint an oil in fifty seconds. Yet today, haste there was. It turned the Constable from a work of promise into mere quantities of pigment awaiting a frame. It is that which first drew my attention.'

'Enlighten me, Holmes, if you will. Why precisely did he need that figure to dry at such a pace? A few hours more or less…'

'… could turn their alibis against them. They had to calculate the possibility something about the death would raise the Peeler's suspicion. This where the figure in the Constable is central. If the figure stayed wet until tomorrow it could throw into doubt the claim a passing stranger – the so-called tramp - was painted in this afternoon and not some hours later. By drying at an exceptional rate, the figure would provide convincing evidence the stranger was alive at three o' clock.'

He paused. 'Nevertheless, I fear I am missing something of immediate importance... something critical to the case.'

I remained quiet, happy to be back to my role as sounding-board while Holmes continued in intense cogitation, his eyes narrowed to slits. 'Was there something in the setting?' he murmured several times, 'the dim-lit mill-attic? A shaft of sunlight through the window playing on the easel...'

As if I were no longer at his side, Holmes continued, 'All that bended knee to history. The meadow where Jack Cade was slaughtered... so much on Cade's death and his severed head on London Bridge I felt I was at a vivisection. In the telegram, Siviter threw in Pevensey as bait, such was the urgent wish to bring us here. He knew we would want to meet the famous artist and view his work, yet consider our host's pains to prevent us from being tête-à-tête. Why so? You saw Pevensey's uneasy stance upon our entry? How soon he took his leave? The glance he gave us on his departure. He may be incidental to the crime - I doubt he would garrotte a tube of Chrome Yellow - but Pevensey's paintings are vital to their alibi. As to taking an earlier train than ours, more likely he wished to avoid a Pullman car containing Holmes and Watson than worry over Third Class compartments filled with colporteurs and market-women with babies!'

'Holmes,' I interrupted, 'if the use of boiled linseed and the sheen so greatly aroused your interest, why did you not bring the matter to Siviter's attention after Pevensey left the attic? Would it not have been of interest to hear what the patron had to say?'

183

'We were not yet acquainted with the report in the *Standard*. I was not in the market for seeking clues. After Pevensey spent a week or more on such a mundane commission – jobbing works in imitation of a Constable or paintings of ruins by moats will not enhance his reputation – he may have decided to complete the work in the quickest time. It would hardly be out of character.'

'Holmes,' I said mildly. 'Isn't that a plausible explanation for his use of boiled linseed oil?'

Holmes' thin lips compressed. His brows drew down, lost in profound thought. He turned in my direction and looked at me with a reluctant expression, as though the investigation had reached its end.

'Watson, it is possible you have been right all along. Perhaps I am simply spinning conjurors' plates. A fifth-rate Counsel might tear my suppositions to rags. As we stand here at this bridge there is insufficient evidence to bring an accusation to their porch or even gain the ear of Scotland Yard. Our ferret-like friend Lestrade would react exactly as you suggest – he would listen in apparent seriousness and snigger the moment our back was turned. While I maintain there is truth in my conclusion, that this is an assassination – and by the Kipling League - I can see they have you firmly on their side and would gain the sympathy and respect of a jury too.'

While sympathetic to my companion's gloom, my heart grew lighter at these despondent words. I gestured towards the carriage. The watchful cabman picked up the reins at the ready. The horses' brass accoutrements jangled. The greys, still grazing the lane verges, pulled forward for a last mouthful of vegetation, dislodging a rabbit from its shelter. With amazing celerity it dashed across the lane, leaping into the nearby field. Successive bounds merged into a long and shallow glide like a porpoise accompanying a Cunard ocean liner. Despite the ever-dimming evening light, the tufted white of the tail was remarkably easy to follow.

With the fear draining from my being, I twitched Holmes' sleeve.

'What would Darwin say about the whiteness of that creature's tail?' I asked gaily. 'It cannot be a warning like the cobra hissing – it has no weapons in its armoury but flight. Surely such a ball of cotton commands the fox to chase it rather than dissuades it? Does this not contradict the *Theory of Evolution by Natural Selection*?'

'It is a paradox,' Holmes agreed.

'And why does the white tuft flash only when its owner is retreating?'

'At the very least it is a warning to its brethren.'

'But what of its own safety as it rushes to its burrow?' I asked, looking expectantly at my companion, keen to engage longer on the subject whilst edging ever-closer to our carriage.

'Then, Watson… as it approaches its burrow what happens?' Holmes responded.

I replied, 'Why, with luck it scurries into the very deeps of Mother Earth.'

'With luck, you say? But can it be just through luck? No species survives over brutish time at the whim of Mistress Luck, not a creature with such a lodestar of a tail.'

'Yet prosper it has. Look at the numbers in this field alone.'

'Indubitably so.'

'So what of Darwin's Theory?' I insisted. 'Surely the rabbit is too successful for the tuft to be mere evolutionary baggage?'

'Darwin could only argue the creature prospers because of – not despite – the whiteness of its tail. Natural Selection permits no other conclusion.'

'By which you mean…?'

'If it raises only when the creature senses danger, it must aid, not endanger its own escape.'

'Holmes,' I pursued, 'I may lack quickness of perception, but how could that be? Have we not this very moment observed what a marker the white tail makes, even in the dusk? Even from this distance our eye tracked it to its lair some forty yards away.'

'Indeed,' Holmes assented. 'Again I ask, what then?'

'Why, as I said, with luck it scurries into its burrow.'

'And I repeat, Watson, we and all things living are lost if Nature depends so heavily on the momentary chance.'

'Then I give up,' I replied, perplexed, shaking my head dolefully at my ignorance, deeply pleased my stratagem was working. With a smile Holmes said, 'Watson, you have aroused my curiosity and led me off from my own pursuit, well done. It is good you keep me flat-footed. We shall take this matter of the rabbit to a logical conclusion. What of the tail's location?'

'Why, Holmes,' I laughed, 'where tails are always located!'

'Meaning?'

'At the very back.'

'Thus when the fox pursues it?'

'In the fox's very eye?' I ventured.

'How would you describe the action of that tail?'

'That it bobs up and down?'

'Watson, bravo! Once more today you have solved a vexing puzzle.'

Perplexed, I stared at my companion. 'Holmes, would you kindly explain how I have solved this mystery?'

'Why, as you suggest, it lies less in the tail than the bobbing.'

'What of the bobbing?'

'At the very least the speed of bobbing would allow a predator to calculate if the creature's agility makes it impossible to catch – but let us assume our fox is in full cry. Whenever life is taken, there is always a decisive moment. Think when that would be for the rabbit.'

'Just as the fox closes in, jaws gaping…'

'… at which point the very whiteness of that tail even in the gloom would now be jigging before the fox's eye… up, down, up, down…'

Dramatically I threw my arms into the air. '…creating mesmeric turmoil in the fox's brain! Of course! Holmes, well done!'

At the very instant I uttered my congratulations it was as though an electric stroke passed through my companion. With an iron grip he took my sleeve, pulling me swiftly from the carriage step. I heard him crying, 'Watson, you have done well! Let us reconsider Pevensey's paintings in the light of the rabbit's tail. Answer me without demur, at the last minute what replaced the dog in the painting of the wagon pond?'

'The passing stranger, Holmes. Surely that could be simple poetic licence? Clearly Siviter wanted a shepherd or woodman in the landscape… why not?'

'No Watson, the figure at the wagon pond, that was the rabbit's tail! That's why Siviter wanted it to replace the dog – it was not only to establish the victim was alive and present at three o' clock, it was to concentrate our attention on it when we viewed the painting in the Mill. But why?'

Never had I seen Holmes rise so fast to such a pitch, save but once, in *The Illustrious Client*.

Suddenly he shouted, 'Daubigny! Landscape With A Sunlit Stream! The other painting! Watson, we must return at once to the Mill-

188

attic!'

Bewildered I demanded, 'What of the other painting?

'It is the other painting – the one they threw aside - which requires our immediate attention. The proof of murder lies in it. Watson, from a most casual look I recall it contains a serious blunder, one which will oblige Inspector Gregory to bring a charge of assassination against the Kipling League!   Rather than confront Siviter openly at his door we must return with the utmost secrecy to the mill. We must at all cost gain hold of the canvas on the floor, the painting of the castle ruin and the moat!'

I stared at Holmes in stupefaction.   A ruined castle in the early-evening light, a sprinkling of azaleas and a moat? How would such a painting help his cause?

By now Holmes was at the sociable, turning to beckon me with an urgent gesture. His voice rang with joy.

'Watson, come with the greatest speed! We've got 'em, by Heaven, we've got 'em!   Your rabbit's tail – it has given us the key. Come, Watson, come!' he shouted. 'With the help of the god of justice I will give you a case which will make all England stand agog.'

Holmes flung himself aboard the carriage.   At his command, the cabman flicked the reins and the greys were away, clip-clopping past an isolated farmhouse signed 'Naboth's Vineyard'. It was the last habitation before Crick's End.   Holmes rubbed his hands and chuckled like a connoisseur sipping a comet vintage. My spirits sank to depths never before plumbed.

CHAPTER TWELVE
We Burn Down The Mill

With the clatter of the horses' hoofs reducing the likelihood the driver could hear our words, Holmes darted an artful glance at me and repeated in a gleeful sing-song, 'We've got 'em. I believe we've got 'em!'

I peered at him reproachfully in the near-dark of the cab's interior.

'Holmes,' I pleaded despairingly, 'please inform me...'

'The canvas on the floor, Watson. Tell me, you mentioned how artists staff such canvases with shepherds and peasants - to create the idyllic? Then what about the stranger in that painting too?'

'Which stranger, Holmes?' I enquired. 'I have no recollection of any figure.'

'Why, at the moat's edge, where else!'

Once more my hopes rose. 'Holmes, I recall no stranger by the moat!'

'No stranger? Then perhaps a shepherd employed by Fusey?'

'Holmes, there was no shepherd in the painting.'

'Then woodman or peasant?'

'Holmes,' I yelled in exasperation, regardless of our driver. 'There was no peasant nor woodman nor hunter nor pig-sticker nor mediaeval knight nor any other figure standing by the moat. I can assure you unequivocally – do you hear me? – unequivocally there was no such figure. If you now expect to base your entire case on...'

'Was there not?' Holmes enquired, grinning over at me in the gloom. His unnatural persistence was irritating me beyond compare. 'You looked at it more closely than I. Surely you observed someone in the painting? Just across the moat from where Pevensey must have placed his easel, perhaps?'

'Holmes!' I repeated, in the tone of voice I would normally reserve for the dangerously insane, 'let me spell it out. There – was – no – figure – by - the – moat - I – am – certain – of - it.' I followed this in a normal voice. 'I assure you, if there had been such a figure, it would have come to my attention.'

To my intense irritation, my companion continued, 'You are completely certain? Surely there was a figure wearing a Tropical hat?'

'There was not, Holmes. Yet again I must inform you, such a figure would without doubt have caught my eye.'

'Especially with such a hat?'

'Especially,' I affirmed.

'As did the figure in the painting on the easel?'

'Precisely as did the figure in the Constable.'

If I had hoped (as I very much did) that at my adamant responses my companion would turn his face to the cabby and order him to return the carriage to Etchingham with us inside, I was disabused immediately. Far from dissuading him from proceeding to Crick's End and professional extinction, Holmes began to sing a ditty in a jog-trot, in time with the clopping of the horses' hoofs, 'The dog that didn't...', with open delight at whatever it was which had struck him so forcibly.

'Holmes,' I began, 'I beg you, you really must explain...'

It was no use. Back came 'The dog that didn't...' in a high falsetto. His voice was quite unlike his usual tones. It was the most eerie trill I had ever heard, as though a Mongolian throat-singer had sprung unbidden from the dusk of the Dudwell Valley and taken over my companion's larynx. I looked back and forth from him to the world outside. The carriage wheels drummed like tumbrels in my ear. While Holmes carolled away like a lark I meditated upon the many-sidedness of the human mind.

Suddenly the grotesque trill stopped and my companion spoke as normal. 'Watson, motive must take a back seat for the present. We must pursue this regardless of their motive - if we can prove opportunity and planning, if we can show an irrefutable connection between moat and corpse and wagon pond, that will suffice for a jury to convict. The President of the Royal Academy is their weakest link. When we threaten him with an appearance in the dock as accessory to murder, the chainmail will unravel like an old wool cardigan. Confront him at the Royal Academy and I guarantee he will buckle. I shall provide you with the evidence of the vital role he played the moment we reach the mill-attic. After that we can, I assure you, put up the shutters on the day and pull a pint of beer. Tobias Gregson will arrest Pevensey in his studio with his customary quiet and business-like bearing. We will let Gregson and Lestrade have a report before tomorrow is out.'

By now very close, the sociable took on an ever-more-cautious pace, reducing the noise of clopping of the horses' hoofs. My companion fell silent. He sat as I recall him at the start of every chase, arms folded, soft grey deer-stalker (though now the ear-flapped travelling cap) pulled down over his admirable forehead, chin sunk on his chest. Although almost paralytic with dread I felt proud to know him. Attired as he was, and with such a pensive mood upon his angular face, he presented a sight that will forever be pictured in the imagination of all those faithful to the memory of the nation's greatest detective, his face so subtle in its play of expression.

The lane straightened as we approached Crick's End head on. The high yew hedges loomed. We came ever-nearer to the wrought-iron gates. Questionable and forbidding though it appeared, it looked at most the setting for a plot of Empire rather than callous murder. To our right lay Donkey Field, stretching up at a steep incline to the village on the ridge. From it, low above the coachman's head, the thick branches of the great oak stretched across the lane, planted when Crick's End was in its youth. Lit by the gibbous moon, Constable clouds bubbled up from the north-west, sinuous wisps like tentacles drifting across the face of the moon. It was a place and hour you might well expect to see Kipling's phantom rickshaw.

The carriage halted. Holmes leaped out, up for the chase. Without a backward look he swept a hand behind him.

'Watson, ask our coachman to return to this precise spot in half an hour. And tell him at all cost not to be seen.'

I passed Holmes' words to the coachman. Without so much as a look in our direction he raised the whip to his hat and turned the greys full circle. The sound of the rattling wheels died away along the narrow lane. We crouched in the dense black shadow of the yew hedges which separated the grounds from the track. Immediately to our left a small sign proclaimed 'Park Farm No Through Road' along an uneven pock-marked stretch of track. Twenty paces along, shielded from Crick's End by the high hedge, we saw a six-bar gate.

'Wait here, Watson,' Holmes instructed.

Over the years Holmes had leapt many a gate. Even at a middling age Holmes maintained his india-rubber ability un-sapped. In some awe of this, Inspector Lestrade of the Yard with momentary wit said Holmes would vault a six-bar gate even when it was open wide. By contrast, cumulative injuries since my days playing rugby, and especially the hardships and wounds of Afghanistan, had left me less athletic.

Holmes turned to the gate like a good horse given cry and rein, and cleared it in a twinkling. A magnificent dog-fox, startled by the human arrival, made a dash for the long grass cover of the Wild Garden. A warm breeze blew from the westward. I stood alone, waiting, heart in mouth, as I had waited in the midst of many a case.

Above the nearby Park Wood the clouds had passed on. The young white moon was visible in a darkling sky. The Sussex Weald at night is other-worldly, full of mystery and sounds. Under the veiled moon, on this late-spring evening, it was possible to conjure in the mind wolves standing eyes a-glowing, howling amid bluebells and wood anemones. Among them, men wearing tunics with a belt, like a Norfolk jacket, over which was thrown a plaid fastened with a brooch, dwelt in the woods, as charcoal-makers or herding swine and small-horned cattle, or tending crops of wheat and barley. The pale moonlight cast deep shadows, turning everyday shapes into menacing creatures from a nether world. The very ground felt treacherous underfoot. My nerves were a-tingle by the time Holmes returned, presaged by his high-pitched whistle in imitation of a woodcock performing its roding ceremony.

'Watson, the moon makes this route too visible. There are two doors ajar, including Dudeney's, and several windows with lights behind them. We shall take the lane and enter unseen from the Mill-pond side.'

In case of need we agreed a civil greeting and a plausible excuse, based on a missed train, a love of moonlight walks and a keen interest in the countryside by night, but unremarked we soon stepped over the turbine with its 14-inch pipe and came once more to the entrance to the mill. Inside the unbolted door Holmes pushed aside his dust-coat to reach into a pocket. He withdrew the stump of a red wax candle, passing it to me with the murmured words 'Please light it only when we reach the attic.'

We clambered in darkness up the narrow stairs, the familiar smell of old wood and rotted oats arriving at our nostrils. Within seconds we regained our former places in the attic. The speed and angle of our ascent left me puffing and blowing like a spavined horse, my old leg wound aching. Tense with excitement, Holmes ordered, 'Watson, first the canvas on the easel. Light the candle and bring it to the painting of the wagon pond.'

I did as Holmes bid, stepping forward cautiously on the uneven boards. My foot knocked against a discarded bottle, spilling its last contents upon the dust layering the floor. The smell of linseed oil rose in the damp air. Holmes joined me at the easel. In the candle's light his forefinger darted at the flamboyant stranger by the wagon pond. 'Look, Watson, see the figure's shadow, painted in so clearly? Note its direction. It indicates the sun was just west of south. And gauge its length - there can be no doubt it confirms the stranger was standing there at three o' clock, sworn so by Pevensey and Fusey if required.'

'Holmes,' I began, in a hoarse whisper, 'of itself, this does not…'

'Offer proof of a conspiracy to murder, I agree! That you shall now have, Watson, did I not give you my word? Come with the candle to the canvas on the floor – my doubting Thomas, you and Scotland Yard are about to have your proof!'

I feel Holmes' triumphant anticipation even now. Even now I hear the ringing timbre of his voice.
I trod with caution across the uncertain floor and took hold of the canvas, lifting it to the level of our eyes.

'This is truly to be my coup de maître, Watson,' my comrade exulted, bending his head towards the canvas. 'Note well, Ruth to my Naomi! Now we can lay an account of the case before Inspector Gregson in its due order. Have your pencil at the ready! You shall have…'

His words came to a disbelieving stop. A cry at once furious and anguished burst from him. Finally he managed a half-gasp: 'Look! Watson, they have done us in!'

I swivelled the canvas towards me. Stare as I might, I could see

196

nothing in the canvas to trigger so dramatic a reaction.

'They have done us in,' Holmes repeated in a strangulated voice. 'The cunning devils! I fear our train has escaped the rails and is now sliding across the landscape. Their alibi is complete. Dudeney did not take Pevensey to the railway station. Siviter kept him back. Now I know for certain they killed the Boer but we can never prove it.'

Violently Holmes turned towards me. 'I have been a farcical blunderer! I have committed the most serious error of my career!'

His agonised gaze returned to the canvas. 'My display of interest in Pevensey's work... Watson, had we been on a case, I would have kept my cogitations to myself. Unintended, my amiable enquiries caused them to conduct an examination of the paintings. They discovered the very oversight I required intact to make a convincing case to Gregory and Lestrade.'

I stood in helpless silence, uncertain how to respond. After a moment, to my surprise, Holmes spoke in a vibrant voice rather than the former strangulated whisper.

'It's all right, Watson,' he reassured me. 'They will know we are here. I warrant there is no likelihood they will come to meet us.'

'But Holmes,' I began, bewildered, staring at the canvas. 'What is there in this painting which...'

My companion pointed to a spot on the inner edge of the moat. His outstretched finger looked gnarled in the flickering light. 'Look most carefully, Watson. Earlier, you swore thrice you had no recollection of a figure in this painting - surely now you see your error. Surely you see the figure of the Boer!'

Panic swept over me. Am I in a nightmare, I wondered, such a nightmare as I suffered after engaging the forces of Ayub Khan at the battle of Maiwand where I was badly wounded? Would I soon awaken at break of day in a fevered sweat? Would I soon be able to dash my face and head in cold water to dispel the magic-lantern illusions of the night?

'I'm sorry, Holmes,' I croaked. 'Where you indicate is just a patch of grass beneath an open sky. I see no Boer.'

Holmes kept his insistent finger close to the moat. 'Nevertheless,' he continued, 'you note the shadow on the bank as of a human standing there, its length and direction indicating early evening?'

I peered again, bringing the guttering candle ever closer to the canvas.

'No, Holmes,' I responded at last. 'I see no human shadow, only that of the overhanging bushes.'

'Then what of the Boer's reflection in the water?' Holmes pursued, increasing my agitation with each successive question. 'Surely you discern his reflection!'

Again I peered where his shaking finger pointed.

I said firmly, in a low but determined voice, 'Holmes, once more, may I make myself entirely clear - there is no human shadow on the bank nor any such reflection on the surface of the moat.'

'That's the utter damnation of it!' my companion cried out. 'On this very canvas this afternoon there was both shadow on the ground and dappled reflection on the surface of the water as of a man standing there - but no figure. I recall still with what meticulous detail he painted the hat's reflection. Clearly he had seen it at close hand. Even now I can visualise the daubs of dark purples, browns and viridescence. He must have painted in the shadow and reflection last evening, waiting to complete the oil today.'

At Holmes' words, a work of art flooded into my mind. In the foreground, below fine trees, a reflection on the surface of a stream picked up the passers-by.

'That's why you shouted Daubigny just now!' I burst out.

My companion nodded.

'Then what...?' I began.

'Immediately on our departure, they returned Pevensey to this attic to examine both canvases for any possible blunder.'

He pulled the painting to him and held it close to his face, sniffing at its surface.

'Poppyseed oil – there you have it!' he cried hoarsely, pushing the canvas back at me. 'Poppyseed oil is not the best medium to over-paint a reflection, let alone a shadow, but it was to hand. It is much too light, yet it has served its purpose.'

Tentatively I dabbed a finger at the spot Holmes indicated. A thin line on the moat's edge, perhaps half as long again as the shadow of the stranger by the wagon pond was tacky to my touch. In the gloom I looked back at my companion's contorted face.

Holmes' words spilled out. 'The presence of a human shadow and reflection awaiting a figure made me the more surprised when Pevensey told us he completed this canvas yesterday. I took it he was in a rush to finish his commissions. He would not trouble himself to paint a figure in or, otherwise, to paint out the shadow and reflection. Now I realise it was an oversight brought on by panic. That omission was what the Sungazers discovered even as we were returning here from Etchingham. The shadow and the reflection were painted out not half an hour ago. Like the sign-post to Wood's Corner, once painted in, the figure would become the gnomon of a sundial, its shadow of a length and direction signalling six o' clock, precisely the time Fusey would swear he saw our Boer standing by the moat had we boarded the three-ten train as commanded.' He added despairingly, 'To be 'found by the woodman in the exercise of his rounds' at seven.'

In the silence of the Sussex night I could hear Holmes' gold watch ticking the seconds by. A grudging admiration was taking hold on him.

'Watson, the mechanisms employed in this extraordinary crime are quite unique. This is the work of immensely skilful men. The wagon pond was a far less satisfactory choice than the moat and indeed makes little sense – adults seldom drown in waters a mere eighteen inches deep. The Sungazers had no option once it was known we were on our way aboard the earlier train - they needed warmer water to stew the corpse. They calculated – correctly – they could rely on the influence of Fusey's powerful testimony on the local constable.

In return, Fusey was happy to take a little disapprobation over the condition of the wagon pond verges.'

Holmes turned to me. 'Watson, it took a mind capable of the most remarkable daring to accommodate such a last-minute change of plan.'

'Siviter's?'

'I have no doubt.'

'And it succeeded.'

'It did. Did he not write 'You must not blink when the wounded tiger comes running at you'?'

After a minute's heavy silence, Holmes continued.

'The cunning dogs have truly covered their tracks.' He pointed to the moat. 'That empty space awaiting a human figure... that was the dog that didn't bark. Had they not been pushed by my innocent enquiries... had I not related *The Adventure of Silver Blaze*... they may not have uncovered Pevensey's lazy blunder. The painting you hold would have led to the unravelling of murder.'

I was disturbed to hear Holmes' voice taking on a quite sinister drawl, rather high-pitched as though, like Dr. Jekyll and Mr. Hyde, he was transmogrifying into an alter ego. Seeing him in the gloomy attic with his head thrown back and eyes half-closed, a chill of fear came over me. I stood uncertain how to react, holding fast to the canvas and candle. I was about to speak some consolatory word, even congratulate him on taking such a violent setback so well, when

– not for the only time on that extraordinary day - something took place which will forever stay in my memory. His face now utterly distorted, Holmes shrieked 'Am I to stand here and chuckle at my own defeat? Put candle to canvas, Watson! Do it now!'

Realising even as he spoke I would refuse to perform this sensational act, Holmes closed with me like a Fury, seizing me with convulsive strength. The ink- and chemical-stained hands able to display an extraordinary delicacy of touch with his experiments now seemed to belong to a Madagascar python. My legs began to sag. Within an instant a hand able to bend a steel poker crushed my fingers, pressing the candle against the canvas. Tiny bluish flames sprang like genies from the surface, licking at my hand. The candle dropped. Spilt linseed oil on the thick dust and tinder-dry wood-shavings caught fire. Within seconds the roar of the burning floorboards sounded preternaturally loud.

We made our exit. Despite the stiffness in my leg from the Jezzail's bullet, I scrambled at speed down the narrow stairs, staying on the very heels of my fleet companion. Once outside, at the small bridge leading to the Wild Garden, for an unconscionable time Holmes stopped to stare in silence at Crick's End. I waited anxiously. Even though the wind had slackened and the night air was cooling fast, I worried that the Aberdeen terriers would catch our scent.
At Holmes' whispered command we re-commenced a withdrawal, as despairing as Napoleon on the retreat from Moscow, passing a statue of Hephaestus, blacksmith of the gods, half-hidden by the Brazilian gunnera, the plant's leaves huge and sinister in the half-moon's light. At the side-gate to the pitted lane I paused to look back through high trees. The mill was a blaze of light. Flames had forced their way through the ancient roof, stabbing into the heavens, like pink feathers from a monstrous flamingo. Alerted by the acrid smell of smoke

202

drifting across open windows and the loud crackle of burning timber, Siviter's staff were running out into the open. Soon the garden would be alive with people. At any second I expected to hear the deep, booming voice of a scenthound on our trail, hunting us as such hounds hunt jackals in Afghanistan.

Ahead of me by some yards, I could see the gleam of the side-lights of our waiting carriage. Holmes was already there. He gave a rapid order to our cabman. Driven by my and Holmes' exhortation, quite as though he had no eye for the flames nor ear for the urgent voices of half a dozen Crick's End staff, our loyal driver used his whip. The carriage surged forward.

CHAPTER THIRTEEN
We Journey Home To Baker Street

The greys clattered at a long trot through a lane so narrow it would have been reckless at a busier time of day. The carriage's side-lights blazed, brushing against the hedges as the carriage swayed and jolted. I listened for the sound of a motorised barouche roaring behind us. We came to the small bridge over the Dudwell River. The horses pulled left and began the steep climb to the ridge on which Burrish's ancient church stood. The atmosphere in the cab was dark beyond all measure. Twice I tried to question my companion but he remained silent, lost in unhappy reflection. The quiet air of command, the incisive voice pitched like the string of a high-strung violin, the subtle, sly, dry humour, all were for the moment vanquished.

'Holmes,' I asked, hoping to lighten his mood. 'What do you say - a year in Pentonville for burning down a mill listed in the Domesday Book? Six months' hard labour for each canvas painted by the President of the Royal Academy?'

Again he made no reply. He was sunk in profound thought, and hardly opened his mouth except to emit a succession of deep sighs. The horses, blowing hard, climbed the last of the steep slope to the village. Once upon the ridge they set off at a goodly clatter round the curve towards the Straight Mile, as eager as I to be home.

After several minutes I determined by insistent interrogation to make my companion break the oppressive silence.
'Holmes,' I both begged and invited, 'I am at a loss on several parts of these most extraordinary events. I would be most grateful if you would answer my questions if, as I believe, we are safely away.'

At last Holmes lifted a hand. 'I see from your determined expression you will brook no denial. Ask on,' he replied gloomily.

Before he could sink back into the state of intense and silent thought from which he had emerged, I said, 'As your Boswell, I implore you, my dear friend, to commence at the very beginning – from the moment you chose to purchase the *Evening London Standard* at the railway station, an act which in itself I found unusual.'

'I shall do as you wish, Watson, although I shall require you to put your pencil down. I do not want it in writing that we have had to flee in such ignominy.'

This was followed with the despairing words, 'Could the fates be turning their faces against me, Watson?'

Once he began to speak, to my intense relief my friend composed himself and commenced a most extraordinary speculation.

'You assume I purchased the newspaper on a whim. Not so. It was one more link in a chain which lengthened throughout the day. From the moment of my return from the Poplar Dock this morning there was a disturbance in the air. A labourer fresh from the countryside with eyes that harked of Hades, standing on the paving within constant sight of our door, purporting to sell hares but refusing would-be clients. The reply-paid telegram from the President of the Kipling League with its imperious tone, delivered by special messenger like a lettre de cachet. The importance they placed on getting me aboard the three-ten train this same afternoon – the further inducement of a hamper and a bottle of fine wine ordered for delivery to a Pullman car. The light rain which we were told was keeping his guests indoors...'

At this Holmes laughed scornfully. 'Would such top guns from many an elephant or tiger-hunting expedition in the Monsoon seasons be so shy of an English mist? The post-script on Pevensey, the reluctant way he was referred to... What was the precise wording, Watson, do you recall?'

I pulled the telegram from my pocket. ''And Pevensey hopes to introduce himself'.'

I looked up at Holmes. 'Why mention him at all if by then, as you insist, he had such a major part to play in the plot you ascribe to them?'

'There was always a chance we might encounter him. Failing to mention a guest of his standing would have been questionable. It was not Pevensey but his paintings they needed. They were the first line of defence in their alibi. In any case, I believe his presence was sheer serendipity. Siviter may have commissioned the painting of a Constable some weeks ago, anticipating the coming of summer. I am certain he had no second oil in mind at the time.'

I itched to use my pencil.

'The Boer arrived a few days ago,' Holmes went on. 'The Sungazers heard him out and determined on his murder. An alibi was needed. The finest alibis are forged utilising whatever tools lie naturally to hand. Pevensey was already present, painting the wagon pond at Scotney Castle. Without his knowledge or consent, this President of the Royal Academy became central to the scheme the Sungazers swiftly put together. Staffing a painting with a passing stranger projecting a shadow as of a given o' clock would persuade even you

206

the victim was alive and well at the very hour the Kipling League assembled at Crick's End, a dozen miles away. Siviter showed true genius. He is a long-admired if distant neighbour of the Fuseys – he would know the Scotney Castle estate almost as intimately as his own, certainly the ruined castle and the moat. He gave Pevensey an extra commission – paint the moat - suggest it would look at its best as the evening-sun began to set, shall we say around six.'

'To include a figure in a flamboyant hat on its bank.'

'Indeed.'

'And all this while their would-be victim was still alive?'

'For just the time it took Pevensey to ready a second canvas.'

Holmes paused. 'Then they attended to the other contrivance – how to prove the plotters were assembled at Crick's End when the so-called drowning took place? What would give them the greatest alibi in all the world? Someone with a sense of theatre, quite possibly Sir Julius, said 'Let's summon down that Baker Street fellow this afternoon', a plan of such impudence it takes the breath away. Hence the telegram you hold in your hand, inviting me to take the three-ten train.'

My companion gave a harsh laugh. 'Imagine Pevensey at the wagon pond after lunch today, intending to return to the moat towards six this evening, ready to complete the canvas with a figure wearing Sir Julius' hat, brushes poised like Pistoian daggers. There he stood, still at the wagon pond, putting the final touches to Constable's dog, when his nightmare commences. Prompted by the news we were on the earlier train, Van Beers and Siviter consulted the Watson Codex.

207

Your tables gave them the information they needed, no longer to prolong the onset but how to hasten rigor mortis. Nothing but an hour or two simmering in warm water would do it. They had no other option but to deposit the body to its very neck in the wagon pond, just the head above the water, the one hand jutting out to offer up the dark glasses. The phantom figure was no longer wanted in the painting of the moat but in the Constable. The length of shadow should show the man alive at three. No wonder Pevensey's nerves were stretched and raw. Our encounter in the mill-attic must have deepened his anxiety a hundred-fold. Worming your way to the Presidency of the Royal Academy is quite different from holding your nerve when you find you are an accomplice to murder. That is why he and that rogue Siviter followed my enquiries so closely. What of my interest in scumbling and hog's-hair brushes? What had I in mind? And the sheen, what was the real purpose of my enquiry? When I asked, why the use of boiled linseed oil, they asked, why this concern from Sherlock Holmes? By now I could hardly discuss the weather or England's chances against Australia without them looking under the covers for a double-meaning.'

He stopped for a moment, staring at me wildly. 'Watson, I could tear my hair in rage. I was merely parading my wares! No thought of a crime entered my head. How could it? On our departure, Siviter and Pevensey hastened back and made careful inspection of both pieces. One or other noted the Boer's shadow and reflection still lay by the moat as of six this evening, awaiting its human figure. At once, Siviter made Pevensey take up his brush and paint out the emanations of a man who was never there.'

'Using the only medium Pevensey had to hand other than boiled linseed oil.'

'Poppyseed oil, yes.'

Suited to our deep depression, from out in the darkening landscape came a land-rail's repetitive harsh cry.

Holmes continued. 'I am certain there was no question of a second painting until this unexpected visitor turns up at their door. When we viewed it in the mill-attic, far from making a pair with to the Constable, the second painting was a distraction – but for what purpose escaped me completely. Now I know the second painting would provide the defence they needed. The deep moat at Scotney Castle, a spot known to every vagrant on his way from Canterbury to Camden Town, was the natural body of water for a tramp to take a wash and drown – and distant enough from Crick's End not to draw attention to the Kipling League. All was on course until we forced a hasty change of plan. It was when the *Evening London Standard* told us a body had been found in the wagon pond despite the propinquity of the moat I knew something was afoot – but what? Our ruse to escape their watchman's eye by catching the eleven-fifty meant Siviter had no further knowledge of our movements until our telegram arrived from Tunbridge Wells less than half an hour away.'

'Three hours earlier than expected.'

'Yes.'

Observing my expression, Holmes continued, 'Watson, you still look dubious. Let us consider the mathematics of this case, so central and so precise it required the most exact administration. According to your Codex, if a body is kept cool there should be a stretch of eight hours ten minutes before rigor mortis takes its grip. Anticipating we would take the three-ten train they dispatched the Boer this morning,

209

the body taken at once and deposited in the moat. That done, all they needed to do was wait. All would go like clockwork. We were to give our talk at six. The woodman would stumble across the corpse at seven, his attention directed to the pile of clothing and the hat. At once the village constable would be summoned. He in turn would assume the victim, arms and legs still limber, might well have died within the hour, a time to be consolidated both by Fusey's sighting and by Pevensey's painting of the phantom stranger showing him alive at six. But think, Watson, what must they do on receiving our telegram informing Siviter we had taken the earlier train? Imagine their agitation! We would be on our feet and speaking not at six but three. Now, rather than retarding the onset of rigor mortis, they need to speed it up for fear the body would stay limber much too long - long enough to lose them Holmes as their alibi. But how does one speed up the natural process? Simple! Refer once more to a famous work on rigor mortis. I am certain from their remedy those who masterminded this crime are well acquainted with the Watson Codex, as Van Beers and Siviter would surely be. They are veterans of many violent engagements where medical men would swarm. Taking their cue from your tables, they rushed back to fish the corpse up from the moat, recover the clothes from a nearby bush, and hurry the body to the wagon pond where the warmth of shallow water even in our early summer would work its wonders.'

He paused, smiling at me grimly. 'Watson, without the scientific information in your Codex the Sungazers could have made a very dangerous blunder.'

I shook my head in wonder. 'You construct a most ingenious theory, Holmes, quite the equal of *The Murders in the Rue Morgue*. If what you say is true... they should have hidden or destroyed the second painting the moment they heard we were on the earlier train.'

'Except that Siviter had no idea that Pevensey, anticipating a change of weather, sketched in the shadow and reflection yesterday, in the evening sunlight, leaving just the figure to brush in today.'

Holmes' mood returned to black despair. He flung his face in his hands. 'Damnably, had I not recounted *The Adventure of Silver Blaze* I believe we could have got them. They were attentive to my recitation solely to discover which gaps might lie in their violent undertaking. Such fiends! They used my vanity against me. To think how I flattered their confounded League by expressing my obligation to their patron.'

When the excess of emotion had drained, Holmes leant forward and looked at me with an accusing expression. His outstretched fingers twiddled before my face in curious fashion, as rhythmic and hypnotic as the antennae of a mantis.

'Watson, after this, your plans for my retirement must change. Were I ever to stand before another audience, I would be asking myself which among these keen and attentive faces is totting up my words for clues to get away with murder – are we once more to be the assassin's alibi!'

'Holmes,' I interpolated, 'we are not done with the day's events. Why would they empty the dead man's pockets of all possessions? It was that which added to your suspicions.'

'He was a foreigner. All such indication would have to be removed in case an overheated constable declared it was the corpse of an enemy agent en route to Downing Street or the Palace. Inspector Gregory would have been called down at once. The League wanted no such intrusion.'

'But Holmes, again I ask, why did they have to disrobe the unhappy man?'

'Fully clad, just his hands and face would have been apparent. In the countryside ruddy face and wind-burnt hands are the norm, even among gentlefolk who could afford this sort of apparel. Undressing him sent a signal to someone in particular, almost certainly in Pretoria, someone who would recognise the clues on offer. Dark glasses, chest and legs burned by Tropical suns from above the calf to just below the knee. And that most brilliant touch, the substitution of the fedora with a hat designed for Tropical climes.'

'Surely, Holmes,' I broke in, 'a Boer, if such he was, would own...'

'... such a hat? Why not! But I tell you, Watson, that was never the dead man's hat. It would prove to be a half-size too large if we could measure his skull. Indubitably it was Sir Julius's. Do you remember in the parlour when I remarked how he had so recently worn a hat a half-size too small? Did you not note the change in his expression at what was at most an inconsequential remark? A man of such standing and wealth would have his own skilled hatter. He would never resort to an off-the-shelf fedora. The report in the *Standard* - the mention of the weathering between calf and knee, the V-shaped sunburn of the chest, the dark glasses especially, even the location so near to Crick's End - would merely tell the recipient of this news their man is dead. Without that hat tossed atop the pile of clothing it might well have been the accidental or self-inflicted drowning asserted by the constable which the newspaper in your pocket reports almost as a fact – a conclusion you yourself are still inclined to, despite my every effort. To someone who knows this Boer, the

212

description of that hat will signal murder. His close acquaintances would know he never owned a hat with such a band. And who else but someone in the Transvaal would recognise the reptile referred to in the newspaper report? In the outside world, how many are familiar with this mud-coloured lizard's skin? No, Watson, certainly 'gentlemen of the road' do steal or are given gentlemen's clothing as hand-me-downs to replace their tattered attire. Think of the watchman in the bowler hat. But when the intended recipient of this news reads the pile of clothes was topped by a crimson hat, 'a yellow and brown spiny snake' for the band, they will know that this was murder.'

At this, my companion knocked out the dottle from his pipe and refilled it with fresh tobacco. I watched with impatience. Unable to restrain myself longer, I broke in, 'Holmes, do go on! What could be the aim of such a killing?'

'It can only be designed....' Holmes responded, puffing hard at his pipe, '...to engineer a third South African war.'

I stared at him in the greatest astonishment.

'Watson, I see you are incredulous. I ask you, who was there to-day?'

'Van Beers for one.'

'South Africa.'

'Wernher...'

'South Africa.'

'Weit.'

'South Africa.'

After a further pause, he continued, 'A lot remains unsettled and at stake from the recent war, not least the Transvaal, bristling with guns and gold, the most opulent state in Africa.'

'Then let me ask again about Pevensey – why did he go along with them and play his part? He has no connection with South Africa. He is not a man known for his commitment to the Empire.'

'Yes...Pevensey,' my companion replied, frowning. 'It is hard to believe he could have been elected to the presidency of the Royal Academy without the Kipling League's most earnest interventions. These men's millions carry weight. He may not be a member of the Kipling League, I suggest he is not, his nerves are too ragged, but he is no doubt much beholden to them. Until the corpse was thrown into the wagon pond and the clothing assembled before him he may not have known the role he was playing. Indeed, I am inclined to think he did not.'

Holmes puffed on his long pipe, a slight crack in the ill-fitting carriage-door drawing the smoke away. 'Watson, had we used him as our principal witness against them, it is not too far fetched to think his life too may have been in danger.'

The gleam of the occasional street-lamp along the ridge road flashed on his features. 'Such hatreds, Watson. Africa is a volcano from Cape to Cairo. I am certain somewhere in this lurks another war.'

While I digested this, Holmes continued, 'Lust for gold could lie behind this. Greed is a human pandemic worse than enteric fever. But if you add pursuit of power ... I am still a child in international affairs and must learn more ... how does one State come out on top? Why are alliances made and broken? Do they aim to unite Natal and Cape Colony with the Boer republics under an English flag - under Van Beers' control?'

The carriage took a bend, straightened and increased in pace down a slight slope. Holmes shook his head. I spied a hint of admiration in his eye.

'Watson, most such plans would go awry with an assembly as large as that which orchestrated today's events. If their victim was an emissary from the Boer High Command, their hate for him would be pretty black.'

After a further few minutes, I said cautiously, 'Holmes, you have built a mighty edifice from to-day's events.'

'That is true, my loyal friend,' he replied.

'Assuming all you say is true, by what means were we so utterly defeated?'

'By tactics I have never before encountered. Never has anyone laid out wares before us in such a clever and understated way – as if each item were entirely inconsequential, like Siviter's medlar jelly tea.'

'They were not ignoble foes,' I offered in consolation.

'They were not. They have overthrown my maxim the only safe

plotter is he who plots alone. Even though we nearly had them, their safety was recovered by a few simple strokes of Poppyseed oil.'

I watched as Holmes again shook his head in reluctant admiration. 'For all his pretty-pretties, Siviter is more deadly than the Gaboon viper.'

Expecting a mocking answer to a rhetorical question, I teased, 'Nevertheless, surely not the equal of the late and unlamented Moriarty, Holmes?'

I was staggered to hear Holmes' response. 'Siviter is his better,' he replied, quietly. 'I would back him 5 to 4.'

'Have we heard the last of them, do you suppose?'

'They are supremely able instruments. There are curs to do the smaller work but these are wolf-hounds in leash. I wager they'll be on the prowl for a long time yet. '

The fresh country air was beginning to press in on me. The gulp of brandy taken from my hip-flask was helping. A pleasant lassitude descended.

'Holmes,' I said in consolation, my now-weary eyes closing. 'Lessons learned will be of great benefit to us.'

The dancing shadows of the flaming mill were far behind us. Crick's End and my memory of it were dissolving into mist. With a tap of a finger I checked the collection of large bank-notes from our day's work tucked safely in an inner pocket. Noting the slight pat of my hand on my wallet-pocket, I heard Holmes say with sudden warmth,

'Was it up to your expectations?'

It was my old friend back to normality.

Above and behind, I could hear the sound of the cabman's voice communing with his greys, for the first time using their names 'Christmas' and 'Easter'. Lulled by the rhythmical throb of the carriage at speed on a decent surface, I settled back for the briefest of naps.

'It was, Holmes. A princely sum,' I replied in satisfaction.

'Then how much?'

'Three hundred Guineas!' I murmured.

'My Heavens,' Holmes responded, in genuine surprise. 'In bars of gold - or a pouch of diamonds?'

'In English Five Pound notes.'

'My Heavens,' he repeated. 'Though not quite five shillings the word, there is money in public speaking! And what of my wager over Marco Polo? Did he forget the fifty guineas?'

'I have them too,' I replied, smiling.

Soon we would be at the railway station. The violence of Holmes' present emotions would fade. Crick's End would become but a remembrance of things past. At any moment I expected Holmes to say 'Watson, take a wire down, like a good fellow.'

In the event I was utterly wrong to believe Holmes and I were to remain in our companionable state, so deep and lasting was his embarrassment at his defeat. Unbeknown to me, after some weeks of intense reflection, he informed the editor of *The Strand* he would refuse outright to have my chronicle ever see the light of day. No Editor would take it. For Holmes the débâcle became the subject of a tabu. He raised no objection when I told him I planned to resume my medical practice. I found fresh premises and we parted. It was clear our long friendship was at its end. Want of capital excluded me from setting up in the Harley Street district of Westminster, famed for the members of my profession who catered for the wealthiest patients. I settled for a ground floor in Paddington. Even then, to raise the money I was obliged to sell my cherished painting of General 'Chinese' Gordon.

ADDENDUM

So great was Holmes' humiliation he abandoned his plan to compile a text-book on crime detection for fear it would invite mockery from reviewers. The years passed. I caught sight of my former comrade only once in all that time. I was taking an evening walk in St James's Gardens. He was entering Buckingham Palace perched in a shabby one-horse shay. I was with him on a previous visit to the Palace when Queen Victoria conferred an emerald tie-pin on him for services above and beyond the call. I discovered later that despite our estrangement this second visit was to ask King Edward if the knighthood His Majesty had offered to confer on him for services to Justice (an honour Holmes refused) could be transferred to me, a request the King rejected out of hand. Was that passing glimpse at the gates of the Palace to be the last time I was destined to see my dear friend, I wondered. I pined for our long lost days as comrades-in-arms.

More years passed. The King died. George V was crowned. Holmes and I may never again have been shoulder to shoulder until death (I had long since gained his word of honour for a grave next to his among the Italian bees) except for a most remarkable and unexpected event seven long, lonely years later.

It was 1912. I stood in the early-morning sunshine outside the front-door of my medical practice. The badge of my profession, the stethoscope, hung from my neck. It was my custom to observe patients before they came limping through my door. Many are the times I have made my diagnosis before they enter my premises or utter a word.

My thoughts turned to my dear dead wife, a striking-looking woman with a beautiful olive complexion, large, dark, Italian eyes, and a wealth of richly-tinted deep black hair. Holmes once opined she was a little short and thick for symmetry, to my mind a quite impertinent remark. With her passing I felt doubly lonely. Of all ghosts, those of our loves are the ones we most want to wend their way back and wave to us.

It was while deep in such thoughts that I had an unexpected interruption. One of the cheaper horse-drawn cabs pulled up in front of me from which our former landlady alighted, the good Mrs. Hudson, clutching her favourite lace-edged parasol. These days I saw her only on an annual basis when I went round to pay for the storage of my tin trunks in her attic and indulge in a few moments of nostalgia over a first infusion of her best tea. She brought with her a most curious and unexpected summons.

'Dr. Watson,' she cried in great agitation, waving the parasol, 'a telegram from Lewes. I must assume it's from Mr. Holmes. I know he never remembers your address. I hope he's all right. Why would he send a telegram when the letter post is so much cheaper!'

Holding out my hand to her with a reassurance I did not feel, I cried, 'Why, my dear Mrs. Hudson, I am sure there is nothing amiss. Holmes never writes when he can telegraph!'

She received my hand in hers, looking up at me with moist eyes. 'I know you've had your differences of late but I wouldn't waste an hour in going to see him, sir, or you may not see him alive.'

To judge by her words and her precipitate arrival, Mrs. Hudson feared (and at the thought my heart beat even harder) his tempestuous life might be coming to its end. A world without Holmes, even a disaffected Holmes? And two years my junior? No.

Unthinkable.

For the past few years my former friend had spent much time at his isolated farm-house on the Sussex Downs, occupied with his hives and building a library. A mutual acquaintance came to tell me Holmes prowled about the purlieus of his farm like the Bengal tiger 'Bert' at the Regent's Park Zoo, as restless, brilliant and dissatisfied as ever. This acquaintance took the chance to tell me that my name never came up.

I slit open the envelope. The message read, 'Early today a cutting from the *Rheinische Merkur* was pushed under my door. Grave events afoot. Come, if convenient – if inconvenient come all the same. S.H.'

I read out the words to Mrs. Hudson. Without waiting for her encouragement (which was soon forthcoming), I resolved to obey my old comrade's ringing command, though the request made it unlikely he was, as I had immediately feared, lying on his bed near death. Nor was there in this summons any hint of malice or retribution.

There was a post-script to the telegram. I should arrive by a circuitous route. This, I was instructed, would be by fast train to Hindhead, in Surrey, where he had arranged for the Station Master to put me on a char-à-banc or electric brougham to Lewes. At Lewes, given the state of the ground after a period of heavy rain, I would find a horse-drawn four-wheeler to take me on the final stage of my journey to the farm near King's Standing. I was without fail to bring the latest Continental Gazetteer. The telegram ended, 'The tsunami has struck,' followed by a mysterious command, 'Spend an hour in intensive study of the Kiel Canal.'

My heart sang at his customary presumption though I was alarmed by the phrase 'The tsunami has struck' and by the order to take a circuitous route. 'What on Earth does all this mean?' I said aloud, after I had twice read over the summons. Should I purchase a carpet-bag and fill it with a jemmy, a dark lantern and my best field-glasses? Or at the very least load two chambers of my Eley's No. 2 with soft-nosed bullets and slip it in a hip-pocket? As to the Kiel Canal, I revolved in my head how to carry out so strange an order in such a short time and decided it was not possible.

I threw myself briskly into country-wear wondering why I should 'without fail' bring the Continental gazetteer. My practice could get along very well for a day or two without me since it was the slackest time in the year. I pinned a note to the patients' entrance asking them to make do with the locum summoned from the St. Pancras Hospital. I promised Mrs. Hudson a supply of black hothouse grapes from Solomon's in Piccadilly on my return and left helter-skelter for the railway station. Soon I was taking lunch on the train to Hindhead.

Shortly after five o' clock that day, with a medical bag and the small portmanteau containing the Continental gazetteer, I was aboard the four-wheeler travelling through the mud and quiet of the Ashdown Forest. Just past Chelwood Vachery I glimpsed Holmes' lonely, low-lying black-and-white building with its stone courtyard and crimson ramblers. From a nearby height Holmes could command a view of the English Channel, close enough as the seagull flies to blast his farm with winter gales. It was clear his respect for Nature had grown with age and familiarity. For many a year it took a little diplomacy to wrest him from London. On several occasions during our days at Baker Street I urged him to go to the countryside for a rest, not least because he could obtain a wondrous view of the heavens. He replied with some asperity, 'Watson, the proper study

222

for my species is my species, not blades of grass or insects and the stars! I shall sooth myself with Nature in my later days. For the moment, it is to the Quadrant of Regent Street and Charing Cross I turn to for recreation and inspiration, amid the sounds and sights of hansom-cabs, omnibuses and dog-carts, wing collars, and the flickering of gas-light, watching the ever-changing kaleidoscope of life as it ebbs and flows through Fleet Street and the Strand.'

As I journeyed closer to Holmes' country retreat, my hearing grew attuned to the clip of the horses' hoofs striking the road's metalled surface. This switched to the crunching sound of the carriage-wheels turning from the highroad into the gravelled drive. The air wafting through the carriage window was suffused with the scent of dried grass. Heralding my arrival at this once-familiar place, we passed the small stand of Holm oaks and a fine 100-foot Lebanon cedar with a small engraved plate pinned to the bark stating 'From a seed sourced in the Forest of the Cedars of God, planted to celebrate the defeat of Napoleon 1815'.

To my relief (given my still-bubbling worry for his health), as the horses pulled the carriage along the final stretch, I saw Holmes pacing up and down. He looked well enough for a man now into his sixties. I observed nothing formidable in his symptoms, except for an increase in lumbago in the lower spine, no doubt worsened by damp air seeping from the nearby woods. His demeanour reflected the tenor of the telegram. While I fumbled for money to pay the cabman, Holmes drummed his fingers on the carriage side. The payment made, with a touch of the driver's whip the horses wheeled and turned away. I could give Holmes my fullest attention.

My host reached a hand across to my shoulder and in the tone of old said approvingly, 'Well done, Watson, prompt as ever in answering a

223

telegraphic summons. I see you have brought the Continental gazetteer.'

'I have, yes,' I responded, suffused with warmth, 'but are you well?'

'My ever-faithful friend, I am. You shall meet Mrs. Keppell once more, she is still with me. Her billeting and victualing are still carried out like army manoeuvres.'

Mrs. Keppell had remarried. Her new husband was the village wheel-wright and coffin-maker, though she kept to her former name when at Holmes' farm. With her came Tallulah, a lively Norwich terrier. Refused entry in-doors by the master of the house, Tallulah spent the two hours as on daily duty, patrolling the courtyard, yapping with unabated excitement whenever Mrs. Keppell waved from an open window.

Now summer was almost upon us, petunias and snap-dragons set the farm ablaze with colour. Wall-flowers protruded from crevices, a favourite flower of mine from a nostalgic childhood holiday spent in Dorset with my mother, taking long walks around Thomas Hardy's birthplace at Higher Bockhampton.

With the carriage gone and my introduction to Tallulah complete, Holmes raised a hand dramatically. Grasped between finger and thumb fluttered a piece of newsprint perhaps five inches square, displaying angular heavy characters. I heard his dry, crisp, emphatic utterance as, with a grim expression, he plunged into the matter without further preamble. 'The tsunami, Watson, the proof of crime – and worse it is than we could ever have imagined.'

'What crime?' I demanded.

224

'What crime?' Holmes expostulated, striding towards the house. 'The greatest crime of our life together!'

At the veranda, he stopped to allow me to catch up. 'Those Sungazer devils, Watson. I should have realised it would not end at the slam of a Lanchester's door. I fear they mock us yet. In the night this piece of newsprint was pushed beneath this very door by person or persons unknown, though I can guess from where the commission came.'

'Were there no clues as to the sender?'

'None, Watson. Would you expect a seal of red wax stamped with a crouching lion? No. You will observe the cutting is pasted to ordinary cream-laid paper without watermark.'

I followed him into the house, Holmes continuing to hold the cutting high, like a tour guide waving a coloured umbrella at the British Museum. Despite the warmth of the air outside, the fire was already burning up, crackling merrily, and sending spurts of blue, pungent smoke into the room, overcoming the perfume from the vases of sweet peas and roses Mrs. Keppell had placed everywhere. Within two hours of leaving London it was as though we were once more back in our old rooms in Baker Street.

'Watson, this clipping torn from the *Rheinische Merkur* contains the answer to the riddle at Scotney Castle. It is turning out to be a greater riddle than either you or I thought. You will shortly agree nothing in our long career as allies in the fight against crime has had such implications.'

Holmes could on occasion resort to exaggeration though never with me, or at least not in private, even in the terrifying case of the Parsee Solicitor. Once inside the low-beamed room, I placed my coat upon a peg. As of old, while I waited for Holmes to settle, I shuffled through the pile of correspondence threatening to tumble from the overmantle. One piece, several months old, began 'Rumour abounds in Titel that Albert Einstein ordered the mercy-killing of his daughter Lieserl...'

I put aside a handsome mahogany Seneca view camera and took its place on a rickety chair. Over the years of regular occupation, white-painted shelves of deal had sprung up on every wall, purchased from a late fellow at Oriel College. One shelf was loaded with modern text-books, another with works of reference, including the much-thumbed Dictionary of London by Charles Dickens' eponymous son, with its guide to Ah Sing's opium den and much other information required of a Consulting Detective. Old friends lined the upper shelves, transported from our rooms in Baker Street. In addition to a two-year-old Baedeker, I spied British Birds, the Dictionary of National Biography, the Origin Of Tree Worship, Poe's The Mystery of Marie Roget, Catullus, Winwood Reade's Martyrdom of Man, several of my favourite sea stories by Clark Russell, The Holy War and, less to the fore, The Physiognomical System of Drs. Gall & Spurzheim with its instruction on reading the faces of Chinamen. A few of the works had accompanied him from far-away University days – Hafiz and Horace, Flaubert and Goethe, Twelfth Night, a copy of E. Cobham Brewer's Dictionary of Phrase & Fable, and the pocket Petrarch.

More volumes lay open on the bear-skin hearthrug, signs of wide contacts among authors, printers and publishers. A French admirer had presented him with a stuffed icterine warbler in a small glass cage. In another glass cage was a human skull the size of a coconut, with an iron-stained mandible. An inscription stated, 'To My Partner In Crime, Sherlock Holmes, the culmination of my work. Chas. Dawson F.S.A'.

One wall was bullet-pocked with the patriotic monogram V.R., the old Queen's initials. My former companion had continued his habit of pistol-practice in the sitting-room, his formidable marksmanship learned from many visits early in life to a range on the sand-dunes in the neighbourhood of Calais, a whole day's shooting for one pièce de cent sous. Though he had undergone no military training as far as I ever ascertained, he was at least my equal with a pistol though less so with something heavier.

'Watson, my dear friend,' came Holmes' voice, interrupting my inspection. 'For just a moment I shall keep you in suspense over this newspaper clipping. Please, first take up the Continental gazetteer and read me the entry for Carl von Hofmeyer. Then we shall indulge ourselves in a cup of Mrs. Keppell's tea.'

He threw himself into his old arm-chair, drawing up his knees until his fingers clasped round his long, thin shins. With a gesture at a box on a low table, he said, 'Try one of Lord Cantlemere's cigars. He dropped them off on his way to the Continent the other day. They are less poisonous than one would expect.'

'Ulrich von Hofmeyer,' I repeated to be certain I had caught the name. 'Who might that be?'

'We shall discover that together if you do as I ask, Watson,' Holmes responded, the old sarcasm evident in the words softened by a slight smile.

227

I turned the pages to 'H' and came to von Hofmeyer.

'Count Ulrich von Hofmeyer (1856-)
Ranked among Germany's most prominent imperialists.
1881 1st Life Guard Hussar Regiment
1888, Founder of Deutsch-Ostafrika, considered the pearl of Germany's overseas possessions.
1891 appointed Imperial Commissioner in German East Africa.
Such is his enterprise and energy, by 1889 he was seen as rival to Henry Stanley.'

Holmes broke in, impatiently, 'The Informal, Watson, the informal!'

He was puffing on a familiar old pipe, the smoke curling up more thickly to emphasise each curious element in the Gazetteer's tale

I moved my finger down the page.

'Apostle of ruthless imperialism. Devoted agent of the Kaiser. Of all the conquistadores in the Scramble for Africa, von Hofmeyer is considered the most pugnacious, his line of march through Africa marked by blackened villages and dead warriors.
Uncomplimentary reports on his activities in Africa have appeared in the British Press (especially the Manchester Guardian).
Said to model himself on Nietzsche's Superman.'

I stopped reading to comment, 'Nasty piece of work, Holmes!'

'Who became a rising statesman at the Kaiser's Court. Read on, Watson, then we'll talk.'

I continued:

'Regarded by Bismarck as a 'flag-waving, buccaneering freebooter'. Describing Africans he is said to have expressed the view 'the only thing that would make an impression on these wild sons of the steppe was a bullet from a repeater'. Among those he is accused of murdering is Swahili sugar-plantation owner Abushiri ibn Salim al-Harthi, chief supporter of the Sultan of Zanzibar.

In 1889 he engaged in a mêlée with Galla tribesmen, killing a sultan and six of his leading men, then pushed on into the Wadsagga country.'

I looked up. 'That's all,' I said. 'But tell me, Holmes, why the interest in this unpleasant fellow?'

''Of all the conquistadores in the Scramble for Africa'...' He turned to me and repeated, ''Of all the conquistadores in the Scramble for Africa.' Watson, what do you make of that?'

'I make nothing of it, Holmes. What should I be making of this murdering ... this...' I looked back at the page. '...flag-waving buccaneering freebooter'?'

Holmes put away the pipe. He pulled a silver cigarette-case from a pocket and pointed with it to the pile of books scattered across the floor.

'As you can see, I am expanding my knowledge as you so often urged. It now strikes me had I not been a consulting detective – or a Naturalist ...' his eyes gave a momentary twinkle, 'I might have

229

become an historian. There are many similarities in our quest for answers.'

He extracted an Alexandrian cigarette and after lighting it resumed. 'I doubt if your gazetteer yet contains the name of another Prussian, Bernhard Dernburg?'

'It does not,' I affirmed after a search.

'No matter.'

Holmes reached for a strip of paper at his side and threw it across to me.

I read. 'Confidential. From Mark Sykes, British Embassy Berlin, 31/V/1912. For the attention of Mr. Sherlock Holmes. Near Lewes, Sussex, England. The 'Hottentot' Election of 1907. 'Parties of Order' gained a solid majority. Arrival in the Reichstag of hardliners such as Count Bernhard von Bülow. Bülow picked a new kind of Hercules to sweep out the Augean Stables (the German Colonial Department), 'a plump young banker with a light brown beard and smiling eyes', as one German newspaper described him, named as Bernhard Dernburg. His message is visionary – economic imperialism is the answer. Germany's African colonies could become jewels in the Kaiser's crown through which the Reich could exploit cheap and secure sources of those raw materials most needed for a strong Defence of the Fatherland – oil, cotton and the rubber, vital to its 'destiny' as the world's second greatest steel power.'

'By strong Defence we must take it Sykes means war,' Holmes remarked.

230

My companion then moved to a mysterious matter alluded to in his telegram earlier in the day: 'Watson, are you *à la page* with the Kiel Canal?'

I replied I was not. At his quizzical look I added I had come across reports from correspondents in the *Morning Chronicle* and the *London Times* but such matters remained at the far margins of my interest.

Holmes nodded. 'I see. My dear Watson, I am about to enlighten you about an unexpected turn of events. As you are seated, if precariously – I must get Mrs. Keppell's husband to deal with that chair – let us examine this newspaper cutting pushed beneath my door. You may not know it from the photograph but the cutting refers to the man I first asked to you to look up in the Gazetteer.'

'The conquistadore in the scramble for Africa?'

He passed me the original cutting. 'Count von Hofmeyer, yes. I have had it translated.'

I looked at the cutting from the *Rheinische Merkur*. It showed a police-type photograph of an unsmiling man wearing dark glasses. Printed by it were several lines in a Teutonic type.

Holmes began to read out the translation.

"Graf von Hofmeyer Declared Legally Dead", he began. "No Solution To The Mystery. It is seven years since Ulrich von Hofmeyer disappeared after departing the French coast at Dieppe by packet-boat for Newhaven on the coast of Sussex on the 24th of May

1904. Nothing has been heard from him since. At the request of his wife the Authorities have declared him legally dead. A figure widely identifiable in Eastern Africa because of his attachment to dark glasses and uncompromising approach to the natives, von Hofmeyer had only recently taken up new, undisclosed diplomatic duties in Berlin after disposing of extensive personal assets in Tanganyika, including three tanzanite mines at Arusha.''

At his words I burst out in a strangulated voice, 'the Boer at Scotney Castle...'

'Precisely, Watson, the dead Boer...'

'... was a Boche!'

'You have it,' Holmes replied, observing me quietly.

A grey mist swirled before my eyes. Everything which had seemed real threatened to tumble around my buzzing head. I felt I would swoon for only the second time in a life not absent of desperate surprises. The first occasion was when Holmes unveiled himself after years during which I thought him dead, though it was a close-run thing during my early weeks in India when a brother officer at my side in the Mess-tent, seemingly at the end of his tether, drew a khukuri and stabbed himself thrice just above the knee with the utmost savagery, screaming the while like a Banshee spirit. After some seconds of this curious display, when no artery was severed and no spurt of blood forthcoming, I realised he had a wooden leg. On both occasions it took me a while to recover.

After several moments I spoke.

'Holmes, the article is so close to an obituary, like you I am certain the corpse was von Hofmeyer's. He may have come intent on discussions on a matter of some moment, but still I say, to be murdered and stripped naked... surely that goes too far?'

'Do you recall how the Sultan Saif Al-Din Qutuz and his generals treated the four emissaries of the Mongol prince Hulegu Khan when they brought a letter demanding instant capitulation?' Holmes asked.

'Why, no, I do not recall,' I responded.

'At Qutuz' command the ambassadors were cut in half at the waist, decapitated and their heads placed on Cairo's great Zuwila Gate.'

'So killing the Boche and stripping off his clothing...'

'Would it not make a considerable point, if short of being halved?'

'It would, Holmes,' I agreed, 'but if he was murdered - and under the circumstance I am obliged to accept it was not suicide or death from accidental drowning - why has no effort been made, as far as we can see, by our Foreign Office or the Imperial German Embassy in London to put two and two together? We know the finding of the corpse was reported in the *Standard*. Particular mention was made of the presence of dark shiny spectacles – they are so much the dead man's signature the *Rheinische Merkur* refers to them in this clipping.'

'I telephoned Brother Mycroft this morning. It transpires His Majesty's Government was fully aware of the Count's journey to Sussex from the moment he left Berlin. Furthermore, von Hofmeyer sent a letter from Crick's End to the Chancellery on the morning of his death using the German Naval code. His letter was intercepted at the Burrish Post-Office. It took Mycroft a mere six hours to decipher.'

'And it said...?'

''Proposals well received. Anticipate arrival of eminent personages from Downing Street within hours'.'

'Why did your brother not let you know of this at the time?'

'The Official Secrets Act 1889 Section 2, 'Breach of Official Trust', that's why. I had no idea Mycroft could be so pedantic. He insisted on reading the entire wretched Act over the telephone like the Sermon on the Mount.'

Holmes threw me a serious look. 'Watson, I had my suspicions even then that the murder was – if not officially sanctioned - at the very least condoned by a bellicose faction inside the Government. Once von Hofmeyer left Dieppe for Crick's End, followed all the while, he had one chance on life to a hundred chances on death.'

'A bellicose faction inside the Government?' I exclaimed. 'Led by whom?'

'Why, the Blenheim spaniel, Winston Churchill, who else? Mycroft has informed me your friend Marsh was forbidden to tell you on pain of his knighthood.'

'But even Winston Churchill could hardly command events at Downing Street,' I protested. 'Ambitious he may be to a fault, but he is not yet Prime Minister. He is not even Foreign Secretary.'

'My dear Watson,' Holmes replied, chuckling. 'Surely you remember our one visit to Downing Street? The labyrinthine layout, the innumerable baroque state rooms, the poky passageways, the hidden courtyards, the secluded offices. It is a wonder we ever found our way out. It only lacks a few suits of armour, oriental robes, curved swords, Ottoman miniatures, Islamic calligraphic manuscripts, murals and a ghost or two for it to be mistaken for the Topkapi Palace. Those are not the corridors of power but mediaeval courts run from broom cupboards, one of which is reserved for Mycroft Holmes but another must bear the label 'Winston Churchill'.'

So it was that for the next fifteen minutes, swiftly by degrees, Holmes took me on a most unexpected tour d'horizon. He launched into his narrative, as strange a story as he had ever laid before me.

'I have given this great thought while awaiting your arrival,' Holmes continued. 'I believe – as would the sender of this newspaper cutting – we are now far too late if we hope to prevent the catastrophe that lies not far beyond the horizon. The Kipling League achieved a triumphant finis to their record in England. Van Beers and Sir Julius are safely abroad. Weit, as you must know, is dead. I can only make sense of this by assuming Count von Hofmeyer came to a conclusion Africa was a blind canyon. His great hope and natural ally, the Boers, suffered a rout and mostly inhabit the bush beyond the Orange River. The boundaries of the Continent, so carelessly drawn, are a shaming legacy of the Scramble for Africa, the mere by-product of some European explorer's wanderings or statesman's puffed-up pride. Take a particular absurdity, the Caprivi panhandle named after the German foreign minister from his mad idea of building a railway from South-West Africa to Portuguese Mozambique - without ever having learned the terrain is most unsuitable. No, Watson. Opportunity for a man as ambitious as the Count no longer lay in Africa.'

'What of this man Dernburg?' I asked. 'What of his concern with Africa?'

'A deliberate diversion, contrived by von Hofmeyer to put England off the track. Dernburg was groomed to replace him, a device to convince us Africa rested at the epicentre of the German Chancellery's ambitions. In that way it would take our eye off the widening of the Kiel Canal while encouraging our War Department to prepare as they always do for the wrong kind of war, a third engagement against the unrequited Boer in Southern Africa.'

'If this contrivance freed von Hofmeyer from Africa, to what aim….?'

'Weltpolitik, my friend! Do you not see, he returns to Berlin, the Capital of the most powerful kingdom of Middle Europe, in time for the widening of the Kaiser Wilhelm Canal at Kiel? I would not have asked you to bone up on the Canal if it was not of the utmost importance to our present discussion. In the past year they have widened it at the cost of 242 million marks, wide enough to take the greatest German battleships. The Canal crosses the Cimbrian Peninsular and connects the Baltic with the North Sea. Prussians would not spend that sum for pleasure yachts on their way to Cowes or Cannes. It saves a ship – a Dreadnought perhaps - 250 miles through the dangerous waters of the Skagerrak.'

Incredulous that this should be a principal topic of conversation, I demanded, 'Holmes, is it simply to inform me of these statistics you send me a telegram which nearly gives Mrs. Hudson a heart-attack with worry, in which you order me to leap aboard a train with more than all due speed - and by a circuitous route - just short of telling me to bring my service revolver and a dozen soft-nosed bullets?'

'Soon the tumblers will fall in place, I assure you, Watson. Von Hofmeyer could see the strategic possibilities for a mighty German Navy. The immense ship canal is the rival of the Suez. The Germans are now free to move from safe and secret Baltic bases to the whole of the world's seas – except for what, Watson...?'

My mind returned to a conversation with Edward Marsh at The Athenaeum where I had repaired one evening for a good cigar and intriguing gossip.

'...that the Royal Navy lies in the way?' I hazarded.

'Indeed.'

In his detached and entertaining way Marsh had related how Britain's First Sea Lord and First Lord of the Admiralty grew panic-stricken as Germany's naval challenge proceeded. Major British forces were withdrawn from far-distant routes to India. Fleets were reorganised based on Malta, Gibraltar and the home ports. Planning began for a new all-big-gun battleship together with the Invincible class of battle-cruiser. The new fleet was to give Great Britain such an intimidating lead Germany would give up all competitive activity from cost alone, let alone a failure of ambition. Instead, Holmes was informing me, far from containment or intimidation, the race for sovereignty of the seas had become sterner.

Holmes continued, 'Count von Hofmeyer knew of Van Beers and

Siviter from his years in Africa. He knew they would have the Prime Minister's ear. They in turn would be well aware of his blood-thirsty history.'

'So he was sent to Crick's End to oblige a humiliating submission? You suggest by murdering this Hun, leaving him stripped of clothing in the wagon pond, the Kipling League sent a signal of the utmost defiance to Berlin?' I paused. 'If that is so, shall we agree what they did in killing this fellow would not be so damnable – there might be honour in the matter?'

'That is the message Siviter would have conveyed to Fusey - and Pevensey - and to the staff at Crick's End and Scotney Castle, several of whom were needed in the running of events, especially the woodman and Dudeney and his motor.'

I stared at my companion.

'You say 'the message Siviter would have conveyed,' Holmes. How otherwise could it be?'

He sat in silence, brow furrowed, without responding to my question.

I went on, 'The Holmes, I beg you at least to put an end to my curiosity on one singular point which has engaged my mind throughout my journey here today and well before…'

'Ask on, Watson,' my companion assented in a most amiable way. 'Up to today I have been entirely unwilling to engage with you on any aspect of this matter but I am the more ready to do so now. Which singular point do you…?'

238

'I have often stood at your side at the start of the chase but never where you came so swiftly to your conclusion or stayed with it to such a bitter end. When Dudeney returned us to Etchingham Railway Station, you heard the newspaper vendor calling out. I recall to this day the speed with which you concluded something grave was afoot. Your exact words were...'

"...the very second I adopted the hypothesis everything seems to fit – or at least nothing seems to contradict it'?' he interrupted.

'Indeed,' I replied. 'I have read and reread that report in the newspaper a dozen times. I have it framed on a wall. What was it which brought you so swiftly to such a conclusion?'

'The first 'scumbling' to catch my eye was the local constable's determination to report the corpse as the former temple of a passing tramp. What could possibly have brought the village bobby to that conclusion?'

'May I let you answer that?' I returned.

'Because Lord Fusey indicated it was so, how else? The evidence itself, right in front of the constable's own eyes, pointed in quite another direction.'

'So why did Fusey offer this opinion?'

'Because it removed all concern for murder – tramps are valued even less than hobos in the countryside.'

'You said it could not be the body of a tramp because the evidence pointed in quite another direction – what in particular, Holmes?'

239

'Were you not struck forcibly by the appearance of the corpse? Remember, it had been stripped of clothing.'

'Which opened to view the scorching of the skin by a Tropical sun... what else was there of interest?'

'The fearful bruising of the body.'

I looked at Holmes sharply.

'The bruising?' I exclaimed. 'Who said there was bruising? Holmes, there were no bruises reported in the *Standard*. It simply said the victim's skin was seared in a particular pattern.'

'Then what of the broken bones?'

I stared at him aghast.

'Holmes, you know full well there was no mention of broken bones.'

'But what of the terrible cut across the nape as from a cutlass, a violent slash which so nearly beheaded him?' Holmes asked, smiling.

'Holmes, you know perfectly well such a wound would have been...'

I stopped abruptly, casting him a rueful smile. This was not an example of Holmes' Socratic method. He was up to his old and familiar trick, scrambling my brain like Mrs. Hudson's Sunday eggs.

'Precisely, Watson!' Holmes continued. 'No cuts, no bruises, no broken bones? How can it be? Why not a brutal slash across the throat to divide the carotid artery?'

I waited in impatient silence while he exchanged the cigarette case in turn for a favourite pipe. He resumed, 'What then, I ask again, what of our cadaver at Scotney Castle? There was no report of any such disfigurement. Did that not arouse your suspicion? Siviter and his cohorts made a serious blunder in prompting Fusey to declare it was a vagabond who killed himself or took a bath in the wagon pond and drowned. That it was a suicide or a chance drowning was not impossible. It was impossible it was the suicide or chance drowning of a tramp.'

He looked at me, the grey eyes narrowing. 'What should that have told you, Watson?'

'I confess I have no answer to your question, Holmes.'

'It proves the act of murder was not long in the soak. Where a crime is coolly planned, then the means of covering it up are coolly premeditated too. Rather than passing it off as a suicide or accidental drowning, they would have thrown me off the scent if they had made it clear it was murder. Siviter should have employed that cut-throat Venucci from Saffron Hill or a murder-gang, or a Smithfields garrotter - or even after the heart ceased beating a bludgeonman with a vigorous arm to crush in the face with three heavy blows of a sand-bag. The Boche should have been deposited in the wagon pond ill-kempt, a half-quartern of gin neat in his pocket, his body covered with contusions or the head horribly mutilated – have I made my point? - why, I might not have given the report a second glance, even with the dark glasses held up from the water like Excalibur.'

241

'So their scheme was endangered because...'

'They were too fastidious? Perhaps.'

'Or?'

'Or they had reached the limit of their ingenuity.'

He paused. 'Then there was the peculiar matter of Dudeney's response.'

'The peculiar matter of Dudeney's response!' I parroted. 'What of Dudeney? His response to what?'

'Cast your mind back to our journey to Crick's End in the Lanchester. Do you recall informing him you had read Siviter's cat-and-rat fable?'

'I did tell him that, what of it?'

'Just when we came through Etchingham and entered the Straight Mile?'

'It was about then I spoke those words, yes.'

'And that you looked forward to viewing Crick's End's electricity at work?'

'That was what I told him, yes.'

'And he responded with?'

242

'He said the mill-pond was low, too low to generate sufficient electricity until replenished by the leat.' I stared across at Holmes with a perplexed smile. 'You considered that to be important?'

'Exceedingly so,' he replied. 'The very fact he informed you of this – did you not find that of curious interest, my considerable friend?'

'Telling me of the level of the water in the mill-pond? Not especially, no. Surely that was entirely inconsequential?'

'Possibly - if he had left it at that.'

'By which you mean…?'

'This conversation struck me as odd. Why did he feel obliged to offer such detail? Even so, my interest and curiosity were subsiding until some minutes later he aroused them once again.'

'By?'

'Did he not tell you the reason the water-level was so low?'

'As I recall, he did,' I replied. 'And?'

'Which was?' Holmes pursued.

'Village children at play had emptied it - by opening the sluice.'

'Yes, Watson, those were indeed his words. And you made nothing of them?'

'Nothing. Neither then nor now. Why should I?'

'If you remember, he proffered this explanation after returning from the cart which shed its load of hay… which was where?

'At the other end of the Straight Mile. So?'

'Some five minutes later. Why did he not give this explanation at once?'

'You have lost me, Holmes,' I replied. 'What bearing does the mill-pond at Crick's End have on the discovery of a corpse at Scotney Castle? What does it matter if the mill-pond was low or if a chauffeur should wish to bring the reason for this to our attention – or when he did so?'

'Not so much the pond was low but the reason Dudeney gave for it being so – village children had opened up the sluice. Why then, hardly one hour later, did our host offer a completely different reason? Twice Siviter told us this same pond was low through the extra demand of visitors. Why did his explanation so oppose the one Dudeney had on offer – unless both were hasty inventions?'

'Then I ask again, Holmes, what of it if the pond was low – or the reason for it?'

'Because, my considerable friend, a case can be put together from such tiny inconsistencies. Where there is a want of consistency we must suspect deception. I repeat, why were we were offered two distinct and contradictory reasons? It can only be each was deliberate, each intended to mislead us, what else? It was indeed surprising the mill-pond was so drained despite the recent rains and the open leat.   Lack of electric lighting left Crick's End deprived of much evening comfort.   Yet if we suppose neither children at play nor the extra needs of guests caused this condition, what other explanation might there be? Why was the mill-pond so empty?'

'If neither Siviter's nor Dudeney's explanation was true...   I am sorry, Holmes, I must leave it to you.'

'I believe the method was connected to Siviter's great love, that turbine-generator.   I suggest its infernal mechanics were rigged to let the water flow at excessive speed, more gallons a minute than we can ever guess, far above the norm.   It spun the wheel so fast the current passing through the victim's head or chest was raised to deadly heights.   The local constable judged it suicide or accidental death by drowning. I would wager my whole fee from the case of the Third French Republic there was not a drop of wagon pond water in the Boche's lungs. Water killed him, but not by filling up his lungs. The fellow died from electrocution.'

Once more the Holmes I knew of old unfurled his wares before me.

'Watson,' he went on, 'you suggest it was no bad thing they murdered him, a Prussian emissary issuing violent threats of war, daring to board a packet-boat to Newhaven to beard the British lion in his very den. Was that the true purpose of his mission? I confess I am undermined by doubts gnawing at me like lionesses disembowelling a buck. Why kill him? An assassination involves grave risk. I ask myself again, for what profit did the Sungazers go to such lengths, at such danger to their far-flung enterprise?'

'That is indeed a point of curious interest,' I interjected. 'Knowing you held it to be murder I too have pondered on it many times.'

245

'To which conclusion, may I ask?' Holmes enquired in a friendly tone, eyes twinkling.

'Alas, none, Holmes. It has proved quite beyond my ability. Such an assassination was without doubt a risky throw even for such a high and mighty League. How do you explain it?'

'An act of desperation, given the stakes for failure. Planned as the clock struck midnight, judging by the late commission of the second painting.'

He stopped, then recommenced. 'Yes, Watson, it remains the most puzzling question of them all - why murder? Why not a clip across the ear and send him on his way?'

'I await your answer, Holmes. I have no solution to that most baffling question.'

'Unless...'

He paused.

'Unless?' I prompted.

'What if...' he repeated slowly.

'Holmes,' I laughed. 'What if what! I demand you cease this teasing!'

'I can assure you, teasing is far from my intent. Watson, consider this. Until this very moment we have taken it for granted Count von

Hofmeyer arrived at Crick's End with threats in mind.'

Again, to my frustration, Holmes fell silent.

'What do you think now?' I urged.

'Surely if what we hold to be von Hofmeyer's reason for visiting Crick's End is true, murdering him would go counter to the interests of the League, yet these are men of the most extraordinary intelligence and experience.'

'So why...?' I commenced.

'The clipping from the *Rheinische Merkur*,' he replied. 'I am certain the Kipling League ordered its delivery to my door, but why so? Why these seven years on? Do we take it they mock us still? What would be the point?'

Once more I turned these facts over in my mind. As I did so, I became aware of a change taking place in my comrade's demeanour. He pulled himself to his feet and strode past me to a window, staring out as though he could see Crick's End on the horizon, like the sinister Spectre of the Brocken we watched in awe during a trip to the Harz Mountains many years ago. A minute passed before he tore his gaze away from the landscape.

'Watson!' he demanded, 'what has taken place out there during our seven years of separation? Quick, tell me!'

Taken by surprise by his intensity, I stammered, 'Why, I have been mostly engaged in my medical practice...'

'Not in your world, Watson! You are a doctor, for heaven's sake. You dispense potions. I mean in the outside world! What of the imminence of war with Germany? The newspapers are filled with it.'

His expressive face had now taken on the agonised look of a man whose heart was collapsing. I was half-way to my feet to retrieve my medical bag from the veranda when he waved me back with an impatient gesture.

'Of course! That was their intention! Watson – once again you have worked a miracle as my sounding-board. This clipping from the *Rheinische Merkur*, I ask you again, what was its purpose?'

'Because they wish to torment us, Holmes?'

'No, I no longer hold to that assumption. That cannot be the League's intention. They have placed the riddle of the sands before us. It is as though Siviter seeks to justify their crime. These Sungazers had this clipping delivered precisely because it provides the answer.'

He stabbed a thin finger towards the sounds of Mrs. Keppell and Tallulah engaging in chit-chat with each other through a back window. 'Come, Watson, let us continue talking in the front-yard.'

At times like this Holmes' finely-cut face glowed with something more than human. He led me out, pausing to pull from the pile of books the newly-published edition of The History of Nineteenth Century Britain. Galvanised by his excitement, I sprang to my feet, the unstable chair tumbling to one side.

'What is the answer?' I called after him as he strode on without a backward glance, like Orpheus leading Eurydice from the Underworld.   With all his old verve recovered he crossed the veranda at speed to an open space beyond.

'Holmes,' I called out again from several yards behind. 'What have the Sungazers offered us with this piece from the *Merkur*?'

'The very answer we have been seeking!' came his reply. 'We have been more stupid than we have ever been! What has become of any brains God gave us? I shall never forgive myself, never! Count von Hofmeyer could not have come with menaces in his pocket. Nations have other ways to display their keenness to fight - grandiose military parades, dreadnoughts at Cowes and other huff and puff. Had he arrived with threats of war he would be alive today.'

'If this Hun did not come with threats of war,' I cried, 'why did they kill him and throw him in a wagon pond?'

'My dear friend, I shall not keep you in suspense much longer.'

He opened the tome he was carrying at a well-thumbed page.

'...listen to these words of Viscount Van Beers on his role in the eruption of the late South African War. These, I repeat, are Van Beers' own words.'

I stood listening at Holmes' side as he read aloud. ''Convinced of the Justice and Necessity of the struggle, I precipitated the Anglo-Boer War, which was inevitable, before it was too late...before the forces ranged against England grew too strong. It is not a very agreeable, and in many minds, not a very creditable piece of business

249

to be largely instrumental in bringing about a big war. In my defence it should be recalled Protestantism in England took root only when Thomas Cromwell had the head of More struck off.'

We walked on past high Rhododendron bushes. Beyond them, at the courtyard edge, well away from the house, we arrived at Mrs. Keppell's miniature herb garden filled with candytuft and lavender. Here Holmes commenced smoking hard, brows drawn down over his keen eyes, head thrust forward in the eager way so characteristic of the man I remembered with such affection from our years together as partners against crime.

'Holmes,' I interjected, baffled. 'What has this to do with murder?'

'Let us look at the facts from a different angle, Watson. We now know von Hofmeyer came on a particular mission to Crick's End, what else? It could hardly be a social visit. We can assume he was murdered and we know the murder was a savage riposte to the Chancellery in Berlin. But what if von Hofmeyer did not come to Crick's End with bellicose intent? What then?'

'Holmes, you have lost me. Why otherwise would the Sungazers kill him?'

'We are assuming the Count was a harbinger of war, a Prussian emissary in search of humiliating concessions... but what if...?'

'...if not to menace England, why else would he come with such stealth?'

'What if he brought an offer of a peaceful resolution to our differences?'

250

'Holmes,' I responded, laughing incredulously. 'A secret offer of peace! If so, why should he be murdered for his pains? What on Earth would make you jump to such a conclusion?'

'Von Hofmeyer was aware that England's hostility to Germany was growing by the day but he knew the German Kriegsmarine was not ready to take on the greatest Naval Power in history. Ships alone, regardless of their 12-inch guns or speed, are not enough. You must train the men. More time was needed. Remember, this was 1904. An offer of an amicable settlement of differences might appeal to an English public averse to war after expenditure of a thousand millions and such loss of men in South Africa. Who better to bring that offer than the poacher adopting a gamekeeper's mask? Yet think how the Sungazers – Van Beers in particular - would respond. With the utmost horror! Such a proposition could slow a build-up of our forces...'

He broke off, encouraging me to supply the ending to his sentence.

'...until it was too late?' I hazarded.

'Quite so. That would be the Sungazers' thinking.'

After a long pause digesting this, I said, 'And that is why they murdered him... not to forestall an outbreak of enmity between Germany and Great Britain but to prevent an outbreak of amity between our two great countries.'

'They kept von Hofmeyer within those high hedges at Crick's End on whichever pretext they invented, lulling him into thinking his mission of peace was being hotly debated in Downing Street and

251

would succeed, while all the while they were devising which way to murder him. That is the only deduction which fits all the facts. They had to make their response indelible. Van Beers and both Gold Bugs were brought up as Germans. They may rightly feel they have special insight into the blood and iron of the Prussian soul. In Van Beer's opinion as a military expert, a war with Germany was and remains unavoidable. Therefore the sooner the better before Germany completes her armaments and hones her gunnery skills. If the Kaiser's emissary had huffed and puffed on Berlin's behalf, if he had arrived with a pocketful of menaces – halt our Dreadnought programme, hand over half our African colonies, internationalise the Suez Canal, stay silent and quiescent over Germany's expansion into the Balkans, or else! - Van Beers would have sent him packing on the instant. The Count would be alive to-day. When he came with an offer of a settlement of differences, he was doomed. The coterie at Crick's End saw it as a ruse to gain time. Already Germany produces a hundred million tons of steel a year to our sixty, second only to America. To the Sungazers, acceptance would mean disaster.'

By now, Holmes' fox was running at full pelt though there was no sign of exultation or satisfaction upon his face.

'It was a serious blunder by Berlin to approach the Kipling League. Other eminent Englishmen would have been far more amenable. It was not the Kaiser's bullying or an open threat of war the Sungazers dreaded. It was the offer of peace. Therefore the emissary must die. In the Kaiser's Germany no cohort of men could act this way without a nod from the highest authority. Think of it, von Hofmeyer done to death, his corpse left to soak naked in a wagon pond. Not even the Imperial Russian Secret Police could kill a foreigner without the Winter Palace's assent. The clear message to Berlin would be Downing Street wanted no entente or 'equitable solution'. Thus

252

Germany redoubled her efforts to build up the Kriegsmarine and train a hundred crews. Thus in response we amplified many-fold our own construction of armoured cruisers.'

'With the result...'

'War is on the horizon, early rather than late. Precisely what Van Beers and the Sungazers wanted.'

Holmes continued, 'Now I see they wanted the discovery of the corpse to catch the German Ambassador's eye. They knew an unclad body would push into the press. As to their success in misleading me... do you recall with what approval they listened when I told them how I deduced you were recently returned from Afghanistan? 'Just returned from some time in the Tropics, for his face is dark, and that is not the natural tint of his skin, for his wrists are fair.' They must have hoped we would note – and be misled by - the pattern in the corpse's skin if by chance we entered the case.'

'Into thinking he was a Boer...'

'Yes.'

'And the Boche's shiny dark glasses, Holmes, as you surmised, a part of the semaphore?'

'It was a signal to the Imperial German Embassy. The Ambassador would inform Berlin their Africa brute turned diplomat was dead - yet the very same clue compounded my assumption the man was resident in the Tropics.'

I ventured, 'The hat with its lizard-skin band...'

'Sheer genius. Again, it fed in to my deduction the crime was some dangerous residue of the South African war while it served a separate purpose. It ensured the Germans understood this was no suicide or accidental drowning. They would realise von Hofmeyer's fedora had been exchanged for someone else's hat. A quick trawl through photographs of the Kipling League would tell them it belonged to Sir Julius.'

'Holmes, now that you have explained it, I confess that I am as amazed as before.'

My friend nodded. 'They are a formidable lot.'

We turned away from the rhododendrons and seated ourselves on a shaded marble bench.

'Suffice to say the skies are black with the clouds of war,' Holmes went on. 'The Sungazers have put us on the path perhaps five years earlier than might have been, though they would argue just in the nick of time. Already the German fleet has gained a complete ascendancy over that of Britain's on the sea-routes to The Argentine.'

He sat beside me discomfited, shoulders bowed.

I asked, 'Have you any thoughts on the offer von Hofmeyer might have brought?'

'I have no doubt free rein for Cecil Rhodes' dream of Africa - British from Cape to Cairo. Perhaps an alliance to wrest the Congo with its germanium and rubber from the Belgians to share between us.'

Holmes turned his head away.

'My naivety in world affairs. We should have seen we were in March Hare and Mad Hatter Land. They were more cunning than the water-fox. Think on it - the suspicious absence of your most popular chronicles in Siviter's study. That was not by chance. They were purposely removed. I am certain Siviter possessed *The Adventure of the Speckled Band*. It is a study of murder known to every Anglo-Indian. It was Siviter who ordered Sir Julius to switch his hat with von Hofmeyer's and leave it a-top the pile of clothes.' Again my companion shook his head with a rueful look in my direction. 'It was wonderfully done. That speckled band sent me scurrying in quite the wrong direction. I wager they already knew *The Hound of the Baskervilles* – no-one shuddered. But there was a lacuna in their knowledge of your chronicles, Watson.'

'*The Adventure of Silver Blaze...*'

'Yes. Once I discussed it, Siviter and his co-conspirators must have sat there wondering was there a dog which didn't bark in their master plan for murder? I wonder which among them re-examined the painting of the moat and saw von Hofmeyer's shadow and reflection lying there still, without a figure? It alone would prove their first plan was to have the body discovered in the moat that evening, and not the wagon pond at 3.'

Holmes sprang up from the marble bench and paced about in uncontrollable agitation, a flush appearing upon his sallow cheeks. 'To have forever on my mind I could have grasped their deception... Look what other clues I had to hand. I noted Sir Julius had worn a hat too small. The hat marks on his forehead were there for all to see.

255

Were it not for the rain that day he might well have cast it in the Rother or the Dudwell. No well-dressed man resident less than half a mile from Lincoln & Bennett's would bring a hat to Sussex half a size too small. Further, Watson, I saw at once it was German, probably purchased from the hatter Möckel, though brought into wider fashion by the old Prince of Wales. The moment I read the *Standard* I should have deduced far faster the hat Sir Julius brought back to Crick's End had previously perched atop the corpse's head while his was the one cast with such guile a-top the pile of clothes.'

With reluctant admiration he continued, 'These Sungazers are not creatures of thin air. They have taught me a lesson I shall not relinquish, Watson. To think I mocked them on our journey to Crick's End. I called them Late Victorians, relics of a bygone age, purblind Empire Crusaders.'

Holmes looked at me almost accusingly.

'Just as Moriarty used so many petty criminals to do his dirty work, I am now inclined to believe the young blighter selling papers was in the Sungazers' pay, a tiny storm petrel of crime. Dudeney could have given him his instructions. I am equally certain Sir Julius and Siviter arranged the Anatolian dish not simply for your delectation but with a purpose, to effect an hour's delay. How otherwise can you – a greater gourmet than I – explain precisely why our stomachs were invited to digest both medlar jelly and Imam Bayildi? Quite contrary to my first assumption, they wanted us to be met by the late edition of the paper into which their corpse had pushed its way. By then it had become an open challenge – they dared to bat against me at my own game.'

A pause followed.

'Damnation, Watson, the horror, the utter horror of it all. Those...unspeakable...those...wretched boulevard assassins. They are the skins cast off by vipers. May they be buried at cross-roads with a stake in their heart ... '

Then, morosely, 'It is lucky I have my bees for consolation.'

A further pause. 'Hanging is too good for them!' And, 'Nevertheless, it is worth analysis. Men of their ilk will not go away.' And, enigmatically, 'We must bow before the oligarchic laws of Nature.'

He continued in a sombre voice. 'I have carried with me one memory from our encounter with the Kipling League which may stalk me for ever, like a doppelgänger sprung at me from the very depths of Hell.'

'Which is?' I enquired keenly.

'The dark glasses,' my comrade responded.

'The dark glasses?' I repeated with some incredulity.

Holmes nodded. 'Even now a shudder runs through my veins.'

'Not your veins, Holmes, surely,' I demurred. 'A shudder is more likely to be a muscular reaction.'

He looked at me sternly. 'I realise your wit must on most occasions have passed me by. Shall we say a shudder runs through my musculature even now when I recall the moment I came to the dark glasses in the newspaper account.'

'I'm sorry, Holmes,' I returned, starting a scornful laugh. 'If I recall the words they were 'A pair of shiny dark glasses was discovered between finger and thumb'. Hardly anything to shudder at, surely? What of Moriarty's ruthless lieutenant Colonel Sebastian Moran? Consider how near we were to a dreadful fate at his hands. Now that is something to shudder at. A pair of dark glasses must rest a long way down the list of horrors we have encountered in our long journey together?'

'It was the cold inhumanity with which they staged the corpse, an arm left jutting above the water so they could pinch the dead thumb and finger around his trade-mark dark glasses, like a Harrods' window-dresser with a mannequin. Your friend Beerbohm Tree could not have staged it better at the Theatre Royal. They turned the Boche into a speechless, sightless, lifeless signpost. It is the grotesque image which stays with me, not the manner of his death itself. I doubt if von Hofmeyer did the St. Vitus Dance ten minutes before the current killed him, a current lethal but less than would burn the skin.'

Silence fell between us. After a while Holmes added, 'Sir Julius chose that hatband well. When threatened, the majestic spiny lizard wedges between the rocks and puffs itself up. It becomes impossible to remove.'

Minutes came and went in unbroken silence. The mystery of the dead Boer had reached its conclusion.

Tremulously I took my chance. 'Holmes, there is one last matter of great concern to me....'

Holmes threw me a disquieted look. 'My dear friend, please go on.'

'Is it possible my... my craven fear of the Kipling League, my unwillingness to offer my knowledge of rigor mortis until you put the matter to me directly...'

'...your reluctance to follow my argument so swiftly assembled at Etchingham railway station?'

'Yes, Holmes. Exactly that. By that did I...?'

'...by your obstructive behaviour did you impede a timely resolution of the affair?'

'That is what I fear greatly, Holmes, yes.'

'And because of that we face a fearful war against the Hun more surely and much earlier than expected?'

'Yes, Holmes.'

'Which may bring about the end of the British Empire?' Holmes pursued.

'Holmes,' I cried despairingly, 'I fear it may be all my fault!'

'Watson, be at rest, my old and faithful friend,' my old comrade chided me. 'They beat us. Like lizards feasting on a wax worm they swallowed me whole. It was I who provided them with the instructions they needed to defeat me. It was I who taught them how to look for dogs which failed to bark. You have nothing whatsoever to answer to the Court of History, though indeed I do'

I waited a while. Then I said, 'Thank you, Holmes, but I am not yet done. There is something further I should tell you.'

'Concerning?'

'The wagon pond painting.'

'Do go on, Watson. You have my ear, I can assure you,' Holmes responded companionably.

'At the time, as you will certainly remember, I was unwilling to add fuel to your assumptions. I was certain you were determined on the path to professional extinction. I was desperate to save you from yourself. I shall regret one deliberate omission of mine for the rest of my days.'

'Which omission precisely, may I enquire, Watson?' Holmes asked, a twinkle in his eye.

'Perhaps the final clue you needed to make a charge of murder stick,' I responded.

Holmes raised his eyebrows. He gave me his full attention. 'Please go on, Watson, this is of especial interest! Do you claim you were privy to a clue which entirely escaped me – and furthermore you kept it hidden? Is this history in the making?' Mischievously he added, 'I said at the time you had joined their camp!'

Ignoring these friendly barbs, I continued. 'You recall the moment Pevensey made his exit from the mill-attic?'

'Indeed I do.'

'And how we both approached the canvas on the easel...'

'I do, most certainly. Go on!'

'And that I asked Siviter why a human figure had been painted standing by the wagon pond instead of the dog in the Constable?'

'I remember as if it were this morning. Do continue.'

'So you will recall his explanation?'

'Watson, well done! You have picked up at last on my method of interrogation. Why, let me think, I must surely remember... let me see. Ah, yes! Siviter said 'To tell you the truth, I don't feel he is at his best painting animals'.'

'Those were his exact words, Holmes,' I responded in admiration.

'What of it, Watson? Why do you wear such an unhappy look? Many painters make cats look like bull-terriers.'

'There is a painting at the Tate which from the day the Gallery opened I and all those interested in medicine repeatedly visit and revere.'

'Which is?'

'It is known by the title 'A Visit to Vediovis'. Venus is consulting the Roman god of healing about a thorn lodged in her foot.'

'And?' Holmes queried, looking puzzled.

'The artist has painted a bowl of luscious fruit at the side of Vediovis...'

'What of it?'

'And by this bowl, painted in minute detail with the finest red sable brush, a wondrously life-like dog lies on the floor.'

'And the painter of this masterly work?'

'Pevensey.'

'Damnation!' Holmes exclaimed, his face darkening. 'Why did you not confront Siviter with this at the time?'

'As you said, Holmes,' I responded, smiling broadly. 'We were still his guests – nor had we been commissioned to investigate the murder of a Hun.'

'Touché, Watson, well done!' Holmes chuckled with excellent grace. The cooler evening air blew from the South-West as we left the courtyard and went inside where Holmes knocked a blaze out of the logs in the grate.

Some twenty minutes later, the sound of bicycle tyres on gravel came through the open window from the courtyard, followed by a sharp pull at the bell. Soon afterwards we heard a creaking which could only come from the hinges of the front door. We listened while Tallulah first, then her mistress, welcomed the rider in their different ways.

As in our former days together, Holmes threw me a look of anticipation. 'A telegram, Watson? What have we? Other than you, only the Foreign Office and the Eastern Department – or Siviter and the Kipling League - know I am here.'

Greatly curious, we rose and went out to the veranda to be met by an excited Mrs. Keppell. Reminiscent of our dear former landlady, she hurried towards Holmes and pushed the telegram at him with a polite bend of the knee. This time, rather than throwing it to me, Holmes pounced forward, taking it swiftly from Mrs. Keppell's outstretched hand. He withdrew the slip of paper from its envelope and began reading it to himself.

He cast the first of a succession of serious looks in my direction. 'Watson, it is a private telegram forwarded by our Foreign Office from a foreign potentate, the Sultan Mehmed V Reshad. You will of course know him as the son of Sultan Abdülmecid.'

'Indeed. What then?' I responded, looking back and forth from Mrs. Keppell to Holmes, trying to contain a smile at this conspiracy.

'The Sword of Osman has been stolen!'

'The Sword of Osman, Holmes?' I responded, biting a lip. 'Tut! What is that?'

'The sword of state used during the coronation ceremony of every sultan,' he replied, throwing me another serious glance. 'The sword is named after Osman the First, founder of the Ottoman Dynasty many centuries ago.'

He read further. Another glance was thrown in my direction. 'Watson, this theft could endanger the Sultanate itself. Clearly it is designed to bring about the collapse of their Empire. Sultan Mehmed V Reshad is the very person we need to woo the Ottomans away from Berlin.'

He looked back at the telegram but continued offering asides gained from his readings on the Ottomans. 'The girding of the sword of Osman is a vital ceremony which must take place within two weeks of a Sultan's accession to the throne. The practice started when Osman was girt with the sword of Islam by his mentor and father-in-law Sheik Edebali.'

I listened in growing admiration at my friend's knowledge and ingenuity as he continued. 'The fact the emblem by which a Sultan is enthroned consists of a sword is highly symbolic. It shows the office with which he is invested is first and foremost that of a warrior.'

'My Heavens, Holmes,' I retorted in insincere amazement. Was this the purest Oscar Wilde or the topsy-turvy world of Gilbert and Sullivan? 'This is a very serious matter. When does the son of Sultan Abdülmecid wish us to start hunting for the dastardly criminals who have nabbed this sword?'

'At once, Watson, at once. He invites us to catch the first ship to Constantinople.'

He paused briefly. 'The Asturias should leave Southampton in one week's time. She can take us to Smyrna via Civita Vecchia, Malta and Alexandria. From Smyrna we can take a line direct to Constantinople.'

I listened in wonderment at how far his imagination had stretched in putting together so bizarre a tale to console and entertain his guest. When would that stern and eager face break into confessional laughter?

'And does the Sultan offer us a reward?' I managed.

He looked back at the telegram. 'He does. Should we succeed in regaining the Sword our reward will be a belt of diamonds and gold. After our arrival at Karaköy we are ordered to take the carriage to the Topkapi and go immediately to meet a bimbashi waiting for us at the Chamber of Petitions, known by the locals as the Arz Odası, behind the Gate of Felicity. Watson, are you with me on this venture?'

'Holmes,' I nodded vigorously, offering a fine smile. 'I am at your shoulder. A belt of diamonds and gold, you say? I trust for such an occasion you will choose again the Poshteen Long Coat and wear your Order of Saint Stanislaus - and your gold watch? For my part, I shall bring my glossy topper with a new side-feather and collect my service revolver and fifty rounds from Mrs. Hudson's. You can never be too heavily armed for Ottomans. I shall meet you aboard the Asturias in Southampton Water in six days' time. Can Mrs. Keppell let the Sultan know we shall require First Class cabins?'

At this we turned and re-entered the farmhouse living-room to partake of Mrs. Keppell's tea. Through that early-Summer night Holmes and I sat together, once more in perfect amity, and doubly strengthened. He pulled at more than one of his favourite pipes. At one point, in a meditative tone, Holmes said, 'You know I feel quite sorry for the Prussian in the coming war – there has never been a race of conquerors and killers more savage and resourceful than you English.'

265

He spoke as though in sympathy and tradition he held England at arm's length, as if his Celtic origins trumped upbringing and country of birth.

He continued, 'And you, Watson, in particular, when roused by the fiery speech of some Army colonel or at my behest or that of friends, you are the apotheosis of an Englishman, redolent of all his virtues, vices, inconsistencies and compassion. When I watch you gaze across this Weald I know you would give your life to defend it.'

I flushed up with pleasure at my companion's words.

That midnight, after a lengthy walk with torches in his woods and fields, we returned to the house where I struck a match on my boot and put it to the fire laid earlier by Mrs. Keppell to ward off the country damp. We watched the ancient hearth blaze up as heartily as in our days in Baker Street, though from the abundant oak, the Weed of Sussex, rather than sea-coal. Together we put together these words as an Addendum to accompany at no extra cost each copy of what a publisher should still call *Sherlock Holmes and The Dead Boer at Scotney Castle*. In that quiet, low-beamed room in deepest Sussex, I jotted down copious notes which somewhat later, after smoothing and modelling and paring-away, would surely become a chronicle selling in the many hundreds of copies in dozens of countries.

Over time, Holmes would publish his learned bibliography titled *The Polyphonic Motets of Lassus* and a collection of bee-farming manuals, including two small blue volumes, the alliterative *The Hibernation Habits of the Hive* and the *Practical Handbook of Bee Culture, with some Observations upon the Segregation of the Queen* and the best-seller, *Bees Foraging on Distant Landscapes*, illustrated in his own hand. In it he deduces how the genus *Apis* communicates sources of forage to each other, indicating by a prancing figure of eight the compass bearing and distance, an opus which has gained widespread respect among bee-farmers in New Hebrides and China.

Our friendship restored and the addendum completed, on the next evening I sat with him in the little summer house he himself had built in an open space on his farm, partially shaded by the branches of a Symonds apple-tree sent to him nine years before by an admirer in New Zealand. We perched on two corn-chests with Tallulah stretched between us, while Mrs. Keppell, specially commissioned for the occasion, served us a repast, filling while not extravagant. She surprised me by laying before us two bowls, one containing very shiny black tea and the other scented green, bought from a newly-established shop in Lewes. It was a rare Holmes who drank tea, yet we each imbibed the contents of two cups of the black.

On the morrow, a quick hansom drawn by a dapple-grey cob took me to Lewes. The carriage rocked and swayed as I laughed uncontrollably at Holmes' kindly effort to cheer me up – like Sindbad we would go on a wondrous voyage, to Constantinople to meet the bimbashi awaiting us at the Chamber of Petitions, tasked with the recovery of the stolen Sword of Osman indeed!

As it was, two weeks later, a powerful windstorm in the Bay of Biscay behind us, Holmes and I sat with the worried Sultan and his advisers in his palace by the wide and beautiful Bosphorus Strait, once more before a table laden with plates of Imam Bayildi followed by Ottoman sweets. A visit to Seraglio Point ensued. From its heights we had a most excellent view to the shores of Scutari, the Sea of Marmara and the Isles of Princes. From where we stood with shining eyes the minarets of the fabled city mingled with sea and shore, light and shade, the softness and the Eastern charm was unequalled anywhere else in the whole world.

We stood transfixed at this Oriental vista. Not far away lay Bulgaria where the knyaz Ferdinand had just declared himself Tsar. That too is a story I itch to publish. There never was nor ever will be a Royal Highness as complex and cunning as Ferdinand Maximilian Karl Leopold Maria of Saxe-Coburg and Gotha-Koháry.

****

POST-SCRIPT

A notice dated 14 June 1904 appeared on an inside page of the Kent & Sussex Courier headed 'Open Verdict Coroner Rules'. It read, 'The Kent Coroner has returned an open verdict following the death of a man late last month. A post-mortem was not conducted. The uncovered body whose identity remains unknown was found partly submerged in a wagon pond on the Scotney Castle Estate, near Lamberhurst.'

Despite being offered Watson's favourable diagnosis of a dozen years more, Alfred Weit died less than a year after the Kipling League meeting with Holmes and Watson at Crick's End. A bridge over the Kafue River, an important tributary of the great Zambezi, was named after him. His obituary in The London Observer read: 'One of the most extraordinary of self-educated men, he assembled a very large fortune in mineral speculation. Long years of unintermitted toil and living in the Tropics culminated in a fever of the brain, under the influence of which he committed suicide.'
In his last Will and Testament he left 500 guineas 'to my friend Dr. John Watson'.

Alfred Weit's business partner Sir Julius Wernher, purveyor of the recipe for Imam bayildi, lived past the First World War.

Early in 1915 Siviter and his wife Charlotte turned most of Crick's End into a convalescent home for officers and retired to a cottage in the grounds where Siviter embarked on his memoires. In his later years, long after the Kaiser's War had come and gone and Britain had begun to accept the loosening ties of Empire, he turned back to his Indian cultural heritage, contemplating the old Hindu custom of giving up material interests to prepare for the spiritual plane, a theme

269

forecast in his story titled *The Miracle of Mengohn Temple.* On his 44th wedding anniversary, three decades after the events described in *the Dead Boer*, Siviter died from a perforated duodenum. He was buried at Poet's Corner in Westminster Abbey. The pall-bearers included a Field Marshall, an Admiral of the Fleet, and Britain's Prime Minister. His tongue and hand sealed forever in death, with Siviter went most of the inside knowledge of the dramatic events surrounding the corpse at Scotney Castle.

1st Baronet Sir Edward Pevensey's reputation in history was hampered by the fact that of the three Victorian Olympians (the others being Frederick Lord Leighton and Sir Lawrence Alma-Tadema) the least is known about him in spite of the fact that he produced some of the period's most revered paintings. He was President of the Royal Academy for twenty-two years. He died a few months after the Great War ended.

In 1922, Lady Susan Townley, wife of a former Second Secretary at the British Embassy in Berlin, in her memoires 'Indiscretions' Of Lady Susan added detail to Sherlock Holmes' speculation on the offer von Hofmeyer might have brought to the Sungazer Gang. She wrote: 'We were once present at a dinner given to the Kaiser at our Embassy when Cecil Rhodes, who was the guest of honour, asked to meet him. At this dinner (it was in 1899, if I remember right) an incident occurred hitherto unrecorded, which I am convinced had great future political interest for both Britain and Germany.

Before the dinner, Cecil Rhodes had been speaking of his grand conception of an All-British Cape to Cairo Railway, the greatest transcontinental line in the world. At that time this scheme was threatened by the lively interest which Germany displayed in African trade development.

270

"If only we could make the Kaiser abandon his African schemes and leave us free to get on with ours," Rhodes said. "But he's so obstinate. Once he has thought out a plan nothing will make him change it ... Unless," he added reflectively, "I could think of some other scheme to put before him that would fire his imagination and lead him off on another scent!"

After dinner the ladies retired, as usual, but my husband told me afterwards how the Emperor and Rhodes fell at once into an animated conversation. In pursuance of the plan that had occurred to him before dinner, Rhodes set to work to draw a red herring before the Kaiser's trail by leading the conversation on to the topic of Mesopotamia.

"If my thoughts were not centred on Africa," Rhodes declared, "that would be the field of development that would attract me most. Not only is it capable of becoming the granary of the world, but it is the obvious route to the Far East and to the undeveloped markets of Persia and Afghanistan. The way to those countries lies through Baghdad!"

I know how much Cecil Rhodes had hoped to gain from this after-dinner talk, and it may be judged with what eagerness I watched for his reappearance. When after a long time the men joined us, his face was flushed with excitement. "Thank God," he whispered, "I believe I have done the trick. I have side-tracked him out of Africa!"

... I am convinced that at that moment was born the idea of the Baghdad-Bahn.'

Whether or not Cecil Rhodes influenced the Kaiser, the Baghdad railway was attempted by Germany at great cost and limited value. A better line for trade with the East would have been via Bucharest

271

and Constanza to one or other of ports on the Black Sea such as Batum in the Caucasus or Trezibond, and onward to Persia.

In 1915 Mrs. Hudson received a considerable accolade for service to humankind. A Belgian lady was sent over specially to reward British canteen workers with the Ribbon of the Order of Queen Elizabeth for the part they played in befriending Belgian soldiers during the first year of the Great War. Though without any strong partiality for expensive outfits, a photograph taken for the occasion shows Mrs. Hudson in a light dress with a boned, high collar and tiny braid buttons from throat to knee, beneath a straw hat tied on by a large bow of white moiré ribbon. She wore child-like white cotton socks with second-hand black buttoned boots, the latter first purchased from Nain Bleu in the Rue St. Honoré 'by a rich lady'.

From modesty Mrs. Hudson made no claim for the medal but for the remainder of her long life the ribbon remained firmly attached to a pin-cushion in her quarters, until finally it shrivelled and dropped off and was swept up, unnoticed, with the dust.

Lord Van Beers died in 1925. With his departure a generation of Victorian men and women not to be equalled again in their reach, self-belief, and ambition for England had gone.

In 1929 Mrs. Keppell came into ownership of Sherlock Holmes' farm and bees in Sussex. No record was kept of her Norwich terrier Tallulah.

As the years passed, Eddie Marsh proceeded through the rites of passage of a successful Civil Servant's career. 'Eddie' Marsh became Edward Marsh, alias Mr. E. Marsh, Esq., transmogrifying into Sir Edward Marsh K.C.V.O. as presence was forced upon him.

272

He retired in February 1937 with a gift of 'an exquisite and convenient inkstand of Sheffield plate', inscribed 'To Eddie, from his friends in the Dominions Office'. In retirement he spent many of his waking hours in the bow window of Boodle's Club in St. James Street or at his cottage in Picardy.

Dr. Watson died in 1939. Conscientious to the end, his last recorded words were, 'Has anything escaped me? I trust there is nothing of consequence I have overlooked?'

A short obituary appeared in his favourite newspaper, *The Morning Telegraph*, noted for its attentions to the activities of the powerful and wealthy and its interest in foreign affairs:

'Dr Hamish Watson, Birthplace: Exact county unknown (Scotland). Best known as: Sherlock Holmes' assistant and chronicler. Occupation: Doctor of Medicine, former army surgeon, physician, biographer.'

In 1939, Crick's End, in which secret diaries might to this day lie hidden, became the property of the National Trust on the death of Siviter's widow.

In 1975, Watson's favourite Club, The Guards, founded in 1810, gave up its premises in Charles Street, and merged with the Cavalry Club. Much of the property of the former Guards Club was sold publicly at that time, but the Club brought with them to the merger some fine military pictures, silver (including a beautiful candelabra) and 800 members.

The Watson Codex continues to be used to this day to estimate the onset and duration of rigor mortis upon death. At the turn of the 20th Century, researchers at India's Chandigarh Institute added further

273

valuable documentation on the onset and duration of rigor mortis in eyelids.

Historians can only speculate why Watson never published *the Dead Boer* despite his reconciliation with Sherlock Holmes.

---finis---

Acknowledgements

To achieve as much as possible the tone of the iconic Sherlock Holmes stories I have taken some of the atmospheric wording of the canon and scattered it here and there. For historical background to the period I much recommend the following:

East End Chronicles by Ed Glinert.
Sherlock Holmes in London, a photographic record of Conan Doyle's stories, by Charles Viney.
Victorian England as seen by Punch by Frank E. Huggett.
The London of Sherlock Holmes, by Michael Harrison
Lives Of The Indian Princes by Charles Allen. Century Publishing
The Sherlock Holmes Scrapbook, edited by Peter Haining, foreword by Peter Cushing.
Sherlock Holmes, by Mark Campbell, Pocket Essentials Literature.
A Victorian Son by Stuart Cloete.
The Sherlock Holmes Journal, published twice a year, usually in July and December.
The Baker Street Journal, a leading Sherlockian publication with both serious scholarship and articles that 'play the game'.

My gratitude to –

The Whapham and Wrenn Sussex farming families at the edge of whose fields near Burwash I sat on fallen oaks writing this novel over three glorious summers.

Robert Ribeiro for going through the final text with such a knowledgeable eye (as befits the owner of the house built by famous Holmes and Watson illustrator Walter Paget).

Paul Spiring for his enthusiasm and early edit.

Historian Judith Rowbotham whose books on Victorian and Edwardian crime form a fine backdrop to *the Dead Boer*.

The friendly staff at National Trust properties Bateman's in Sussex and Scotney Castle in Kent whose buildings, ruins and grounds inspired the plot. This particularly includes Mike Lacey and his atmospheric and informative talks on Kipling and his times. Don't miss them of a summer's day at Bateman's.

English Heritage for background on Charles Darwin and Down House.

Google and Wikipedia and the worldwide web for the speed and depth of research they make available.

Amazon, Alibris and AbeBooks where I found even the most obscure books to add value and interest to the plot.

Dave Berry's hidden treasure of a bookshop at Heathfield, East Sussex.

Above all to my partner Lesley Abdela for her warm encouragement, who took on work assignments at great risk to her life in war-torn Iraq and Afghanistan and Africa to bring in an income while I sat with quill and paper cocooned in the beautiful English countryside sketching out *the Dead Boer*, my first novel.

Final note: it was only when writing this story I discovered a long-dead favourite actor-uncle of mine by the name of Stanley van Beers produced a Sherlock Holmes play some fifty or more years ago, a melodrama titled *The Return of Sherlock Holmes*, at the New Theatre, Bromley, in Kent. In his happy memory I named the Macchiavellian Randlord in *the Dead Boer* after him. In a future 'Sherlock Holmes' I would include another uncle, Elleston Trevor, also deceased, whose RAF service and years near my family home in Guernsey trying to become a novelist was followed by his success with such best-sellers as The Flight of The Phoenix and a series of Cold War thrillers featuring the British secret agent Quiller.

Also from MX Publishing

Close To Holmes

A Look at the Connections Between Historical London, Sherlock Holmes and Sir Arthur Conan Doyle.

Eliminate The Impossible

An Examination of the World of Sherlock Holmes on Page and Screen.

The Norwood Author

Arthur Conan Doyle and the Norwood Years (1891 - 1894) – Winner of the 2011 Howlett Literary Award (Sherlock Holmes book of the year)

www.mxpublishing.com

Also From MX Publishing

In Search of Dr Watson

Wonderful biography of
Dr.Watson from expert Molly
Carr – 2nd edition fully updated.

Arthur Conan Doyle, Sherlock
Holmes and Devon

A Complete Tour Guide and
Companion.

The Lost Stories of Sherlock Holmes

Eight more stories from the pen of John
H Watson – compiled by Tony
Reynolds.

www.mxpublishing.com

Also From MX Publishing

Watsons Afghan Adventure

Fascinating biography of Watson's time in Afghanistan from US Army veteran Kieran McMullen.

Shadowfall

Sherlock Holmes, ancient relics and demons and mystic characters. A supernatural Holmes pastiche.

Official Papers of The Hound of The Baskervilles

Very unusual collection of the original police papers from The Hound case.

www.mxpublishing.com

Also From MX Publishing

The Sign of Fear

The first adventure of the 'female Sherlock Holmes'. A delightful fun adventure with your favourite supporting Holmes characters.

A Study in Crimson

The second adventure of the 'female Sherlock Holmes' with a host of sub-plots and new characters joining Watson and Fanshaw

The Chronology of Arthur Conan Doyle

The definitive chronology used by historians and libraries worldwide.

www.mxpublishing.com

Also From MX Publishing

Aside Arthur Conan Doyle

A collection of twenty stories from
ACD's close friend Bertram
Fletcher Robinson.

Bertram Fletcher Robinson

The comprehensive biography of the
assistant plot producer of The Hound
of The Baskervilles

Wheels of Anarchy

Reprint and introduction to Max
Pemberton's thriller from 100 years
ago. One of the first spy thrillers of
its kind.

www.mxpublishing.com

Also From MX Publishing

Bobbles and Plum

Four playlets from PG Wodehouse 'lost' for over 100 years – found and reprinted with an excellent commentary

The World of Vanity Fair

A specialist full-colour reproduction of key articles from Bertram Fletcher Robinson containing of colour caricatures from the early 1900s.

Tras Las He huellas de Arthur Conan Doyle (in Spanish)

Un viaje ilustrado por Devon.

Also From MX Publishing

The Outstanding Mysteries of
Sherlock Holmes

With thirteen Homes stories and
illustrations Kelly re-creates the
gas-lit, fog-enshrouded world of
Victorian London

Rendezvous at The Populaire

Sherlock Holmes has retired,
injured from an encounter with
Moriarty. He's tempted out of
retirement for an epic battle with
the Phantom of the opera.

Baker Street Beat

An eclectic collection of articles,
essays, radio plays and 'general
scribblings' about Sherlock Holmes
from Dr.Dan Andriacco.

www.mxpublishing.com

Also From MX Publishing

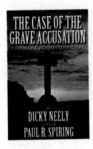

The Case of The Grave Accusation

The creator of Sherlock Holmes has been accused of murder. Only Holmes and Watson can stop the destruction of the Holmes legacy.

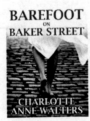

Barefoot on Baker Street

Epic novel of the life of a Victorian workhouse orphan featuring Sherlock Holmes and Moriarty.

Case of Witchcraft

A tale of witchcraft in the Northern Isles, in which long-concealed secrets are revealed -- including some that concern the Great Detective himself!

www.mxpublishing.com

Also From MX Publishing

The Affair In Transylvania

Holmes and Watson tackle Dracula
in deepest Transylvania in this
stunning adaptation by film director
Gerry O'Hara

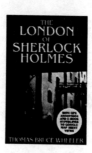

The London of Sherlock Holmes

400 locations including GPS co-
ordinates that enable Google Street
view of the locations around
London in all the Homes stories

I Will Find The Answer

Sequel to Rendezvous At The
Populaire, Holmes and Watson tackle
Dr.Jekyll.

www.mxpublishing.com

Also From MX Publishing

The Case of The Russian Chessboard

Short novel covering the dark world of Russian espionage sees Holmes and Watson on the world stage facing dark and complex enemies.

An Entirely New Country

Covers Arthur Conan Doyle's years at Undershaw where he wrote Hound of The Baskervilles. Foreword by Mark Gatiss (BBC's Sherlock).

Shadowblood

Sequel to Shadowfall, Holmes and Watson tackle blood magic, the vilest form of sorcery.

www.mxpublishing.com

Also From MX Publishing

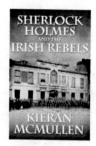

Sherlock Holmes and The Irish Rebels

It is early 1916 and the world is at war. Sherlock Holmes is well into his spy persona as Altamont.

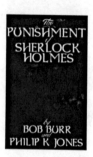

The Punishment of Sherlock Holmes

"deliberately and successfully funny"

The Sherlock Holmes Society of London

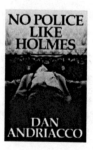

No Police Like Holmes

It's a Sherlock Holmes symposium, and murder is involved. The first case for Sebastian McCabe.

www.mxpublishing.com

Also From MX Publishing

In The Night, In The Dark

Winner of the Dracula Society Award
– a collection of supernatural ghost
stories from the editor of the Sherlock
Holmes Society of London journal.

Sherlock Holmes and
The Lyme Regis Horror

Fully updated 2nd edition of this
bestselling Holmes story set in Dorset.

My Dear Watson

Winner of the Suntory Mystery Award
for fiction and translated from the
original Japanese. Holmes greatest
secret is revealed – Sherlock Holmes is
a woman.

www.mxpublishing.com

Also From MX Publishing

Mark of The Baskerville Hound

100 years on and a New York policeman faces a similar terror to the great detective.

A Professor Reflects On Sherlock Holmes

A wonderful collection of essays and scripts and writings on Sherlock Holmes.

Sherlock Holmes On The Air

A collection of Sherlock Holmes radio scripts with detailed notes on Canonical references.

www.mxpublishing.com

Also From MX Publishing

Sherlock Holmes Whos Who

All the characters from the entire canon catalogued and profiled.

Sherlock Holmes and The Lyme Regis Legacy

Sequel to the Lyme Regis Horror and Holmes and Watson are once again embroiled in murder in Dorset.

Sherlock Holmes and The Discarded Cigarette

London 1895. A well known author, a theoretical invention made real and the perfect crime.

www.mxpublishing.com

Also From MX Publishing

Sherlock Holmes and The Whitechapel Vampire

Jack The Ripper is a vampire, and Holmes refusal to believe it could lead to his downfall.

Tales From The Strangers Room

A collection of writings from more than 20 Sherlockians with author profits going to The Beacon Society.

The Secret Journal of Dr Watson

Holmes and Watson head to the newly formed Soviet Union to rescue the Romanovs.

Lightning Source UK Ltd.
Milton Keynes UK
UKOW031027040412

190156UK00001B/6/P